NOT MY HUSBAND

BOOKS BY CATHRYN GRANT

Welcome to the Family

NOT MY HUSBAND

CATHRYN GRANT

bookouture

Published by Bookouture in 2026

An imprint of Storyfire Ltd.
Carmelite House
50 Victoria Embankment
London EC4Y 0DZ

www.bookouture.com

The authorised representative in the EEA is Hachette Ireland
8 Castlecourt Centre
Dublin 15 D15 XTP3
Ireland
(email: info@hbgi.ie)

ISBN: 978-1-80550-418-4
eBook ISBN: 978-1-80550-417-7

*For my readers—thank you for spending time with my characters.
You light up my life every single day.*

ONE
CHELSEA

My mom was worried that I hadn't known Jay long enough to be marrying him, but my mom had always been a worrier. I'd never understood why. Now, especially, she no longer needed to worry. For me, all the painful events of the past two years were now a blurry, dissolving memory. Today was the happiest day of my life.

Since Jay was from Southern California and I'd grown up in the San Francisco Bay area, he suggested we should have a destination wedding on neutral territory. That way, neither one of our families would feel the other was favored. When he showed me pictures of a lush garden overlooking several water-falls on The Big Island of Hawaii, I was reminded again why I'd fallen in love with this man. He was absolutely perfect for me. It seemed as if he knew my heart better than I knew it myself.

Now, the ceremony was over. The photographs had been taken, and the limo had driven us down beautiful roads past palm trees and breathtaking views to the resort where we were hosting our reception and spending our honeymoon. We'd sipped champagne while our closest friends lifted their glasses in toasts that made us laugh and glow with the warmth of their reflected love. Both my parents spoke heartfelt words that brought tears to my eyes, their voices filled with love for me, and respect for Jay. There wasn't a note of reservation regarding their belief in our future.

It wasn't as if I were a child, leaning on my parents. At thirty-two, with a six-year career in the tech industry behind me, and now, a year of law school under my belt, I wasn't exactly looking to Mom and Dad for approval in everything I did. But at the same time, we were a close family. I cared about their feelings and considered their opinions. They'd never steered me wrong.

Now, most of our guests were dancing. The sun was sinking into the ocean, casting pink and orange streaks across the sky as the rays spread through a thin layer of cloud on the horizon.

Jay was dancing with his best friend from high school while I took a short break. I'd discarded my silver heels an hour ago and had been enjoying the cool feel of the dance floor on the soles of my bare feet. Now, I stretched out and admired the pale pink polish on my toes, peeking out from under my wedding gown. I sipped champagne, loving the slightly tipsy feeling and this absolutely perfect day.

Bella, my maid of honor, was dancing with my dad. My mom and her best friend, Katherine, were standing by the bar, whispering, sharing their secrets, and laughing as they had all their lives. How had I gotten so lucky?

My life hadn't always been so perfect. I'd left my job under horrible circumstances, but that had led to something better— my decision to go to law school. I'd had to take a break from school following my accident and I couldn't wait to get back to classes once Jay and I settled into our new condo after the wedding.

The song ended. I saw Jay reach into his pocket and pull out his phone. I couldn't imagine who might be calling him. Nearly everyone we were close to was right here. We'd discussed having a no-phones policy but in the end, we decided it might be off-putting to some of our guests. Too controlling and judgy.

He left the dance floor, taking long strides, giving the impression the call was urgent and he needed to get quickly to someplace quiet. He pressed the phone hard against his ear, drawing attention to his freshly trimmed dark hair, the tiny curls I loved that had grown at the back gone so that he looked sharp for our wedding photos. No matter what he did with his hair, Jay was gorgeous. My heart beat slightly faster watching him walk toward the patio where wicker chairs and tables and a koi pond provided a comfortable setting for quiet conversation.

As he turned to step out of the path of a server carrying a tray of champagne flutes, the expression on his face startled me. He looked worried, or something else. Frightened?

I sat up and smoothed my dress over my legs as I watched him disappear onto the patio.

I picked up the tiny purse that held my lip gloss and phone. Despite my brief desire to have a phone-free wedding, it was hard to let go of that always available device. In my heart, I knew I'd want to post a photo or two on social media. How could I resist? Jay and I looked our absolute best. And not just because of his tux and my strapless gown with its three-foot train, my cascading curls and perfect makeup, carefully applied by Bella. Our happiness was spilling out of our eyes and shimmering in our smiles.

I hurried after Jay, ignoring my shoes in my rush to catch up.

As I drew closer, I couldn't quite hear what he was saying above the hum of voices around me, and the next song starting up, but the tone of his voice was clear. His words were sharp. Maybe he was annoyed that someone had bothered him at our wedding with something trivial. It must be a work call.

But there was something else. A note of anxiety.

I pulled out my phone, texting him as I walked.

Everything okay?

I thought he might turn to see where I was, but he didn't. Instead, he continued walking, faster now. I stared at my phone waiting for a response, turning to skirt the edge of the koi pond.

I felt a sharp jab to my upper arm as I crashed into someone who seemed to appear out of nowhere. My phone flew out of my hand and splashed into the pond.

I gasped, watching it sink into the dark water. Immediately, four large orange and white fished rushed to investigate, blocking it from my view. I wanted to grab it out, but the thought of sticking my hand into the midst of those fish with their mouths opening and closing, convinced that someone had tossed them a delicious treat, made me hesitate.

"Oh no! I'm so sorry, Chelsea. What a klutz I am." I looked up to see my mom's friend, Katherine. "I guess neither of us were looking where we were going. These phones. Right?" She laughed, waving her own phone. "I'm really sorry. Let me get it for you." Without a hint of squeamishness, she plunged her arm into the water past her elbow. The fish scattered.

She grimaced. "I can't reach the bottom. I didn't realize it was so deep." She pulled out her arm, dripping with water.

I took a step back, pulling the skirt of my gown close to my body.

"I'm so, so sorry," Katherine said. "I'll replace it, of course."

I glanced toward Jay. He was no longer on the phone. He started toward us, smiling as if everything was absolutely fine, as if he wanted to convince me that I'd misread his hurried departure, his tense shoulders, his sharp tone.

He came toward me and kissed me.

"Is everything okay?" I asked.

"Of course. Why wouldn't it be?"

"You rushed out. You were on the phone."

He slid his arm around my waist. "I didn't rush out. Let's dance." He kissed the edge of my ear.

As he guided me smoothly toward the dance floor, he was moving with the same determined strides with which he'd left the reception room moments earlier. I felt rushed. I felt as if he wanted me to stop asking about the phone call.

I felt an unwelcome thought puncture the fizz of champagne bubbles inside me. Who was on the phone and why was Jay lying to me? Maybe my mother was right. Were there things I didn't know about my new husband after all?

TWO
CHELSEA

Jay told me the phone call was nothing. A complaining parent from the elite private high school where he taught history and coached the boys' golf team. Concerned calls were the norm nearly every day of the week with his students, many of whom had overly involved, highly competitive parents.

I wanted to ask more. I wanted to hear the details, to be assured he was telling me the truth. His reaction to the call hadn't entirely matched what he was telling me now, even though he had mentioned the upset father of one of his students just before we left for Hawaii. But this was our wedding night. Not the time to be talking about our jobs, or grouchy parents of high school kids, or phones that had been fished out of koi ponds and declared dead.

Before the party started to wind down, Jay and I slipped away to our suite overlooking a swimming pool on one side, a garden filled with large leafy plants and exotic flowers on the other, and a view of the ocean beyond the garden. The resort had gifted us another bottle of champagne and some chocolate-dipped strawberries. It was cliché, but neither of us cared. They were delicious.

The next day, we met our families and the members of our wedding party for a late brunch. Of course, there was more champagne. And so much food.

As I nibbled a spring roll, I leaned toward Bella, whispering in her ear. "I know I shouldn't be thinking this on my honeymoon, but I'm honestly not sure how I'm going to cope without my phone." I laughed, then took a sip of champagne.

She patted my leg. "You'll manage."

"I wanted to take pictures of all our adventures."

"You can probably find a kids' digital camera in the gift shop." She clicked her glass against mine. "You should tell Jay to leave his phone at the front desk. Ask them to lock it up. You two can completely disconnect from the rest of the world. It will be bliss. A romantic high."

It did sound nice. Especially thinking about the tightness of Jay's face, the way he'd walked away from the dance floor the night before. It had almost felt as if our wedding celebration ended in that moment.

"Or we could take a drive to Kona, and I could get a new phone."

She laughed. "That's not healthy. Thinking you can't live for two weeks without your phone."

"I know."

By the time Jay and I had hugged everyone goodbye, I'd decided Bella was right. I mentioned the idea to Jay.

"I don't know, Chelz," he said. "Not being able to communicate at all doesn't sound like a good idea."

I linked my arm through his as we crossed the garden, headed toward the beach. "We have a phone in our room. Landlines still exist."

He laughed. "Sure. But if you had to reach someone, how many phone numbers do you know?"

"We won't need to reach anyone. Let's just try it. The more I think about it, the more I love the idea. No checking social media, no texts we feel obligated to respond to right away."

"But no one knows we're doing this. If we don't respond to anything for two weeks, people will worry."

"We're on our honeymoon! People will totally get it."

He opened the gate, and we started down the path toward the beach. The lounge chairs were all occupied, cabana sides drawn to shield people from the mid-afternoon sun. We walked down to the edge of the water and waded into the surf up to our knees. It was warm and frothy. It truly felt like paradise.

Jay pulled me close, then turned and kissed me slowly.

After a few minutes, we moved away from each other. "Let's do it," he said. "Who do we need to talk to on our honeymoon? This is a once-in-a-lifetime experience."

We put our arms around each other and gazed at the ocean. I was the luckiest woman on earth. Would I ever stop feeling that? I could stand on this beach forever. But we didn't, we walked along the shore for about half a mile, zigzagging in and out of the lapping waves, feeling soft sand between our toes, then turned back. We drank piña coladas on one of the restaurant patios, then returned to our room, showered, and made love. We slept, woke, showered again, and got dressed for dinner.

By the time we fell asleep that night, I was already adapting to life without a phone. I felt calmer, knowing that the person who had disrupted our wedding reception with an unwanted phone call, putting that look of panic on Jay's face, could no longer reach him. Part of me wanted to ask him about it again because something poked at my stomach, telling me it was more than an upset parent, but I didn't want to spoil the evening. For now, I would accept the answer he'd given me earlier.

It was nice, not constantly pulling it out of my pocket or my purse, checking to see what everyone else was doing, all the people who weren't with me. I hadn't spent time trying to think of something clever to say about our wedding or my new husband. I talked to Jay and enjoyed the flavor of the piña coladas instead of trying to take a picture of our drinks, arranging the tiny paper umbrellas just so.

I was completely absorbed in each moment, and I was really liking it.

In the morning, I woke slowly. The bed was soft and comfortable. The sound of the ocean and the breeze rattling the palm fronds drifted in through our open balcony doors. I smiled before I opened my eyes.

I turned onto my side and felt for Jay. My hand brushed his back. It was warm, his muscles firm. He turned slightly. I opened my eyes.

As he turned toward me, I felt as if he'd punched me in the face. The man looking at me, smiling as if I were the most beautiful woman on the planet, was not Jay. I was looking into the eyes of a complete stranger.

I shoved myself to the side of the bed, screaming.

THREE

CHELSEA

Trying to untangle myself from the sheets, scrambling to the edge, I almost fell out of bed. I was screaming, covering my breasts with my arms. Tears spilled out of my eyes, burning behind my lids—the result of champagne and the sickening shock that was pounding my body. It felt as if my brain was being shaken inside my skull.

The man propped himself on his elbow, smiling at me. He reached out his hand, his expression changing to one of concern. "Hey, Chelz. What's wrong? Did you have a nightmare?"

I grabbed the hotel robe off the bench at the foot of the bed. I shoved my arms into the sleeves, wrapped it around me, and yanked the belt around my waist.

"Who are you? Where's my husband?"

He laughed softly. "What do you mean? I'm Jay."

"Get out of my bed. Get out of my room! How did you even get *in*? Where's my husband?" I pressed myself against the wall. My hands shook and my legs were so weak I wasn't sure I could remain standing. What was happening? I felt sick. I didn't know what to do first. My phone! I didn't even have my phone. I couldn't call for help. Where was Jay?

I lunged toward the bed. I yanked off the comforter, pulling it onto the floor. The strange man lay there exposed, his face still wearing an expression of concern, now laced with something that looked like hurt. What the hell was wrong with him?

"Get out!" I wanted to call security, but the phone was on his side of the bed, and I didn't want to go near him. What if he grabbed me? What if he tried to hurt me? I could hardly think. My breaths came in loud, painful gasps, as if I'd been running at full speed for miles. "Who are you?"

He sat up. "Please. Stop yelling."

"No! I want you out of here. Now. Sooner than now!"

"Please don't," he said. "Tell me what's wrong." He moved to the side of the bed and swung his legs over the edge. He wiped his hands down his face, pulling gently at his skin, then let them fall to his lap.

"How did you get in here?"

"I came in with you, Chelz. After that incredible lobster dinner."

I stared at him. How did he know that? How did he know Jay's nickname for me? "Don't call me that." I shivered, moving my arms to shake off the chill. It was an obvious nickname. It didn't mean anything. "Get out of my room."

I went to the dresser to grab shorts and the rest of my clothes so I could take a shower. I needed to report Jay missing. I could call from the phone in the room, but I needed to do this in person. My heart was pounding, my whole body trembling with fear, but at least my brain was starting to think.

"Hey. I don't know what's going on, but it's me. Jay." He climbed out of bed and moved toward me.

"Don't." I held out my hand. "Don't come anywhere near me."

"But I—"

"I'll scream." I went to the dresser and yanked open the top drawer where Jay had put his wallet the night before. It wasn't there. Another wallet, slightly different, was in its place. I grabbed it and flipped it open. I pulled out the driver's license. Jay Davis. The address was correct—the apartment he'd rented when he moved to Palo Alto. But the photo was of this man. What was going on? I closed my eyes, then opened them. Yes, it was definitely him. How could he have ID with all my husband's information and his photograph? It didn't make any sense! I felt as if I was losing my mind, as if I was in some kind of bizarre reality show, being filmed while an audience was laughing at me. Or maybe an episode of *Black Mirror*, some kind of weird, distorted future state where my brain had been manipulated, or reality itself had.

Could this really be my husband? Was I having a mental breakdown? Had I gotten married too soon after my accident, before I'd healed completely?

I pulled out the credit cards. Jay's credit cards. I tossed the cards and the driver's license on the floor, spinning around to face the stranger sitting on the edge of the bed. "Who the hell are you? How did you get all this? A fake ID? What did you do to my husband?"

"I haven't done anything. Please believe me. I don't know why you're doing this. I wish you'd come back to bed so we can talk. Why are you so upset? Did you have a nightmare?"

"Let me see your phone." He could have a fake ID, but he couldn't fake the data in his phone. Could he?

"I turned it into security. Remember? We said we were going to spend our honeymoon without our phones."

I did remember. Now. It wasn't the first thing on my mind, waking up next to a total stranger. My husband, the love of my life, had vanished as if he'd never been here, as if our wedding had never happened. The ring on my finger was the only evidence that I wasn't completely out of my mind. Maybe this creep had overheard us talking about our phones. But how did he know so many other things about me? I wanted to scream. I wanted him out of our room.

Was this Jay and I was hallucinating? No. No. It was too real. It felt too real to be my mind playing tricks on me.

And this stranger was the only connection I had to Jay right now. I couldn't even text him because I didn't have my phone. I turned back to the dresser, yanked open the drawers, grabbed my clothes, and went into the bathroom. I locked the door and turned on the shower.

While I brushed my hair and teeth and waited for the water to get to the right temperature, my thoughts spun in useless circles. Tears bubbled out of my eyes. Where was Jay? Had he left me? Had something happened to him? I couldn't even get my phone. I could call him from the room phone, but I wasn't sure I remembered his number. My whole life, my connection to almost every part of my life was locked inside my phone, that was now utterly useless, sitting like a broken piece of glass in the drawer of my nightstand.

After a quick shower, I came out of the bathroom to find the man still sitting on the edge of the bed, dressed in shorts now.

I grabbed my purse and started toward the door.

"Aren't you going to wait for me?" he asked.

"No. I need to find out what happened to my husband." I flung open the door and stumbled out of the room, terrified of spending another minute alone with that man, whoever he was.

FOUR

CHELSEA

As I walked along the outside corridor, my pounding heart didn't match the gently swaying palm trees surrounding the swimming pool below, or the soft whoosh of the ocean in the distance. I wasn't sure if I was having a panic attack or a heart attack or a nervous breakdown.

This couldn't be happening. It didn't feel real. How could this total stranger have gotten into my room, into my bed? How had he slept beside me all night without me knowing? It made my skin crawl to know he'd been inches away from me, his body brushing against mine in the darkness. Had he touched me? I had no way of knowing.

I didn't understand how he'd gotten into our room. He must have done something to Jay. He had Jay's credit cards. He must also have his key card for our room. I walked faster, almost running now. I reached the stairs, scampered down, then along the path that wound through lush gardens, past a man-made stream, and into the open-air lobby to the front desk.

No one was waiting to check in at this hour. I rushed up to the first of three receptionists. Her smile was eager and helpful. Her hair was oiled and pulled into a tight bun, her face made up as if she had a modeling gig coming up soon, but still, she looked beautiful, not overdone. She wore pearl stud earrings that enhanced her large, round dark eyes that looked like onyx stones set in cream. She wore a lei of plumeria flowers around her neck.

"Hi. I'm Chelsea Davis. My husband and I checked in Thursday. We had our wedding at the Hibiscus Garden Waterfalls on Saturday and we're on our honeymoon." Why was I telling her all this? Maybe it felt important to explain everything because once she heard what had happened, she was sure to think I was crazy, or making it up. She might think I was high.

"Congratulations!" she said. "Ho'omaika'i ana."

"Thank you." I tried to smile, but it didn't work. Instead, I started crying.

"Oh no. What's wrong?"

"I woke up with a man in my bed who's a total stranger."

Her eyes widened, as if she were watching a TV show she couldn't believe. Her lips formed into a tiny circle.

"I know it sounds unbelievable. I've never seen him before. And my husband's gone!"

"Did you call him?"

"I can't! I dropped my phone in the koi pond at the wedding." I laughed hysterically. Why did I sound nervous? That wasn't right. I wasn't nervous at all. I was scared. Terrified. I didn't understand what was happening. Nothing made any sense. My eyes were so full of tears, I could hardly see her face now. "I couldn't call because my phone's dead. I have no idea who this guy is. He's trying to pretend he's my husband. And he has a driver's license with my husband's name. And my husband's credit cards. He keeps talking like... He knows things about me. He doesn't talk like he knows things. I mean he *does* know things. I need to call the police! Something happened to Jay."

I wasn't sure when it had happened, but as my eyes cleared

slightly, I realized she'd taken a few steps back from the counter. Her eyes were still wide, but her lips were no longer shaped in a circle. She glanced toward the receptionist to her left. He was typing on the computer keyboard. "I should get the manager," she said. "I'll be right back." She left so quickly, I didn't have time to say more.

I stood at the counter, feeling helpless and alone. I wanted to text Bella. I wanted to call my mom. I shoved my hand into my pocket, feeling the place where my phone would usually be pressing against my hip bone. I pulled it out. I grabbed my left hand, feeling the press of my diamond ring against my palm. I twisted it around. I leaned against the counter. It felt as if the few people passing through the lobby all slowed to stare at me, wondering why I was standing at the reception desk, crying, all alone, no one there to help me.

It felt like an hour had passed before the young woman returned. It was probably five minutes. Maybe less. I was crying again, the single tissue I had in my purse wet and limp inside my fist. A young man was with her. He didn't seem much older than the receptionist. How would they help me? Did he understand their security system? Would he have the courage and authority to stand up to the man who had planted himself in my room, insisting he was my husband?

He didn't look confident. He looked uncertain. I wondered what the woman—Kim—had told him. His name badge read Shep. The name didn't fit him at all. He was slender and tall, with black, close-cropped hair and dark stubble on his jaw which did not help him look older, if that was his intention.

"I understand there's a problem with your room," he said.

My room? The problem was so much bigger than my *room*, I couldn't find words to respond to him.

"Is it possible you somehow returned to the wrong room after going to some clubs last night?"

"No!"

"Is this a prank?" Shep grinned.

Kim also gave me a nervous smile, looking slightly relieved, as if she didn't mind that she'd been made to look ridiculous, as long as I was okay.

"It's not a prank and I didn't go to any clubs." I explained the story again, giving less background this time.

"Are you sure?" Shep asked.

"Sure of what?"

"That you're in the right room? That the driver's license..." He stopped, as if he realized that his question sounded as crazy as my story.

"Yes. I'm sure." My voice was shrill. It carried through the large space, over the tiled floor, up toward the high ceiling, across the casually arranged wicker furniture surrounded by potted plants out to the patio area. A couple sipping coffee at a small table glanced in my direction. I hadn't meant to be shrill or loud, bordering on hysteria. But the question was so insulting.

I knew it was difficult to understand. I was having trouble myself, but his job was to treat his guests with respect, not to immediately question my integrity, my sanity. He acted as if I'd gotten so drunk, I'd gone home from one of the resort bars with the wrong man on my honeymoon!

I took a slow breath. "Yes. I'm sure. I know it sounds crazy, but I went to sleep with my husband, and I woke up with a strange man beside me. He keeps insisting he's my husband but he's not and my husband is missing. My phone was destroyed at my wedding—it fell in the water, so I need you to call the police and tell them he's missing."

Shep nodded. He glanced at Kim, then back at me, looking slightly ashamed, as if he hoped I hadn't noticed.

"And who is the man staying in your room?"

"I don't know! I've never seen him before!"

Shep nodded. "Okay. Well, let's try to sort this out." He

pulled out his cell phone and studied the screen as if he wasn't sure what to do with it.

Tears welled up in my eyes again. I felt my heart racing. "Will you call my room and tell him to come here? It's room 322."

"Sure. Sure, I can do that." He looked relieved that he'd been given something to do that didn't involve telling a preposterous story to a police officer." He grabbed the handset on the counter and punched in the numbers for our room. "Your wife asked—"

"I'm not his wife!"

"The uh... the woman from your room would like you to come to the front desk so we can sort out a misunderstanding," he said.

"It's not a misunderstanding," I said.

He was quiet for a moment. "Thank you, sir."

My tears dried quickly. I didn't like the tone of that. This man came into my room uninvited. Slept in my bed. For all I knew, he'd beaten up, and possibly killed my husband. And the resort manager was calling him sir. It didn't give me a good feeling about how this was going to unfold.

I felt a wave of fear wash over me. It was the first time I'd had a coherent thought about Jay, that I'd allowed myself to think he might have been murdered.

How else could I explain what was happening?

If the man in my room hadn't killed Jay, he must know something about what had happened.

A few minutes later, I saw the stranger from my bed walking toward us. He had a warm, casual smile on his face, as if we were meeting for a scuba diving or surfing lesson.

"How can I help?" He extended his hand to Shep. "Jay Davis."

"He's not," I said, my tone sharp but trembling with anxiety, which had the effect of making me sound as unstable as I felt. "He's not Jay."

The man smiled at Kim. He extended his hand to her as well. She shook it, smiling at him, then looking at me apologetically before quickly easing her fingers out of his grasp. The man moved closer, putting his arm across my shoulders.

I shoved him away. Hard.

"Whoa," Shep said. "Let's calm down. May I see your ID, sir?"

"Sure." The man pulled out his wallet, flipped it open, and displayed the license.

Shep tapped a few keys on the computer. "This matches the reservation for room 322. Booked for—"

"Of course it does," I said. "It's a fake."

"Okay." Shep gave me a patient smile. "So, let's see." He stared at the computer screen as if the answer might be hidden inside.

"Just find me another room," I said. "I'll pay, for now. I don't care. And call the police. I don't have a phone."

"Yes, you mentioned that." Shep paused, glancing at the man beside me, then looking to my left, avoiding my gaze. "The problem is, we're fully booked. It's the height of tourist season."

"There's nothing?" I asked.

"No. Sorry."

"What about some of the other resorts?"

"I can try. But it's unlikely."

"I can't believe there's not a single room on the entire island."

"I said, I can try."

"There must be a room somewhere. But first, I need you to call the police. Every minute we stand here is another minute that no one is looking for my husband."

"Yes. I can do that for you." Shep looked relieved. He was probably happy to hand this off to the police.

As I waited for him to place the call, I thought about the other resorts and began to wonder if that was the right decision. What if Jay returned? What if he'd been injured, or was unconscious and he woke up and came looking for me? I didn't have my phone. If I left, how would he find me? Maybe I should stay here. But that man—

"Chelsea," the man said.

I couldn't bear the sound of my name on his lips. I wanted him to stop talking to me. At the same time, I wanted to know what he knew. I wanted to know what kind of game he was playing.

"You said you loved this place because your parents celebrated their twenty-fifth anniversary here. You said it had good vibes for a long marriage. Don't you think we should—"

"How do you know that?" I turned to face him, looking into his dark, infuriatingly kind eyes. "How the hell do you know that?"

"You told me."

I had not told him. I'd never spoken to him at all, never laid eyes on him before this morning.

FIVE

CHELSEA

It took thirty-five minutes for the police to arrive. The situation was not an emergency, Shep told me, while Kim nodded, trying to look empathetic to my situation and supportive of her boss at the same time.

Kim resumed her place at the counter and Shep led me and the strange man to a small room behind the counter. I didn't like being confined to a conference room designed to hold six people, crowded into the windowless room with Shep and the man who wouldn't stop calling himself Jay. I could only imagine how claustrophobic it would become once the police arrived.

The man chatted with Shep, telling him how impressed he was by the resort—praising the food and the service, going on about the easy access to the beach, the beauty of the three swimming pools, the incredible bars. You'd have thought the guy was a salesman trying to pitch an event to Shep. After he was done gushing about the resort, he began asking questions about Hawaii, and the Big Island in particular. He wanted to know how long Shep had lived there, what it was like to live on an island, and whether he thought he would remain for the rest of his life.

Shep was obviously charmed.

I felt sick. He sounded like a nice guy. How could he be so nice and so malicious at the same time? This man was not my husband, and he refused to stop pretending he was. It was making my head ache, watching how he placed his hand on the table near where I was sitting, as if he wanted to project a calming presence. He offered me kind, concerned smiles every chance he got. He acted as if he *was* my husband. It was sickening and dizzying and frightening.

Finally, Kim opened the door and stepped aside, directing a single uniformed police officer into the room. He introduced himself as Officer Almi but didn't take a seat.

Was he not planning to stay long?

"What seems to be the problem?" Officer Almi asked. "We have a report of a missing person?"

"My husband and I were married two days ago," I said. "When I woke up this morning he was gone. And this man was in my bed."

The cop laughed.

"It's not funny." My voice rose. "It's not funny at all."

"Apologies." He arranged his face into a neutral expression. "It's an unusual story, you have to admit."

"It's not a story. Please don't—"

"Okay." He held up his hand like he was stopping cars. Maybe he'd been a traffic cop, and this was out of his league. "Let's start with the obvious. Let me see your ID." He held out his hand to the man beside me.

"The resort manager already checked," I said. "So did I. You're wasting time. It's fake. It has my husband's name on it."

"Let me see it," Officer Almi said.

The man pulled out his wallet and placed it on the table.

The cop picked it up and opened it.

"Your husband's name is Jay Davis? You reside at 723 Parkside Avenue 21, Palo Alto, California?"

"We just bought a new place together. That's where he was living. He hasn't updated—"

"Okay."

The officer turned toward the man beside me. "What's your story, sir?"

"I'm Jay Davis. Chelsea and I were married at the Hibiscus Garden Waterfalls on Saturday. We had a family brunch yesterday and everyone went home. Then—"

"Stop! That's all lies. I mean, that's what we did. But it was with my husband, not this man. Why don't you believe me?"

The cop looked at me. He narrowed his eyes slightly. "To be honest, I'm not sure what to say here. You're telling me Jay Davis is missing, but I can't take a report on that."

"Why not?" I shoved my chair away from the table and stood.

He looked helplessly at Shep and the man sitting there giving me a look of grave concern. The man reached out his hand as if he wanted to take mine, but I moved away from him.

"Because all the information I have right now tells me that this gentleman is Jay Davis," the cop said. "A lot of mainlanders come here to get married. The parties get a little wild. Lots of drinking. I know the resort curtails that, but you said you didn't get married at the resort."

"Our reception was here. And we didn't go *wild*. What does that even have to do with it?"

"Sometimes there are drugs. Did you take anything? Could you be"—he cleared his throat—"could you be hallucinating?"

"I'm not hallucinating. There's nothing wrong with me! This man is not Jay."

"His ID says otherwise. And he says otherwise. I don't know what to tell you."

"You believe him but not me? You think I'm high or crazy?"

"His ID says—"

"You've never seen a fake ID?" I asked, my tone sharp and condescending.

"Sometimes brides put themselves under a lot of pressure for their wedding, they—"

"I'm not having a mental breakdown. I did not have stress put on me. Not by myself or anyone else. I'm a second-year law student. I was a manager at a well-known high-tech company. I'm not a nut case. I don't use recreational drugs. This is not the man I'm married to. He's a complete stranger."

"If you say the man you married disappeared—"

"I don't *say* he disappeared. He did."

"We can check the security cameras. Can you make those available?" Officer Almi looked at Shep, who nodded eagerly. "We'll see if there's any record of someone leaving your room. Or Jay entering your room late—"

"He's not Jay."

"—at night. That's about all I can say right now. Do you have anyone else who can verify your story?"

"It's not a *story*. The rest of my family and friends flew home yesterday."

He nodded. "Jay here seems like a nice enough guy. And you seem—"

"He's not *Jay!*"

"—and you seem really stressed out, if you want my take on the situation."

"I don't want your take. I want you to find my husband and get this man out of my room."

"I don't have any authority to do that, ma'am. There's no crime here. Unless you have someone else who can corroborate what you're telling me."

"So, that's it?" I asked.

"You can stay and see if your memory clears and you feel better. Or you can return home."

"Return home?" I laughed, hearing the hysterical tone rising in my voice again. "I'm not returning home without my husband."

The officer nodded. "We'll check the security footage. And be in touch."

"You can't do it right now?"

"It will take some time. We'll be in touch. Why don't you have something to eat. Relax a little and enjoy this beautiful island, and I'll get back to you. What's your number?"

I explained about my phone, and he assured me he would call my room when he'd finished reviewing the security footage. Until then, I was trapped in my room with this stranger.

SIX

CHELSEA

Shep followed the cop out the door, looking as if he was in a hurry to escape. I stared at the man who knew things about me that he shouldn't. The man who refused to tell me who he was or what he wanted from me. I said nothing. He gave me a tentative smile. There was something about his smile that, for half a maddening second, reminded me of my husband. I shook my head hard to get rid of the thought. I had a strong urge to smack his face.

Instead, I walked out of the room. I heard his footsteps behind me. I crossed the lobby, headed toward the patio and the path back to the building where my room was located. All the suites were located in two-story buildings, the ground floor units with private patios, and the second-floor units with balconies large enough to hold a small table and chairs as well as two lounge chairs. The more conventional rooms were in four high-rise towers.

I felt the man close behind me, and soon he was beside me. I tried to outpace him, but I couldn't take long enough strides. I would have had to run, and I imagined he would probably be able to run faster than I could. He was about the same height as

Jay and a similar build, which creeped me out further than I already was. It gave me the sensation that my husband was indeed walking beside me, especially when I didn't turn to look at him, because his physical presence felt eerily similar.

As my head cleared from the chaos of trying to get the resort manager and the cop to take me seriously, new thoughts rose to the surface. I stopped suddenly.

"Let me see your phone," I said.

"I don't have it. Remember? You asked me to give it to security so we could enjoy our honeymoon without any interruptions."

I felt another icy chill run down my arms. How did he know so much about me? About my conversations with Jay? About our plans, our wedding? It made me feel as if he'd been in our room the entire time, listening to our conversations. But it was more than that.

Of course, he wouldn't show me his phone. He wouldn't be able to explain why nothing in his emails or text messages was connected to Jay's life. He would be faced with the fact that he didn't have a single photograph of me on there.

I also wanted his phone so I could talk to someone who wouldn't make me feel like I was deranged. I needed to talk to my mother, to Bella, to my mom's best friend, Katherine, who was like an aunt and cousin all wrapped into one person. To someone back home who would help me sort this out and figure out what I should do. If the police weren't going to do anything to look for Jay, aside from glancing at images from a few security cameras, how would I find him? He could be lying on a beach, unconscious. He could be injured in the bottom of a canyon, calling for help. He could be trapped between rocks in a hidden cove near a secluded beach. I couldn't even think about the other possibilities.

Walking faster, half running after all, I left the man behind as I hurried the rest of the way back to my suite.

The moment I was in the room, I grabbed a bottle of water out of fridge, twisted off the cap, and went to the phone on the nightstand. I dialed my mother's cell phone, one of only two phone numbers I knew by memory. I also knew the landline number my parents hung on to for the house where I'd grown up, but I wanted to be sure I reached her.

My mother answered on the first ring.

"Chelsea! You're not supposed to call your mother on your honeymoon."

The sound of her laughter eased some of my fear, but not enough that I could join her. I poured out the whole confusing, terrifying story, my words tripping over themselves as I tried to put the senseless events in logical order. When I was finished, she was silent for several seconds.

"Is he still there? In your room?"

"Yes." He'd used the key card he must have stolen from Jay to follow me into the room. He was now on the balcony, gazing out at the ocean as if he had a right to enjoy the beauty surrounding us, as if he belonged here. He behaved as if he'd paid for this room and was relaxing on a blissful holiday with his bride.

"You need to get him out of there. Call security."

"Didn't you listen to anything I said?"

"Yes."

"They won't make him leave. They don't believe he's not Jay, because he has ID."

"Then you..." Her voice trailed off as the details of my story began to fit together in her mind. She coughed softly. "Do you think Jay was meeting someone?"

"Are you saying he's cheating on me? On our *honeymoon*!?"

"No. I meant, you haven't known him very long. I just wondered if he had other business there... or something. I don't know. It's so bizarre."

"That doesn't explain this guy in my room. And Jay and I

don't keep secrets from each other." I knew I sounded petulant, but I resented that she was bringing that up again, implying I didn't know the man I'd married. Her toast at the wedding had sounded heartfelt. Had she been acting? I didn't think so. But the moment something wasn't absolute perfection, that was where her mind went.

"Okay. I'm sorry. I was just asking. I wish I could come back. To be with you. But—"

"I don't need you to come back. I'm not a child. I just need to figure out what to do."

"And your dad—"

"I know. It's fine. I don't need my parents to rescue me."

"But it's so awful. Maybe you should come home."

"Without Jay? Absolutely not. Will you give me Bella's number?"

"Will you ask her to come? I really think you need someone there with you."

"I just want to talk to her. Maybe she'll have some good ideas about how I can get the police and the resort to listen to me. Give me Katherine's number too. It's insane that we don't know anyone's number without our phones."

After she gave me the numbers, she was quiet again. Finally, she spoke in a soft voice. "I'm scared, Chelsea. I don't like this. I think the most important thing is to keep yourself safe. If you insist on letting him stay in your room—"

"I'm not *letting* him. I already told you what happened."

"Yes. Okay, but you need to stay safe. Protect yourself. Keep the door to the bedroom locked. Always. And instead of trying to get this man to tell you what he's up to, focus on Jay. Keep your attention on finding him."

I felt my heart, and everything else, soften at her words. Hearing her speak calmed me. It made me feel as if I could actually accomplish what she was suggesting.

Before we hung up, I asked her to open my laptop and gave

her instructions for looking up my email password. Once I had it, we said goodbye and I called Bella.

The call went right to voicemail. It took me a few minutes to remember—she was attending a two-day orientation for her new job. How could I have forgotten? At the same time, it was easy to see how I had. I was surprised I'd remembered now.

If Bella knew Jay had disappeared, she would absolutely think that was a good reason to forget about her new job. For now, I needed to follow my mother's two-point plan. Keep myself safe and focus on finding out what had happened to Jay.

I grabbed my purse and quietly opened the door, slipping out of the room with my gaze fixed on the man's back to be sure he didn't see me leaving. I closed the door as softly as I could, then ran along the corridor and down the stairs.

Skirting the edge of the pool area, I glanced over my shoulder several times to be sure he wasn't following. Inside the main building, I headed toward the wing with dress shops and jewelry stores, a children's toy store, high-end gift shops, and others that sold souvenirs.

I entered a store that Jay and I had visited on our first day. It carried more expensive gifts that had an island theme such as glass sculptures of sea life and beautifully carved bowls from native woods. In a glass case was a selection of daggers with Hawaiian-themed designs on the handles. I chose a medium-sized one that was still small enough to fit into my shoulder bag. It came in a polished wood box. The moment I was out of the shop, I removed it from the box and tucked the knife into the bottom of my purse.

I walked slowly back to my suite, my head filled with white noise. I had no idea how I would even begin to go about finding my missing husband when the resort manager and the police didn't even believe he was missing.

SEVEN

CHELSEA

With the knife tucked securely inside my purse, for now, I crossed the massive open-air lobby and turned down the hallway leading to the business center. The room was deserted. I wondered why they even had a business center. Did anyone come to a resort in Hawaii and spend part of their day in this windowless room working at a computer?

I sat at one of the five computers, entered the password they'd given us on a small card when we checked in, and opened a browser. The moment I brought up my email page, I realized I couldn't email Jay's best man or his parents to ask whether anyone had heard from him. My connection with them had been through text messages. I didn't have a single email address. I would have to ask my mother or Bella to get those for me.

Thwarted before I'd started, I began searching local news sites, looking for stories about accidents. The cop that had come to talk to me probably hadn't thought to do this. I wasn't even convinced he'd made looking at the security footage his top priority. He seemed satisfied that the man who had let himself into my room in the middle of the night was Jay, simply because he had a California driver's license that said he was, and a few credit cards to match.

I wasn't sure if the cop was lazy, disinclined to take a woman's word over a man's, or if my story was so incredibly absurd, he just couldn't accept what I'd told him. It did sound unbelievable. Every time I listened to myself tell it to someone new, I heard how it sounded. Crazy. Unbelievable. Weird.

The only news articles regarding accidents were for a twenty-two-year-old guy who'd crashed his motorcycle into a fruit stand, a tourist who had been run over by a jet ski, and two children who had fallen out of a treehouse and broken a few bones. Still, I couldn't stop looking. I combed through blog posts and social media pages. I looked at the online site for the local newspaper.

Searching the social media profiles for other resorts, surf clubs, and tourist attractions, I went down rabbit holes as I studied candid photos, desperately hoping I might see Jay. Even as I clicked through hundreds of pictures, I knew this was a futile effort. He'd only been gone overnight. There wasn't a chance he would show up in a random photograph for a snorkeling expedition. He'd been with me the entire time since our plane touched down at Kona airport.

As I looked at photographs of strangers, knowing I was wasting time, my brain began to feel numb and slightly foggy because I had no idea what to do. My thoughts drifted back to the early days of my former career where I'd spent hours scrolling for stock photos, before I'd walked out the door in a fit of ethical pride, ready to take on the injustices of the workplace by going to law school with the goal of becoming an employment attorney.

My three years as a manager had ended horribly when I'd come face to face with the reality of corporate politics.

A vice president at our company had it in for a man on my team. It became my job to micromanage this unwitting man through a *performance improvement process* with deliberately impossible objectives. When he inevitably failed, I was the one tasked with terminating his employment.

When he sued the company, I was required to meet with a team of lawyers who prepped me to tell the company's side of the story, ensuring the executives were protected and the game they'd played wasn't exposed. That's when I knew I had to quit to pursue a new career.

The experience was horrible, but the outcome was positive. Going to law school felt like I was finally pursuing a career where I was doing meaningful work, not simply interesting work.

Was there any hope that my current nightmare could turn into something good like other horrible experiences in my life had done?

I turned my attention away from the search for something that didn't exist and looked up the name of the nearest hospital. I left the computer and went to the table where a single landline sat ready for the rare creature who might require the business center's services but didn't possess a cell phone.

When I finally reached a live person at the hospital and asked whether a patient by the name of Jay Davis had been admitted to emergency, I was told privacy laws prevented them from providing that information. As I hung up, I thought about calling a cab to take me to the hospital and walking through the emergency room looking for Jay. Would they allow me inside without giving the name of the person I was visiting? I would have to persuade the cop to do this for me. But first, he had to believe Jay was missing.

I was right back where I'd started. I didn't even know how long he'd been gone. I could feel the minutes ticking past— wasted and pulling him further away from me.

I walked out of the business center, defeated and out of ideas. But maybe the diversion had reset my brain. Looking at the long expanse of the reception desk, I recalled the stranger's refusal to ask for his phone back. Because I'd been so deeply unsettled that he knew Jay had turned his phone over to security, it hadn't occurred to me that the phone in security belonged to Jay, not this stranger.

I almost ran to the counter, approaching a middle-aged man with a shaved head and a smile that looked genuine.

"Hi. My husband and I were trying to have a phone-free honeymoon, but he needs to send a few messages after all, so we have to break our rule." I gave him a defeated smile. "Will you get his phone for me? It's under the name of Jay Davis. We're in room 322."

The smile stayed broad and genuine, but his words were like a sharp pin, puncturing the joy that was filling my chest.

"He'll need to come ask for it himself. I'm sorry, I can't hand it back to you."

"I'm his wife. I can show you ID." I pulled my purse up and placed it on the counter, tugging the zipper open.

"Sorry, ma'am. I can't do that."

"Why not?"

"It's not your phone. You didn't ask us to hold it. Mr. Davis needs to request the phone himself." With each statement, his smile broadened.

I wanted to tell him to stop smiling. I wanted to tell him to read the room, to consider lining up his appearance with his words. But none of that mattered. I wasn't getting the phone.

As I walked away, it occurred to me they would readily hand it over to the man claiming to be my husband, no questions asked. If I wanted it badly enough, I would have to enter into his charade so I could convince him to ask for the phone. Doing that felt like a betrayal of the man I loved.

EIGHT

CHELSEA

The moment I stepped into the bedroom and closed the plantation doors behind me, locking that man into the sitting area of the suite, I saw it. The solid navy blue of the comforter made it stand out.

Lying on the center of the bed was a single white rose. A scream filled my throat, but I kept it inside, almost gagging with the effort. I forced my brain to consider it calmly. White roses were not uncommon, although in Hawaii people tended to give tropical flowers more often. There weren't that many rose colors to choose from. White could have been a lucky guess.

Still, it brought up that visceral reaction, a scream that echoed inside my skull.

White roses were my favorite flower. There was something so perfect and clean about them. They made everything feel fresh. I loved them, and Jay knew this. He often gave me a single white rose for no reason at all.

This could be a lucky guess. It must be a lucky guess.

But we were in Hawaii. It didn't feel like a lucky guess. It felt as if this man would have chosen native flowers. It felt like he knew.

I wanted to tear the petals of the perfect blossom, just starting to open. But even in my anger and creeping fear, it felt wrong. I couldn't destroy something so beautiful. At the same time, I couldn't put it in a vase and admire it as if I appreciated his gesture. What was I supposed to do? More importantly, what was he doing? And how did he know?

The tip of the stem was in a plastic vial with a small bit of water, so the rose would live for a short while as it was. I placed it on the dresser and went to the doors that opened onto the balcony. He was sitting on one of the lounge chairs, his back to me. I was sure he'd heard me come in, but he wasn't trying to look into the bedroom, which I supposed I appreciated.

I took the knife out of my purse and tried fitting it into my pocket. It was too large. I put it back into my purse and went into the main room where the bifold doors were open and stepped out onto the balcony.

"You've been gone a long time," he said. "I missed you."

"I'd like to enjoy the balcony. Will you please go inside?" I said.

He gave me a wounded look. "I know you're stressed out. But we can relax together. We don't have to talk. Unless you want to talk about law school. I'd love to hear about what you'll be studying when the new quarter starts. I know you can't wait to get back to it."

I felt my body sway. I looked to the side, longing for a door-frame to grab onto to steady myself. Each time I moved past something that chilled me deep in my bones, he managed to spin me around again. I felt as if I was constantly losing my balance, always on the verge of passing out.

"You should sit down. You look pale." He stood. "Let me get you some water." He stepped around me and went to the mini fridge.

"If you think this is getting you into my bed, you can think again. That's never happening. Not ever."

Again, he looked wounded. More than wounded. He looked devastated. "That's not what I'm after, Chelsea. I'm sorry if there's anything I've done that gave you that impression."

"The rose on my bed, not to mention crawling into my bed when I was asleep. Coming into my room. Gaslighting me. We'll start there."

"I know how much you love white roses. That's all." He moved toward the doorway. "Do you want water, or something else to drink?"

Vodka and cranberry juice would have been really nice, but I wasn't about to let him think I appreciated the offer, or to let him do anything for me. Now that he was standing in the room asking me about my drink preference, I didn't want him even grabbing a plastic bottle out of the fridge. "I'm fine. I just need some peace and quiet. Alone."

"Sure." He went inside, sat on the couch, and picked up a paperback thriller that was splayed on the coffee table.

I settled on the lounge chair and closed my eyes. I wished I had my sunglasses. I wished I had something to drink. But I wasn't moving. I didn't want him to know I needed anything, especially not from him. I didn't want him to know a single thing about me or what I was thinking. Seeing no way out of having him in my room was the worst. I preferred not to speak to him or even look at him. I wondered how we would arrange sharing the bathroom. In a few minutes, I would go into my room and get my sunglasses. I closed my eyes.

When I finally opened my eyes, the sun had moved closer to the water and the pool area below the balcony was half-covered in shade, although the air was still warm and the breeze soft. I was shocked I'd been able to sleep. Since I'd woken that morning I'd felt as if every nerve in my body had become a sharp pin, stabbing at my organs and blood vessels, keeping me constantly anxious, my mind racing in frantic circles.

I sat up, then felt the edges of my vision go slightly dark at the sudden movement. I leaned back, placed my hand on my forehead, and waited for a few seconds. A moment later, I sat up more slowly and swung my legs over the side of the lounge chair. I stood and went to the railing without looking into the room behind me. I had a sense that the man was watching me, but I didn't want to know. I longed to turn around and see that he'd left my room, but I knew that wasn't the case.

Leaning on the railing, I gazed at the people relaxing on cushioned lounge chairs, sitting on the edge of the pool with their legs in the water, standing around the shallow end talking and laughing, and swimming through the narrow channel that led to the swim-up bar.

As my attention drifted across the people enjoying a fabulous vacation, undoubtedly some of them honeymooning couples like Jay and I had been less than twenty-four hours ago, a man wearing a white baseball cap caught my eye. As he walked toward the garden, he turned slightly so I could see the logo on the front.

It was the distinctive, unmistakable gold and brown hawk from the private high school where Jay taught. I felt my heart begin pounding wildly as I gripped the railing. I called his name, but the man kept walking. I shouted after him.

"Jay! Jay!" I waved my arm, leaning over the railing. Several people looked up at me, then turned, trying to see who I might be calling out to.

He must not have heard, with all the splashing and loud talking, as well as the music that played into the pool area.

I flung open the sliding door into the bedroom, grabbed my purse and flip-flops, and raced out through the living area.

"What's wrong?" the man asked. "Where are you going?"

"Stay here." I was out of the room and halfway down the corridor before I heard the door close behind me.

NINE

CHELSEA

By the time I reached the pool area, despite being able to run fast because I was barefoot, the man in the white hat had disappeared. I dropped my flip-flops to the ground and stepped into them. I walked around the pool, weaving in and out of lounge chairs and peeking into covered cabanas. I walked under the canopy of pygmy palms to the pool bar and looked at each person seated there. I went to the garden and searched the entire area, going into private groves with benches where couples sat expecting privacy, not a jittery woman asking if they'd seen a man in a white ball cap.

No one had. I wondered if they would even remember. I wondered if they would tell me, preferring not to get involved.

For the next hour, I wandered around the garden and pool, and walked out to the beach. I searched for the man in the white hat, knowing it couldn't be Jay, because if it was, he would have come to our suite immediately. He would have taken me in his arms and held me so close I would hardly be able to breathe. He would have kissed me long and deep and told me everything that had happened. He would have thrown that man out of our room, called the police, had him arrested.

Then we would have locked ourselves away for the rest of our trip—treasuring what we had more than we'd ever dreamed possible.

Instead, I was stumbling around like a zombie, like a woman trolling the pool for a man to hook up with.

How had someone gotten ahold of Jay's hat? The chance that another person from Jay's school was staying at this resort was beyond believability. Unless someone from our wedding had stayed longer without mentioning it? I didn't think so. Was his hat still in our room?

I hurried back up the stairs and along the corridor.

Inside, I heard the shower. I went into the bedroom and opened the closet. I searched the shelves and Jay's suitcase. I went through the dresser drawers. It wasn't there. I returned to the living area, but all the tables were open with a single shelf or no storage space at all. There was no place else it could be. When Jay left, wherever he'd gone, he'd worn the hat.

I flopped onto the armchair, not wanting to sit on the couch where the man would be sleeping.

When he came out of the bathroom, his hair was wet and combed. He was freshly shaven. He wore cream-colored slacks and a white collared short-sleeved shirt. "Our dinner reservation is at seven. I thought I'd shower now so you can have the bathroom to yourself."

Of course, he knew. He seemed to know everything. Jay and I had reservations for a luau that evening, including a show with music and hula dancing.

"No."

"You haven't eaten all day. I'm worried about you," he said.

"You have no idea what I've done all day." He was right. I hadn't eaten, but he didn't know that. And thinking about it, I was now famished. Maybe I wasn't thinking clearly because of it. But there was no way I was sitting across from this stranger, good-looking as he was, and letting him pretend we were married, letting him feed me stories from my life that he'd managed to steal from my text messages or social media or something, so he could present himself as my husband for some reason I couldn't begin to understand.

And all the while, I looked into those eyes with their veil of false kindness and wondered if he'd done something horrible to Jay. If he'd murdered him in cold blood. And when I had those thoughts, I wondered if I was out of my mind to let him stay in my room. But what choice did I have? It was that or return home. And I wasn't going home without Jay.

"Are you okay?" he asked.

I glared at him.

"You look scared."

I walked into the bedroom, closed the door, and locked it. I lay on the bed, staring at the slowly rotating ceiling fan, letting my lower legs hang over the end of the bed. I placed my hand on my belly and felt it rumble. I needed to eat. If I went to dinner with him, was it possible I could break through his cast iron wall of pretense? Maybe a few glasses of wine would throw him off his game.

Without giving it much thought, I grabbed a dress out of the closet. I went into the bathroom, locking the door that opened into the living area as well as the one to the bedroom, just to be sure. By the time I was showered and dressed, I was so hungry, I wasn't sure I could walk to the restaurant. There were snacks in the minibar, but I didn't want to admit to him how hungry I was. I returned to the bathroom and drank a glass of tap water, hoping it would keep me going until we were seated at our table and I could eat a slice of bread, if they even served bread for a luau.

There wasn't any bread, but they served poi as a starter. It wasn't the most appetizing dip on the planet, if you could call it dip. It had a gritty, bland taste. But I was famished, and to me, it tasted like the creamiest, most flavorful dip I'd ever enjoyed.

As we made our way through kālua pig and chicken long rice, Molokai sweet potatoes and so much other food it rivaled the most lavish Thanksgiving dinner, I kept our wineglasses constantly full. As he gazed at me like a lovesick puppy, I hammered him with questions.

"Where's Jay?"

"Do you like the pork? I think it's the best I've ever tasted."

"I asked you a question," I said. "Where's my husband? Is he hurt?"

"I'm right here." He gave me a tender smile.

"Why are you pretending to be my husband? It's driving me insane. Do you think I'm stupid enough to believe you?" I took a large swallow of wine, letting it soothe the frustration that grew with each question to which I received a non-answer. I took another sip of wine. I wanted to drown my thoughts, wash away my feelings and my fears with wine and maybe a few more drinks after that.

"Let's enjoy our dinner," he said.

"How do you know so much about my life? Did you hack my social media? Or—"

"Why can't you relax?" He placed his hand on the table, reaching for mine.

I pulled my hand well out of his reach. I took hold of my wineglass and swallowed all that was left in the glass. I picked up the bottle and splashed in some more.

"I'm worried about you. I hate seeing you so stressed out. It isn't supposed to be like this."

I took another sip of wine. The room around me was slightly blurred. Even the man's face was blurring before my eyes. I squinted. Was I stressed out? Was this Jay, and I was losing my mind like the resort manager and the police officer said? It didn't seem possible. I would know my own husband. I laughed.

He smiled, as if my laugh meant I was relaxed.

I felt like I was living in some strange alternate reality, talking to someone who couldn't hear what I was saying and was responding to different questions than those I was asking.

He ordered another bottle of wine. I knew I should say no, but it tasted so good, it felt so good. It made my thoughts stop racing like wild, screaming rats, tearing at my sanity. It did help me relax. He was right. I needed to relax. No one believed me, and if I sounded hysterical, they never would.

After the bottle was opened, a resort photographer came to the table wanting to take our picture. I declined. The man said yes, absolutely. He moved his chair around closer to mine. I leaned away and turned my head so the back of it was facing him.

"Is this a bad time?" the photographer asked. "You must be in trouble, man." He laughed. "What did you do to make this beautiful lady treat you this way?"

His voice was loud, cheerful. The couple at the next table looked at us. I wasn't sure whether I wanted to make a scene to draw attention to the fact that Jay was missing, or if I was worried that something might happen to me—would they force me to leave the resort if I did?

I turned slightly and offered a tiny smile to the camera. The photographer snapped three pictures. He promised to send prints to our room.

When he was gone, I poured more wine and took a large gulp. Maybe the photograph would be useful at some point. I could use it with the police if they found anything on the security footage showing Jay. Or I could get my wedding photos sent. The thought made me feel better and I took a few more sips of wine. My shoulders relaxed. I felt the tension easing away from the muscles in my face that had been rigid as iron bands all day. My gritted teeth eased away from each other.

"I have something for you." The man smiled and placed a

small box wrapped in dark gray paper with a black bow in the center of the table.

My jaw tightened again. I nudged the box away from me. "No thank you."

"I bought it for you."

"I don't want it."

"You don't even know what's inside."

"It doesn't matter."

"Please open it," he said.

I took another sip of wine and looked toward the area where the hula dancers were gathering for the show.

"Chelsea."

I ignored him.

He sighed. From the corner of my eye, I saw that wounded, hurt puppy look again. "I'll open it for you." He pulled the ribbon loose, letting it fall onto the table in a way that seemed seductive. Had he intended that?

He tore the paper to reveal a small jewelry box. He popped open the lid and showed me a black pearl necklace on a gold chain.

In spite of myself, I gasped.

I'd spent fifteen or twenty minutes admiring the black pearl jewelry the day after Jay and I had arrived at the resort. If Jay had given me this beautiful necklace, it would have brought tears to my eyes. Two days ago, I would have lifted it out of the box with tender care, opened the clasp, and placed it around my neck. I might have worn it every day for the remainder of our honeymoon. It was breathtaking. The thought that Jay had known the one piece of jewelry in the several shops we'd visited that touched my soul would have taken my breath away.

Now, I felt a tremor of fear run through me.

"Do you like it?" the man asked.

I couldn't speak. I loved it. I hated it. I hated him. I wasn't putting it on. I wouldn't even touch it. I wanted to break the pearl off the chain and toss it into the pool of water that stood between our table and where the hula dancers were now swaying gracefully with the music.

I wouldn't give him the satisfaction of knowing he'd chosen the exact necklace I'd admired. I wouldn't give him that power over me. Yet, he already knew I loved the necklace. He already possessed all the power.

TEN

CHELSEA

The moment we entered my room, I told the man he needed to use the bathroom because I would be locking the door after that. I thought that might cause him to push back in some way, to let his kindhearted, solicitous demeanor slip with a fleeting look of disgust. I was wrong. He looked sad, disappointed, slightly hurt, even. But there wasn't a trace of anger that I could detect.

Once I was in the bedroom with the bathroom, bedroom, and balcony doors secured, I got ready for bed. Before I slipped beneath the covers, I placed the knife I'd bought under my pillow.

I'd hoped all the wine I'd consumed with dinner, along with so much heavy food, would lull me to sleep, at least for a little while, but as my head sank into the pillow, my eyes opened. I found myself watching the blades of the ceiling fan turn slowly, their outline barely visible in the darkness.

Without a doubt, this had been the most horrifying day of my life. How had I gone from the best to the worst? Even my accident wasn't this awful, painful and terrifying as it had been. All that I'd gone through in my job—the pressure to go against everything I knew was right, the utter lack of concern for the employees in our company, the way they were treated like easily disposable robots, while I was expected to eviscerate my own humanity, didn't come anywhere close to this.

Was the cop right? Had there been drugs at my wedding? Our wedding was the first time I'd met Jay's friends from Southern California. Had one or two of them introduced drugs into our drinks without me knowing? Was it possible they lingered in my system and I was suffering an elaborate hallucination? But I didn't feel off in any other way. I'd been tipsy from champagne. Other than that, I was lucid through our entire reception and all through our wedding night. So that couldn't be it. Unless Jay himself had slipped something into my glass when we drank champagne in our room.

But why would he do that? Could he be the one behind *all* of this? Was this man who had woken up beside me a friend of Jay's? All of this a horrible, unbelievably cruel prank? That would explain how this man knew so much about Jay, so much about me. But Jay would never. He wasn't that kind of person. Was he? And wouldn't I feel something if I'd been drugged? Other than unrelenting fear and a constant state of confusion, I didn't feel any different than usual. I couldn't believe that about the man I loved. Despite my mother's fears and anxieties and downright paranoia when I'd first met him, I knew Jay. I'd gotten to know him extremely well during the weeks we'd chatted online. We clicked the moment we met in person. I'd visited his family in LA when we got engaged. We'd spent time together in the real world. Ours wasn't an online-only relationship where he could have easily duped me.

I refused to believe he was keeping secrets from me, refused to believe he was behind this. Even though a prank sort of made sense when I thought about all the things that had happened since I'd woken up hours ago to the most horrifying moment I'd ever experienced.

Maybe it was my brain itself. Some sort of lingering setback from my accident. Had the stress of the wedding caused the damage from the concussion to somehow temporarily rewire my brain? Was I in some delusional state, thinking the man in the other room wasn't Jay, when indeed he *was*?

Exhausted by my thoughts, not wanting to believe any of the things I was considering, I got out of bed. I slipped into leggings and a T-shirt. I grabbed the knife, my purse, my flip-flops, and slipped quietly out of my room through the bathroom and out into the moist night air.

In the resort lobby, I found one bar still open. I ordered a vodka and cranberry juice. I went out by the pool, sat on a large wooden chair, and took a sip of cold, soothing liquid. I leaned back and closed my eyes. The tropical air brushed the skin of my face and arms.

After a few minutes, I opened my eyes. I sat up straighter and took a few more sips before placing the drink on the table beside me. The thoughts that had been swimming in my head while I tried to sleep pushed their way back to the surface. I ignored them as best I could. I didn't want to believe Jay would do any of those terrible things. And I didn't want to believe my own brain was tormenting me. Not now. Not after all this time.

I looked up at the balcony outside my suite. The glass doors were dark. I was glad I hadn't woken the man when I'd left. It was hard to move around the rooms, to find any solitude with him constantly trying to please me, asking how I was feeling, behaving as if we were a couple on our honeymoon. I wanted to smack his face and tell him to stop acting like I was the most clueless woman on earth. Did he really think I was so stupid I'd believe he was the man I'd married?

I picked up my drink and took a long swallow of vodka and cranberry juice, feeling it rush through my body, calming my thoughts for a moment.

As I stared at the deserted balconies of my building, some of the rooms still softly lit, I tried to focus my thoughts on what I should do next. I was upset that I hadn't heard back from the police officer. Had they even started looking at the security footage? I supposed there might be a lot of it. I had no idea how many cameras might be on the property. I'd seen some near the lobby door and I could see one now directed at the pool area, but I hadn't made a survey of the entire resort.

I also needed to get to a store so I could replace my phone. Soon.

I picked up my drink and took a few sips. As my vision blurred, a light came on in the main room of my suite. I saw the man's shadow moving around inside. He approached the bifold doors, opening one and looking out at the night sky. I took another sip of my drink, squinting up at the shadowy figure.

There was something about the way he was standing. The man was more muscular than Jay. At least I thought he was. Maybe not. I couldn't be sure. The figure at the window was slimmer, his build identical to Jay's.

Was it him?

ELEVEN

CHELSEA

One Year Ago

Jay gave me good vibes the moment I saw his photo, read his profile, and then did a quick Google search. The photo, the name, and the things he'd written all checked out with what I read elsewhere. He was who he said. It was close to miraculous in this world of catfishing and other malicious games.

From the start, it felt as if Jay and I had a connection. Both of us cared about helping other people. Confined to my childhood home while I recuperated in bed and then went through grueling physical therapy after my accident while doing my fair share of moping that I'd had to take a one-year leave from law school, my laptop and phone felt like my only connection to the world. It was felt as if I'd been tossed back to the days of the pandemic, interacting with people through a screen, except for my parents, Bella, Katherine, and my physical therapist.

Every time my mother knocked on my bedroom door to ask if I wanted a cup of tea, a snack, or to tell me dinner was ready, she had a comment to make about my online activity.

He could be a serial killer, Chelsea.

She seemed to think serial killers were behind every tenth social media account, and chatting with unsuspecting women like me was the way they chose their victims.

What if he's after your money?

"I didn't post our family's financial profile on my account," I told her.

He can figure it out. He knows where you live.

I explained that I hadn't told him right away. We'd built up a level of trust. We knew each other. We'd had long, deep, sometimes intense conversations. We hadn't just chatted about movies and pop culture. We'd talked on the phone. For hours. We'd had video calls. I could read his expressions.

You can't know for sure.

And my favorite. The one that was so insulting, and really had no logical response—*Are you sure it's smart?*

Apparently my college degree, my career in high tech, and my acceptance to law school along with a successful first year, had left my mother thinking I might not be very *smart*.

My mom and I were so close. I respected her opinions, hers and my dad's both. But I was especially close to my mom. Maybe partially because I was an only child, but also because she was easy to talk to. She'd always supported me, listened to me without judgment, and since I'd turned eighteen, she'd treated me, more or less, like her peer. Except for this. Since I'd left for college, we'd been like friends more than mother and daughter. She used the internet and email. She used social media on a somewhat regular basis. But some aspects of the online world baffled her, and meeting a potential life partner was one of them.

"It seems so risky," she said.

"No riskier than meeting someone in real life. Anyone can lie to you."

She agreed this was a possibility, but I could see in her eyes she didn't truly believe it.

"Why is he looking for a relationship on the internet?" she asked. "Why can't he meet women at work? Or in his other activities?"

"I'm doing the same," I said.

"You're confined. And honestly, I don't like that you're doing this. After such a bad breakup, maybe you need some space."

"Maybe. I only did it for fun. But Jay and I clicked. I'm not going to walk away from that."

"It seems like you're getting so serious with someone you don't even know."

"I do know him."

"You don't. Not really. Eighty percent of communication is non-verbal. Haven't you heard that?"

I had. "We video chat."

"It's not the same, Chelsea. You're a smart girl. Don't blow smoke at me."

I laughed. One minute I was not smart, now I was.

"Maybe we should do a background check. If you can get a few—"

"I'm not doing a background check."

"Why not? It seems reasonable. In fact, if he has nothing to hide, he shouldn't mind that. Would you object if he wanted to do one on you?"

"I wouldn't like it."

"Why not?"

"It's obnoxious."

"I think it would be the smart thing to do. Just to be safe. The internet is a dangerous place. You've seen those documentaries about—"

"I've seen the documentaries, Mom. I trust him. And I'm not marrying him. Yet." I laughed.

She gasped softly. "Are you thinking about it?"

"Obviously, I would meet him first. Spend time together."

"Oh, Chelsea. I don't know."

I closed my computer slowly and firmly. "What don't you know?"

"On a schoolteacher's salary. I worry he might be interested in our money." She sat on the foot of my bed, smoothing the comforter that didn't need smoothing. She pressed her fingers into the soft, feather-filled fabric as if they were sinking into a nest. She looked down at her hands, studying the two-carat diamond on her left ring finger. "Can you see that?" she whispered.

"I don't see that at all. He didn't know we had money when we started talking."

"You don't know that. You have no idea what he knew about you when you met. Maybe he'd already searched for you. Maybe he'd looked into *your* background. It just makes me uncomfortable."

"This is how people meet now. It's perfectly safe. Bella met her last two boyfriends online."

"And look what happened."

"Lots of people break up. No matter where they meet. Kristi met Jake online."

She said nothing. She couldn't because my friend from high school, Kristi, who lived three houses away, was getting married in two months. And Kristi's whole family loved the guy. My mom had met Jake at their engagement party, and *she* loved him.

"I just worry." She stood and moved toward my bedroom door. Seeing her standing there as she had when I was teenager, me sitting on my bed doing homework as I was now, without the homework part, made me feel frustrated that the accident had so completely derailed my life and all my plans. I didn't like living at home, but I'd needed their help with cooking and dressing and overall life tasks. I hadn't been able to drive for three solid months after the accident.

"Why don't you trust me? Wait until you meet him. And then decide what you think. It's not fair to be so suspicious when you don't even know him. You're basing all your fears on the worst stories you've heard. And those stories aren't from people you know. They're from strangers."

"Fair enough." She smiled, trying to make her face appear relaxed and accepting. She failed with her expression, but at least she succeeded with her words.

"Just be careful. And maybe don't spend so much time online."

That was easy for her to say. She wasn't taking pain meds that forbid her from getting behind the wheel of a car. She wasn't sitting around all day knowing her classmates were moving on without her, headed toward degrees and the bar exam. She wasn't tormented by crazy dreams, dreams that sometimes lingered into the day, taking on the form of reality, the result of a terrifying accident, a concussion, and those same drugs that kept me trapped in the house unless I asked my mother for a ride. But a ride to where?

TWELVE

CHELSEA

The pounding inside my chest made me certain my body was telling me the shadowy figure I saw in my room was Jay. This was a visceral reaction to seeing the man I loved. Even though my mind was full of doubts and questions, my body knew.

I grabbed my purse and flip-flops and skittered around the edge of the pool. Once I was out of the pool area, I ran as fast as I could, my bare feet slapping the concrete, then sliding across damp grass as I cut through the palm trees to shorten the distance back to the building where my room was located.

I took the stairs two at a time and raced along the corridor. I shoved the key card into the slot too hard. The electronic eye couldn't read it. I pulled the card out and tried again, more carefully this time. The light turned green, and the lock clicked.

Inside, the room was dark again. I pressed the switch, flooding the room with light. No one was standing at the window. The stranger was lying on the couch, the blankets pulled up to his chest, breathing deeply. Was he faking sleep? I'd thought I made a lot of noise fiddling with the door, but his breathing remained steady, and his body hadn't shifted at all.

I went into the bedroom, turning on the light. The room

was empty, as was the bathroom. I stepped onto the balcony, even though I could clearly see no one was out there. I returned to the bedroom and collapsed onto my bed, crying.

Either I'd been hallucinating, or the man had woken, looked out at me, then gone back to bed. I didn't want to bother checking whether he was faking sleep. What difference did it make?

After all my tears had spilled out, I got up, turned off the light in the main room, closed and locked my bedroom door, and tugged off my clothes, dropping them onto the floor. I crawled into bed, taking the knife with me. I tucked it under the pillow and lay in the dark, waiting for my heartbeat to return to normal. I wondered if it ever truly would.

* * *

The sky was just starting to turn light when I woke. I found my fingers curled around the knife handle. When I released it, they were stiff and cramped. The nightmare of the previous day hit me as if someone had punched me in the face the moment I was conscious.

I got up and went out to the balcony, gazing at the ocean, stunned by the contrast between the beauty surrounding me and darkness inside my mind. I couldn't believe this was happening to me. I didn't understand if it was something inside my own mind, or some elaborate game or prank someone was playing on me. Did someone hate me this much they would want to destroy my honeymoon, my sanity?

I took a deep breath, inhaling the aroma of tropical flowers, and went back inside, determined once again to do everything I could to find out what was going on without allowing myself to dissolve into tears and despair.

Before I could get to the bathroom, I heard the shower running. He was up, ready to torment me again with his gentle smiles and concerned eyes. I rolled my own eyes, smiling at myself. At least I still had my sense of humor. I gathered my clothes, then picked up the handset on the bedside phone.

It was three hours ahead back home in California. I dialed Bella's number.

"Hey. It's Chelsea."

"Hi. Are you still... What's going on?"

"Yes. That guy is still pretending he's Jay. He must think I'm a complete idiot."

She laughed, although she sounded nervous, as if she wasn't sure I thought it was funny. I didn't.

"Will you stay on top of your email?" I asked. "As soon as I have my shower and some coffee, I'm going to email you the resort manager's contact info so you can send some pics of me and Jay. I need something to prove to them this guy isn't Jay. Because of his fake ID, the cop, and the resort staff, don't believe me."

"Absolutely," Bella said. "I'm glad I can help. It's so awful. I don't even know what to say! I'll find some photos right now so they're ready to go."

I hung up quickly. I wanted to tell her everything, but I didn't want to be overheard. And I wasn't sure I could tell her how I was feeling without breaking down again. I needed to focus on trying to make something happen. She wouldn't be able to make any more sense of it than I could. If she was there, if we could sit down with a glass of wine, or three, it would have made me feel so much better, but trying to talk over a landline, tied to the nightstand by a cord, knowing he was on the other side of the doors, knowing she might be interrupted at any minute, I just couldn't.

When I was ready to leave, I opened the doors into the other room. He was seated on the couch, the blankets folded neatly at one end. He wore a Hawaiian-print shirt, black shorts, and flip-flops.

"What should we do today?" he asked.

"Nothing."

He smiled. "Did you have a rough night? Maybe after breakfast you'll feel better." He stood. "We can decide what to do while we're eating. I thought we'd—"

"I'm not having breakfast with you. And I'm not spending the day with you. I have to find out what happened to my husband. Unless you're planning to tell me. That would save a lot of time."

He shoved his hands in his pockets. "Aren't you hungry?"

I went to the door and walked out. I wanted it to slam closed behind me, but it was designed to close slowly and softly, so I let it do its thing.

After stopping at the front desk to pick up a business card for Shep, I grabbed a large coffee and a croissant from a kiosk. I took them to the business center. The sign on the door said no food or drinks, but the place was empty, so I took my mini breakfast inside, glad that I'd picked up plenty of napkins to catch the flakes that would inevitably fall off the croissant.

Within five minutes of sending my email to Bella, before I'd eaten half the croissant, she'd sent an email to Shep, copying me. Attached to her message were four photographs of Jay and me. Two were taken at our engagement party—one with us and my parents, one with his parents. There was a shot of us with Bella at an outdoor restaurant, shaded by an umbrella. We'd all taken off our sunglasses for the photograph. I appreciated her attention to that important detail. The last was a close-up of Jay and me taken right after we were married.

She was brilliant. If she was beside me, I would have thrown my arms around her and kissed her hard on both cheeks. I logged out of the email, grabbed my food and went to look for Shep.

I had to wait fifteen minutes before he was available to see me. He studied the photographs for several minutes. He closed the email and looked at me, his eyes full of sympathy.

"I don't know. They both—"

"They don't *both* anything. Do I need to go get him so you can compare?"

He held up his hands. "Please calm down. I just don't think it's clear. People can look different in photographs, and he said—"

"Are you out of your mind? You need to call the police. This isn't the same person."

The man in my room had the same hair color as Jay, and from a distance they might look similar—the same skin tone, and a few other traits that made them resemble each other at a casual glance, but that was it.

Forty-five minutes later, Officer Almi arrived. He looked at the photos. "It's hard to say. I need—"

"I'll go get him." I started to leave the room.

"Hold on," Officer Almi said. "That's not the only issue here."

"What's the *issue*?" I asked. Watching their expressions, I felt a headache puncture the left side of my head, a sharp, sudden stab of pain. It spread across my scalp. The alcohol from the night before seemed to flood back across my brain, making everything foggy. What were they seeing in those pictures that I couldn't see? I rubbed my eyes, trying to think. "Have you finished looking at the security footage?" I asked.

"One thing at a time," he said.

He and Shep moved away, studying the images on Shep's phone. Their heads were close together as they spoke in lowered voices. Were they deliberately trying to prevent me from hearing?

What did they need to discuss? The man in my room was not Jay. If they couldn't see that in the photograph, they should be asking me to get the man and bring him to the lobby. The police officer should be talking to *me*. He should be explaining what they were going to do to get him out of my room. He should be discussing the investigation into looking for my missing husband.

Finally, the police officer walked back to where I was standing.

"What's going on? Why are you whispering?" I asked. "I don't appreciate how I'm being treated. My husband could be lying in a ditch, unconscious, or—"

"We aren't whispering," he said. "I was simply checking to see that the credit card on file at the resort belonged to Jay Davis. I wanted to ask about the reservation and check-in. We're still trying to verify your story, so you need to be patient."

"Don't patronize me! I've been patient. My husband is missing and a strange man snuck into my room. Into my bed! You're acting as if it's nothing."

"Unfortunately, we still can't verify your story, Mrs. Davis. The photographs don't prove anything. They—"

"I'm literally wearing a wedding gown standing next to a man in a tuxedo who is not the man in my room!"

"That doesn't prove he's Jay Davis. You might have been married before. We have no way—"

"There are dates in the photos' metadata!"

"Yes. We can have our technical experts check that. But even if that's the case, it does not prove this man is Jay Davis. The man I've met presented ID for Jay Davis, and credit cards in that name. At this point, I have no reason to doubt he's who he claims to be. He's calm and respectful and pleasant. To be honest, Mrs. Davis, you've come across as a little overtired and confused. You have to understand; your story is very difficult to believe. I'm sorry."

"Are you going to look at the security footage?"

"Yes, ma'am."

"Are you going to look for the man in these photographs? He's missing."

"I can't do that, because I don't have a name."

I'd promised myself that morning I wouldn't cry. I hadn't promised I wouldn't scream, and that's what I wanted to do. At the same time, I didn't want to get kicked out of the resort. Or worse, arrested. And this cop was so stubborn and full of himself, absolutely certain he was right, it wouldn't surprise me if he chose to do exactly that.

THIRTEEN
ANONYMOUS

It was easy to lure the groom out of the honeymoon suite.

When you know a lot about a person, it's not that difficult to pull a few strings and get them dancing like a marionette. If you're good at it, no one else can see the strings. Their legs kick and run. Their arms wave and their head bobs. Their entire body moves to your will. They come to life, looking as if they're moving of their own volition, hardly realizing themselves that you're tugging gently on one string and then the other.

All it took was a simple phone call, a suggestion of a problem, planting a seed of fear.

I knew he would willingly wake himself in the darkest hour two nights after his wedding. He would creep out of bed, leaving his bride in a blissful dream, unaware that she'd never see him again.

He would pull on his jeans and a T-shirt. He would sneak out of the room to the most important meeting of his life, the final meeting of his life.

I saw him walking toward me long before he saw me.

He knew who he was meeting, of course. He wouldn't have come if I hadn't given him a very good reason. He thought he knew what I wanted, what I was going to tell him. But he had no idea what the truth was.

He wasn't as naïve as the bride, of course. But he didn't know what he was walking into.

I liked knowing I could surprise him.

I've had too many surprises in my life. Now, it's my turn to deliver surprises to others. It makes me feel in control. After a lifetime of feeling like everyone else controlled my life and the things that happened to me, I'm finally the one calling the shots.

FOURTEEN
CHELSEA

The cop put his hand on my arm in an attempt to guide me to the small gate that led behind the reception counter. "Why don't we call your husband and—"

I shrugged his hand off, batting at it like a large tropical insect was creeping up my arm. "He's not my husband."

"Let's get the *other party* down here and we can wrap this up."

"I don't want it wrapped up. My husband is missing and you're treating this like I'm hysterical and don't know what I'm talking about." I hated the shrill tone in my voice. Every time I spoke, the volume and panic in my voice gave them more evidence that I was the one who was unstable and not to be believed.

"Okay. Take it easy. Let's go into the back where we can have some privacy and we'll talk about the security footage."

I shrugged his hand off for a second time, then marched ahead of him and into the small conference room where we'd met the day before.

"Please take a seat," the cop said.

"I'll stand."

Shep had followed us. He was on his cell phone. Calling my room, I assumed.

"Hi. This is Shep Campbell, the resort manager. Yes. Good morning to you, sir. Your wife is—"

"I'm not his *wife!*"

Shep continued as if I hadn't shouted over him. "—the police have reviewed the security footage, and it would be helpful if you could come to the conference room where we met yesterday." He paused, longer than necessary.

I wondered what the man was saying about me. I wanted to grab the phone out of Shep's hand. The silence continued, increasing my rage.

"Okay. Thanks. See you in a minute."

After the man arrived and we were seated at the table, I learned immediately that the trip to the conference room, closing the door, and sitting down, had all been completely unnecessary.

"There were no images captured of the man you say left your room at some time between midnight and seven a.m.," Officer Almi said. "There are no images of any solitary men."

"That's not possible."

"With all due respect, Mrs. Davis, your response is evidence that you're having an... I guess I would call it, I'm not a psychiatrist, or an expert by any means, but a psychological episode of some kind. You're arguing with solid evidence. There were no images on any of the security cameras we checked."

I managed to hold back the tears gathering behind my eyes. "Did you check all of them?" How could Jay have vanished into thin air? It wasn't possible. I wanted to accuse him of lying, but that would make things worse.

The man tried to place his hand over mine.

I yanked my hand away as if he'd placed a glowing piece of coal on the back of it.

"That was a poor choice of words on my part," the officer

said. "Yes, we checked all of them. There are no cameras outside any of the guestrooms, but we checked all the perimeter cameras."

"The day after our wedding, Jay and I had brunch with our families. We enjoyed the first day of our honeymoon. When I woke the next morning, Jay was gone and this guy was in my bed! Why can't you understand how serious this is?"

"Your husband mentioned you haven't been sleeping well."

"He's not my *husband*! He was only in my room, *my* room, for one night, half a night. He knows nothing about how I slept."

Shep stood. "I should get back to work. Can you handle this from here?" He looked at the officer, acting as if I no longer existed. The officer nodded and Shep went out, leaving the door ajar, to signal we should be wrapping things up soon.

As if the resort manager hadn't kicked me to the curb, and as it were an agreed-upon fact that I wasn't sleeping well, the officer continued. "And you haven't been eating. Lack of food and sleep can sometimes cause hallucinations. Jay suggested he would take you to an urgent care clinic for an assessment regarding whether you're experiencing a stress reaction." He stood, pushed in his chair, and began backing toward the door.

I leaned over the table, placing my hand on it, palms down. "My husband is missing! He could be dead!"

Officer Almi cleared his throat. "I know when my daughter got married... young women spend their lives looking forward to and planning their weddings. When the event arrives, their stress is off the charts. And—"

"Stop," I said. "Stop talking. That's not what this is. I'm not a child. I'm not a little girl playing princess."

"I understand. But I've exhausted our resources."

"This is unacceptable," I said.

He held up his hands. "I know you're frustrated and upset. But without any solid evidence, I've done all I can. If you can provide some proof of identity or a missing person report from the mainland…" He backed into the doorway. "I hope you can relax and enjoy our beautiful island." He gave me a grim smile, turned, and walked out the door.

The imposter moved closer to me. He reached out as if he meant to put his arm around my shoulder. "Maybe visiting a drop-in clinic isn't such a bad idea. They could give you something to help you—"

"Stop talking." I shoved past him and walked out of the room, taking long strides that made my legs feel strong and purposeful, even if the rest of my body felt as if all my bones were collapsing.

I went to the business center, leaving my paper coffee cup on the conference room table and the man sitting alone with his fantasy that I would trot along after him to a clinic where someone could assess my stress from getting married. It felt as if this cop had just stepped out of the 1800s. Did he think I had the vapors? Would he advise the resort to provide a fainting couch in my suite?

With adrenaline driving me harder than the shot of caffeine from my extra-large cup of Kona coffee, I opened the email from Bella and printed all four photographs, agreeing to the cost presented on the screen before I could print a color document on the high-quality printer behind me. I also printed a copy of the man's fake driver's license that the police officer had sent me only after I demanded it.

I took the photographs and went out to the pool closest to the building where my suite was located. I flopped down on one of the few remaining lounge chairs. The area was filling quickly now that it was mid-morning on another picture-perfect day. I placed the printouts face-down on my lap and closed my eyes.

It was unlikely many of the guests would have seen Jay,

since we'd only been there a few days before the wedding, but it wasn't impossible. If Shep hadn't conceded his responsibilities to the cop, he should have suggested showing the photographs to the entire staff. But like the cop, he clearly didn't believe what I'd told him. I refused to call it a *story*, which they kept labeling it, even in my own mind.

This wasn't a story. It was my life. It was something that happened to me, something that was happening still. A horrible series of events. Jay was missing, definitely injured and unable to get in touch with me, most likely unconscious, and possibly dead, although I was trying with all my strength not to think that. I couldn't think that. I was not going to allow myself to entertain those thoughts. I was going to focus on finding him, as my mother had suggested. I was going to give him all my positive energy and thoughts. There was nothing to be gained in thinking the worst before I was forced to.

At the same time, the police officer and Shep should have been taking this seriously. Just because that man had one piece of ID, because he was calm and gracious and good-looking, they assumed every word out of his mouth was the truth. They assumed every word out of mine was the shriek of a hysterical female, a bride who was stressed out and strung out from the thrill of wearing a white dress and having a ring slipped onto her finger.

I opened my eyes and felt immediately that my luck had changed.

The server standing at the foot of my lounge chair had worked at our wedding reception. She smiled. "Can I get you anything to eat or drink?"

"Hi." I sat up so I could see her name tag more clearly. "Hi, Alison. Remember me? Chelsea? Jay and I were married here the day—"

"Of course, I remember you. You were such a beautiful

bride. I loved working at your wedding. It had a great vibe. You two are..." She pressed her hand to her heart.

I placed the printed photographs of Jay on the lounge chair. Beside them I placed a printout I'd made of the false driver's license. I told her the insanely complicated story as quickly as I could, glancing around to be sure no one was trying to get her attention for a drink or a morning snack.

She put her hand over her mouth as I talked. When I was finished, she took it away. "That's terrible. And so scary." She spoke in a whisper, as if the man might be standing nearby, ready to attack both of us. "That's the weirdest thing I've ever heard. I've heard a lot of really weird stories here, but yours is almost impossible to believe. So scary." She looked over her shoulder.

"Do you see that this guy isn't the man I married?"

"Absolutely." She nodded her head several times. "So creepy. I don't see how that could happen. I wonder where your husband is? It's hard to believe this guy could pretend he's your husband."

"You believe me, right?"

"Oh, absolutely. You were the cutest couple. I wouldn't forget you that fast." She laughed. Her voice trembled slightly. "What are you going to do?"

"Maybe you can help me."

She took a step back. "I don't see how."

I wasn't sure how she could either, now that I'd said it. What did I expect her to do? It felt good having someone believe me. At least I didn't feel like I was losing my mind. At least one other person on this island admitted to having seen Jay. She wasn't acting as if he was a figment of my imagination.

"Yesterday, I thought I saw him. He teaches at a private school. And I saw someone wearing a baseball cap like his, from that school. Which would be a huge coincidence. Have you seen anyone wearing a white hat with a gold and brown hawk?"

She shook her head.

"You're sure?"

"I don't remember that. But when I get busy, I don't always notice every detail about people. It's so scary. And so creepy that that guy is in your room. I'm sorry there aren't any other rooms. I wish I could help. But no one listens to the serving staff." She gave me a defeated smile.

"I'm glad you believe me."

"Of course, I believe you. It's so terrible. I hope your husband isn't—" She put her hand over her mouth again.

My throat felt so tight, I couldn't say anything.

She took my silence as an opportunity to take a few more steps away from me. "Did you... Do you want something to drink? You could probably use a cocktail." She laughed.

"An iced coffee would be good."

"Sure. Absolutely. I'll get that right away." She turned and hurried away.

I leaned back against the chair and closed my eyes. When the coffee came, she didn't ask for my room number. She placed it on the table and whispered *good luck* before hurrying away so fast, it looked as if she was running.

SIXTEEN

CHELSEA

When every gram of caffeine had been sucked out of my iced coffee, including crunching the ice with the milky residue clinging to the small cubes, I placed the glass on the table and left the pool area. I went out to the valet drop-off area and asked them to call an Uber.

Inside the car, I requested a ride to a mobile phone store.

It took a little over an hour to get set up with a new phone, my data downloaded from the cloud, including a backlog of missed text messages, social media updates, and most importantly right now, my photographs from the wedding. Even if no one else believed me, it helped me feel like I was on more solid footing, scrolling through the hundreds of selfies and wedding photos of Jay and me.

Each one of those moments had been real. Jay was real. Our marriage was real, and no matter how many facts this stranger had about our lives, it meant nothing. Even though I couldn't make any sense of what this strange man was doing, whether this was some elaborate con I couldn't figure out, or something even darker, he was not going to manipulate me and break down my sense of reality until I doubted myself and believed his version of the truth over my own, as if this were some kind of brainwashing exercise. He almost seemed to believe that if he repeated his story often enough, with a calm and gentle demeanor, I would start to believe him.

With my new phone tucked inside my purse, my digital life locked behind the security of facial recognition and an access code, I ordered another Uber back to the resort. This time, I was able to relax into the comfortable back seat and look out the window, enjoying the flashes of sparkling sapphire ocean as we passed by the water and the open, sometimes barren landscape burned by lava flow.

The car pulled under the covered entrance and stopped. I opened the door and stepped out, the ride already paid for, the driver tipped and rated the best simply because he'd left me alone in a bubble of silence to enjoy reconnecting with my life and sense of stability.

I closed the car door and started across the driveway, holding my phone in front of me like a precious treasure. As I moved toward the curb, I saw a flash of something racing toward me. I moved to the side, half tripping over my left foot. A young girl on an e-bike, hair flying behind her like ribbons, came so close, the strands of her hair brushed my arm and her elbow, smacked the side of my arm, knocking me farther off balance. I stumbled and my foot caught the curb. My flip-flop twisted, and I fell hard, slamming my shin against the concrete edge. I landed on my hip, gripping my phone, refusing to let it leave my hand. I was not losing two phones as the result of two clumsy people in the space of three days. I would not be that unlucky.

As the pain jolted through my bones, the phone remained solidly between my curved fingers. I smiled at the dark screen, pleased that even though I ached so badly that tears pricked my eyes, I felt semi-victorious. The first good thing that had happened to me in nearly forty-eight hours.

I looked up to see the man from my room standing over me before I heard his voice.

"Where did you go?" He extended his hand to help me up.

I ignored his gesture and his question, adjusted my flip-flop, then pushed myself painfully to my feet.

"Are you okay?" he asked.

I nodded.

"Let me take you to a clinic. I think you should—"

"No." I brushed past him, limping and shuffling toward the entrance. My hip hurt and my shin felt like it had snapped in half, but I knew that once I got moving and the blood flowing, I would probably be fine.

He came up beside me, putting his hand on the center of my back. I twisted away from him. "Don't touch me."

"I want to be sure you didn't seriously injure yourself."

"Jay would not use that word," I said.

He laughed and shook his head. "Let's sit down. You were so lucky. Very lucky."

He looked truly shaken. He tried to guide me toward a bench. "You don't know how seriously you can be hurt from the slightest incident."

"It's not—"

"People become paraplegics from the most minor... even quadriplegics."

I laughed.

He looked as if I'd smacked his face. "It's not something to laugh about."

"I'm not laughing at someone's disability. I'm laughing that you're so upset about a minor bike accident. You need to calm down."

"I want to be sure you're—"

"I'm *fine*." I limped through the opening, past small potted palms, and quickened my pace across the lobby, the man dogging every step as if he was determined to trip me again.

"You should at least visit the medical office here. You need to make sure you didn't break anything."

"I would know if I had."

"Please don't be stubborn."

I was used to pain. This was nothing like the pain I'd lived with in the past. I was certain nothing was broken. At the same time, maybe my bones were more fragile because of my previous accident. I didn't want to admit he was right, but he was. I turned and began walking toward the wing where the business office, resort staff offices, and the medical center were located.

To his credit, he didn't say anything about my change of heart.

The nurse practitioner on duty didn't have X-ray equipment to check out my leg properly, but she didn't believe it was fractured based on the description of my fall and my ability to put weight on it as well as the lack of swelling. A bruise was developing, and I had some abrasions, which she treated. She told me to ice my hip and take ibuprofen if I was uncomfortable, which I could have figured out on my own, but I smiled politely and thanked her for her time.

The man walked beside me as I limped back toward the building where my suite was located, trying to take my elbow in a show of support with every step I took. Finally, I told him he was going to cause another fall with his constant interference.

As I paused on the stairs to rest my legs, he moved to the step above me and looked down. Gone was the charming, easygoing expression he'd worn since I'd first seen his face. His eyes were dark and menacing. "It's not safe for you to leave the resort without me," he said. "Don't do it again."

SEVENTEEN

CHELSEA

Forcing my sore legs to keep moving, I pushed past the man, climbing the stairs one painful step at a time. "Don't be ridiculous. Of course it's safe to leave the resort without you. I'm safer without you than I am with you. My husband didn't go missing until you showed up."

"You need to listen to me. It's not safe."

I laughed. "The e-bike hit me *on* the resort property."

"I'm not talking about the e-bike. It's not safe to leave. You shouldn't go out again unless I'm with you."

We were on the corridor leading to the rooms now so I could move with more ease. "I'm perfectly capable of taking care of myself."

"I want you to stay with me. We're married now, and we should be together."

"We're not married and I'm not staying with you. I have no desire to be with you. The only reason you're in my room is because you refuse to leave and there are no other rooms available for me."

"Please don't leave again without me."

I stopped and faced him. "Why? Is there something you're not telling me?"

"You need to trust your husband."

"Well, you're not my husband. So that argument means nothing." I continued walking, moving as quickly as I could with my bruised shin and aching hip.

When I was a few feet away from my room, I saw a white envelope lying on the mat outside the door. At first, I assumed it was something from the resort, reminding Jay and me of one of the upcoming day trips or special events we'd booked.

Then, as I drew closer, I saw only my name written on the envelope in large blue script. I picked it up.

"What's that?" the man asked.

"How should I know?" I unlocked the door.

I went to the balcony and sat down. Because the man slept in the sitting area, it no longer felt like that part of the suite belonged to me. The balcony, maybe because I wasn't confined by walls and ceiling, felt like neutral territory.

I slid my finger into the opening at the edge of the seal, tore open the flap, and pulled out the card.

EIGHTEEN

CHELSEA

My hands shook as I read the words written on the card.

Chelsea—

I'm so sorry I had to leave you like that.
I know you must be scared, and the last thing I ever want to do is frighten you.
Please trust me. Everything will be okay, just be patient.

Love you forever, J.

With my finger pinching the card so tightly it was creasing across the center, an enormous sob pushed its way out of my chest. I bent forward pressing the card to my chest, wrapping my other arm around myself as I cried with relief. He was alive! He was okay. I had no idea what was going on, no idea where he was or why he'd disappeared from our bed in the middle of the night, but he was alive!

I held the card out and read it again. Then again, my tears falling on the ink, making some of the letters bleed slightly.

Then, a tremor of doubt shot through me. How did I know it was from Jay? It occurred to me that I'd never seen his handwriting, except when we'd signed our marriage license, but that was only a quick scribble of his signature, and I hadn't paid much attention. I'd been filled with excitement, thinking about our reception, distracted by the wedding band I'd slid onto his left ring finger only an hour before. I pushed the doubt away more firmly. Of course it was from him. Who else knew he was missing, aside from the hotel staff and the police officer? The stranger in my room knew, but he was doing everything in his power to convince me *he* was Jay.

The short phrases in the note and the tenderness sounded like Jay.

As my relief that he was alive settled into the core of my heart, questions bubbled up in my mind. Why had he written so few words? Why hadn't he explained anything? Why was he sending a note? I wanted to know where he was, why he'd left, what was going on. It was all so confusing and senseless. If he was in a position and condition that he could write a note to me on expensive stationery, why hadn't he come back to our room himself? In some ways, the note left me even more confused.

That man, standing just a few feet away from me, watching me clutch a notecard as if my entire future rested on those words, sobbing my heart out over this thin offering of hope, knew so much more than he was willing to say. Somehow, he'd gotten ahold of my husband's credit cards. He'd managed to acquire a fraudulent driver's license well before he'd snuck into my room and slithered into my bed while I slept in blissful ignorance.

"What is it?" he asked.

"A note from Jay."

He gave me a kind, but mildly pitying gaze.

"You need to stop this game right now," I said. "Tell me who you are, how you got into my room, and what you know about my husband. Everything. I want to hear how you know so much about us. I want you to tell me what's going on. I'm sick of this game, sick of the gaslighting."

"There's no game."

"I'm not an idiot."

"Of course not."

"Then tell me what's going on."

"I think you're confused. I'm not sure why, but I want to help you."

"You're not helping me. Every minute you refuse to tell me what you know, is another minute my husband could be in more danger. It's another minute that you're making my life more difficult. And when this is over, it won't go well for you."

He leaned his hip against the railing, folding his arms across his chest. "The note isn't from Jay."

"How can you know that? If you know that for a fact, then tell me who wrote it. Tell me where Jay is. Tell me everything right now."

He squatted, placing his hands on my knees.

I twisted violently to the side. "I told you not to touch me."

"Whoever wrote this note is trying to hurt you."

"Meaning, you? Are you saying you wrote it?"

"No. I'm Jay. I wish you would trust me. But I didn't write this. I didn't leave you. I'm here, as I have been all along."

"Don't bullshit me!"

He stood, sighing as he did.

"I'm sick of this!" I shoved myself out of the chair, ignoring the pain that shot through my hip.

"Be careful."

I ignored this warning as well. I turned and rushed through the room, grabbing my purse off the breakfront in the entryway as I went. I flung open the door and burst into the open corridor, breathing deeply, glad to be out of his presence.

I walked down the stairs as quickly as my broken body

would allow and scurried past the pool area. I went out the gate and along the path to the beach.

When I reached the sand, I kicked off my flip-flops and let my bare feet sink into the soft, warm sand. It comforted me, making me feel as if the earth was taking care of me, reassuring me there was something solid beneath my feet, that the waves in front of me and the swaying palms and the constantly moving breeze was carrying me along, clearing the lies and confusion out of my head.

I went to the edge of the water, feeling damp sand and then the water that was such a pleasant temperature compared with the frigid ocean in the San Francisco Bay Area. I walked along the shore until I came to some large, scattered rocks where tiny crabs ran around, trying to hide from my enormous shadow.

Perching on a dry spot on one of the rocks, I stared out at the ocean, losing track of time. I didn't bother to take my phone out of my pocket to check the time or catch up on emails or messages from home.

When I returned to the room, I felt calmer. I desperately hoped he'd gone out as well, but of course, he hadn't. He was still on the balcony. Waiting.

In my rush to escape, in my rage at his refusal to give up the pretense, I'd left the note from Jay behind. And now, it was gone.

I planted my hands on my hips. "Where's the note from my husband?"

"What note?" he asked.

Inside, I felt a cry of grief and rage that wanted to pour out of me, but I was so tired, it couldn't take shape. I turned and went into the bedroom. I closed and locked the door and collapsed onto the bed. My only evidence that Jay was still alive was gone. That man had destroyed it. Now, he was lying to my face, trying to make me believe that the note with Jay's reassuring words had never existed.

NINETEEN
CHELSEA

After crying softly for quite a long time, I finally fell asleep. When I woke, I was curled into a ball in the center of my bed. I went into the bathroom, washed my face, and went out again without speaking to the man.

I was shocked to find the bruise on my shin was dark purple, but the pain was significantly less. The pain in my hip had also lessened even though I'd failed to ice it. Maybe the rest had done it.

In the lobby, I went to the counter and asked to speak to the head of the housekeeping staff. After more discussion than necessary about what I wanted, I was directed to her office. I asked who had been responsible for making up my room that day and explained why I wanted to speak to her.

It was nearly an hour before I was able to connect with Lani. When I asked if she'd seen anyone leave the envelope on the mat outside my room, she shook her head in a firm no. I asked if she would check with the others who cleaned the guest rooms. She said she would, but if anyone had seen a note addressed to a guest, they would have placed it in the room, so she didn't think it was likely they had.

She seemed anxious to get back to work. She sounded as if she didn't want to think or talk about any note that might have been misplaced, worried about being accused of taking something, concerned she or one of her co-workers would be blamed, even though she wasn't sure what for. She kept shaking her head and glancing toward her work cart, edging away from me.

It was the same reaction I'd had from the server who'd worked at our wedding reception, as well as from Shep and Kim. The same response I'd had from the police officer. No one wanted to talk to me. I was a leper to them, a woman who had a cloud of tragedy, or more likely, delusion drifting around her. A woman with a bizarre story that no one truly believed. If it was true, it suggested a crime. It suggested someone stalking me, trying to hurt me. It suggested possible kidnapping, even murder. I gave the impression of being mentally unbalanced. None of those things made anyone want to get involved in my life.

I returned to my room. When I saw the man wasn't there, I breathed a sigh that made my whole body feel at ease. I took a can of tomato juice from the fridge, poured it into a glass, and went onto the balcony. I sat on the lounge chair and opened my phone, feeling comforted by the sight of my text messages and photos, the history of my life in digital form. I felt grounded and real. This wasn't my imagination. That man was *not* my husband!

I opened an email and tried to reconstruct the note. I wanted to remember Jay's words. I wanted to be able to see them in black and white whenever I felt like it. I wanted the comfort of having them readily available so I could remind myself that the note had been real. I'd seen it. I'd read it. I'd heard from Jay, and he'd reassured me he was alive. He had an explanation for what had happened, and soon, he would give me all the details.

After a few tries, I felt like I had most of it. The note had been short, the sentences brief, as his sentences were when he spoke. It wasn't precise, I could feel that it was missing something. Not having the actual document in my hands gave me a creeping anxiety that made it difficult to sit still. But I had most of it, and the act of writing it down reminded me how I'd felt when I'd seen the large white envelope on the mat, how I'd torn it open, how my heart had raced as I'd read the words and known deep in the pit of my stomach that Jay was alive. No matter how crazy I felt and how inexplicable the situation was, everything would be okay.

I emailed the re-created note to myself.

Next, I started a text to Jay's best friend, telling him, in as few words as I could manage, what had happened. I asked if he'd heard from Jay since he'd returned home from our wedding.

He replied immediately.

Not a word.

I gripped the phone, staring at his response. The text message, glaring back at me, shining clearly on the screen cut through all the good feelings I'd had trying to recall the details of Jay's note. If there was something going on that he couldn't yet tell me, if he had some kind of issue with work, or with his family, wouldn't Sean know about it? How could he have heard nothing?

"I thought we agreed we would give up our phones?" The man's voice was loud behind me.

I fumbled the phone but managed to keep my possessive grip on the new device that I wanted to cling to like it was a life preserver, pulling Jay back to me.

That man shouldn't know about our vow. It angered me that he did, and it angered me that he was pretending, yet again, that this was something he and I had done together. I brought my phone closer to my face, tapping through my email, deleting old items just to have something to do.

He moved around so I couldn't avoid seeing his bare feet and tan legs, the hems of his khaki cargo shorts. I kept my head bent low, so I didn't have to see the rest of him.

"Why are you doing this?" he asked. "We're in paradise. Look up and see what's around you."

"I don't need a lecture from you about paradise. You know nothing about me, and I have no interest in anything you have to say."

"I'm worried about you. Is it possible you took your pain medication, then forgot and accidentally had a few drinks? Maybe that's causing your delusional—"

"What?" The phone slipped out of my hands and onto my lap. He couldn't know about my pain medication. It wasn't possible. That meant he knew about my accident. But even more than that, he knew I still had a prescription. And he knew that I'd brought the pain meds on my honeymoon. No one knew that except me and my mother. I hadn't even told Jay.

Those white tablets were a security blanket. I didn't need them anymore. It had been over a year and a half since my accident. With my diligent focus on following the instructions of the physical therapist, with my careful moderation of my medication, never taking more than was advised, and weaning myself even faster than they'd recommended, I was proud of myself. But I still had some intermittent pain. I'd been told that was to be expected.

"I said—"

"I heard what you said."

I'd heard. But how did he *know*? Was this man really Jay and something was so broken inside my brain that I didn't recognize him? Was it possible I was experiencing some completely inexplicable ongoing hallucination? It wasn't any more bizarre than the story I'd been telling every single person I spoke to, including my own family.

It certainly explained why he was so consistently calm and seemingly gentle with me. He was dead certain he was Jay Davis and that I was his wife. But despite the nagging fear that I might be having some kind of delayed brain trauma causing extreme confusion, I refused to believe my perception of reality was that distorted.

Surely there would be other signs. And that made me realize someone had put in a tremendous amount of effort to make me think I was crazy.

TWENTY

ANONYMOUS

It's a proverb that's centuries old.

Revenge is a dish best served cold.

The first time I heard that phrase, I knew it was meant for me. I felt as if someone was whispering it directly into my ear, telling me to be patient. To wait. Telling me I would get my chance. Life could be fair after all. There was justice in the world, even if it didn't seem like it right away. Even if you had to wait a long time.

Revenge that's taken in the heat of passion only satisfies a person's blood lust. Immediate revenge makes the body feel content, but it doesn't offer lasting peace. It fades when your heart rate returns to its steady beat and your breathing slows to a gentle, even flow.

The kind of pleasure that comes from revenge served cold, calculated for a long time, with careful planning and a clear mind and without the madness of rage, puts the mind at ease. It brings a kind of rest, a sense of finality. The victim suffers for their sins, and that is a pure form of justice.

For revenge to be served cold, a person needs to cultivate patience. I've done that.

Living through great pain provides the source material needed to create great art. Some use that material to produce beautiful things—music, literature, sculpture, and paintings. They design stunning pieces of architecture or breathtaking gardens. But for me, and others like me, pain takes a dark turn.

The creative urge is expressed by bringing to life a finely crafted punishment.

I've been preparing this dish for a while.

TWENTY-ONE
CHELSEA

Walking into the restaurant felt like walking onto a stage. It wasn't as if I was a young, inexperienced teenager, going on my first date, or meeting a boy who was taking me to my first prom. But in some ways, I felt as uncertain as if that's exactly what I was doing.

Jay was both real and not real.

I'd seen pages of photos of him. He'd shared pictures of his childhood and high school, and college shots of him playing golf. I'd done the same. We'd talked about everything from our first crushes to our career aspirations, the way we'd been raised, even our religious beliefs, non-beliefs, and all the films and books and music we loved and hated.

I was certain I knew him inside and out. I believed he knew me in the same way. We'd talked on the phone, and we'd had plenty of video calls.

But this was different. It was almost stranger than meeting someone in a bar. Because we knew each other so well, it felt awkward to think about shaking hands and saying hello, looking into each other's eyes for the first time in a three-dimensional world.

Would we kiss? Would it happen right away? I wasn't sure I wanted that, with the eyes of other diners on us. Shouldn't we sit down and talk first? Maybe order a glass of wine? But we were a couple. It felt strange not to say hello with a kiss. Everything that was about to happen was something I'd never experienced before. I had no way to prepare, nothing to compare it with.

When I saw him seated at a table in the back corner near a window facing the garden, all my thoughts about how I would behave and how the evening would flow faded as if they'd never been there. It felt as if we'd stepped out of our virtual world and into the real one in a smooth, seamless transition that was utterly natural. There was nothing awkward, nothing that required overthinking or second-guessing.

He stood and took my hand, we kissed, and it felt amazing. He'd chosen a table against a banquette, and we sat beside each other. We talked throughout our delicious meal, holding hands and eating, the conversation flowing as easily as it had when we chatted in text messages or a video call.

It was the most incredible evening I could have imagined. And when he asked if I wanted to go his hotel room, I didn't hesitate for a moment.

The following day was when the trouble began. I had a foreshadowing of it the night before, during dinner, but I'd brushed it aside because everything was so perfect. *He* was so perfect. All the things I'd loved about him in our online relationship were even better in person. I felt the same connection, more deeply now that I could touch him and hear his voice and look into his eyes when he spoke. The attraction was there when we sat close to each other. We laughed together easily.

Then, he casually suggested we go sailing the following day.

"A friend of mine has a small sailboat he keeps moored in

San Francisco Bay. He's a good sailor. I'm not too bad myself."
He squeezed my knee. "So, if you don't have experience, it's not
a problem. Anna, Ken's fiancée, has been out a lot, and she can
get you acquainted with what to do. And you're a good swim-
mer, so there's nothing to worry about." He laughed. "Not that
we're planning to capsize."

I put a forkful of pasta in my mouth so I couldn't respond
right away. I didn't want to go anywhere on a boat. Not the
following day, not ever. Boats and I were no longer friends. We
would never reconnect.

San Francisco Bay had rough, choppy water at times. It
could be almost like the Pacific Ocean itself. Not that I would
be much happier on a calmer bay or even a lake. But I was crazy
about this man. I was close to thinking I was in love with him. I
might already be at that point. How could I say no to the second
date he'd ever asked me on?

He went on talking about Ken's sailboat and the perfect
sailing weather that was forecast for the following day. He
talked about how he loved the water and boating of all kinds.
He told me about memories of sailing with his father while I
wondered why none of this had come up when we'd messaged
about our childhood vacations or appeared on his profile. Then,
I would have had time to prepare a response without him
studying my expression.

I didn't want this to end. It wasn't that I thought he was so
shallow he would walk out of the restaurant because I refused
to step onto a swaying, drifting sailboat. But it would dampen
something that was bursting into flames between us. I desperately wanted to tell him, but I couldn't. He knew about my
boating accident. Somehow, he just hadn't made the connection
that it had left me with a dreadful fear of boats themselves.
Maybe because telling him about the accident had been part of
our initial encounter, it had faded to the back of his mind. Or
maybe because my accident had happened on a speedboat.

* * *

The next morning, after making love and knowing without a doubt that we were compatible in every possible way, except skimming across the surface of the bay, at the mercy of the wind and the person in control of the boat, I let him take my hand as I stepped down onto the sailboat.

We motored out of the harbor. Jay stood near his friend, talking about the conditions of the wind and the water, while Anna told me about ropes and the boom and how thrilling it was to let the elements control your destiny. I disagreed, but I smiled and tried to feel her enthusiasm.

Once we were clear of the docks, Ken turned off the motor. While I perched with clenched thighs and calves, my stomach equally knotted, Ken, Jay, and Anna went to work pulling ropes to raise the sails. As the white nylon and canvas fabric rose along the mast, it flapped wildly, then held. The sails bowed out as they caught the wind and we began skimming across the surface of the water, waves splashing at the sides of the boat.

Already my legs ached from keeping my muscles clenched. My knuckles were white from gripping the sides of the boat or whatever piece of equipment I could find nearby. As the boat raced forward, the wind whipped my hair and tried to pull my baseball cap off my head. Fresh air washed across my face. It should have felt glorious, but all I could think about was the water and waves surrounding us, the shore moving farther and farther away. The bottom of the bay so far below I couldn't see it if I tried.

After a while, Jay came and sat beside me, putting his arm around me and pulling me close. "Are you cold?"

I shook my head.

"You look like you are."

"I'm fine."

"Let me know if you need a blanket."

"Okay."

He squeezed my shoulders, then turned his face to the wind. We sat quietly for a while, then he released his grip on my upper arm. "I don't mean to abandon you to wind and waves, but I should help Ken."

"Sure." I nodded. He didn't seem to notice that my body was stiff. I didn't want to spoil his fun. I'd agreed to this, I couldn't start complaining about it now. I was exhausted from the effort of trying to hang on. I knew I didn't need to cling so tightly, to keep my feet pressed so hard against the bottom of the boat. It wouldn't help anyway, if we capsized, but the memories of the accident, even though it had been a motorboat, were embedded in my bones and muscles, and they seemed to be making choices that overruled my brain.

I remained in my spot, straight as the mast, my neck aching from twisting my head to stare down into the dark water, hoping it wasn't going to wash up over the sides of the boat that was starting to lean precariously to the side where I was seated. Jay, Ken, and Anna were on the opposite side, giving weight to balance us, but it seemed to be having no effect. I hoped they wouldn't ask me to join them because I didn't think I could navigate the tilted bottom of the boat to get there, even with an outstretched hand to pull me across.

Closing my eyes, I wondered how long it would be until they decided to turn back. I wasn't even sure how long we'd been out here. Time had dissolved into a state of constant terror.

A moment later, I felt someone beside me.

"Isn't it spectacular," Anna shouted into my ear.

I nodded stiffly.

"You look a little nervous." She laughed and rested her hand on my thigh. "Don't tense up. You need to move with the boat."

I ignored her suggestion. There was no way I could will my muscles to relax. They were following their instincts.

"Jay loves sailing. I'm so glad you're willing to give it a try.

It's probably a deal-breaker for him." She laughed. "He's that passionate about it. I'm sure he'll end up buying a boat of his own at some point." She squeezed my thigh, then leaped up and crossed the boat to sit by Ken, moving as easily as the gulls who sat on the waves in the distance, rising and falling with the swells, taking flight whenever they pleased without putting forth any effort.

I looked at Jay and saw the pure ecstasy on his face. I wondered if he saw the terror on mine.

TWENTY-TWO
CHELSEA

I left the man and went into my bedroom, locking the doors behind me. I pulled my carry-on bag out of the closet. I opened it and unzipped the pocket on the center flap where I'd secured my medication. The bottle was still there.

That didn't mean the man hadn't gone through my bag when I was out of the room, but that didn't make any difference. Because I hadn't wanted Jay to know that I was bringing the pain meds with me on our honeymoon, I'd emptied the bottle into another prescription bottle. If the man had gone through my bag and read the label, he would have assumed these were for a stomach problem, unless he was some kind of expert in pharmaceuticals, and he recognized the drugs simply by looking at the pills. But that seemed highly unlikely.

Sitting back on my heels, I stared at the bottle, trying to figure out how he knew so much about me—my love of white roses, the necklace I'd adored in the gift shop, things about my relationship with Jay, even private conversations we'd had.

I stood and placed my bag at the back of the closet again, behind my larger suitcase. I closed the door and got my black bikini out of the drawer. I changed into it, put on a cover-up dress, stepped into my flip-flops, grabbed a canvas bag with sunglasses, a hat, and sunscreen, and left the room, carrying my phone.

The man was still on the balcony in the same spot where I'd left him.

I went to the pool closest to my suite and found an empty cabana covering two lounge chairs. I was lucky to find one available now that the patio around the pool was filling up. It made me want to cry, thinking that I had such good luck with a tent and a lounge chair, while the rest of my life was crumbling around me.

Settling on the chair with my bag on the table beside me, I put on my sunglasses and hat and called my mother. She answered before the second ring.

"Did you find Jay?"

"No."

"Oh, Chelsea. What are we going to do? Should we—"

"Did you tell anyone at the wedding that I brought my pain meds with me to Hawaii?"

"What?" She laughed. "Why would I do that? I'd almost forgotten you had. Why would I *tell* anyone? What are you talking about?"

"The man in my room knows I still use the pain meds. And he knew I had them with me."

"He probably went through your bags. This is getting dangerous. It was *already* dangerous. You need to get him out of there. I can't believe the resort isn't doing anything about this. They're a highly rated—"

"My pain meds weren't in the prescription bottle. I put them in the bottle for the prescription I had for my stomach problems when I was recovering from my accident because I didn't want Jay to know I had the pain meds with me. Even if the man went through my bags, he wouldn't have known it was pain medication. But somehow, he knows! I don't understand how. He knows everything about me. About Jay. About our relationship. I don't understand it. I'm scared."

"Why won't they get him out of your room? It's not safe. Do I need to call them?"

"Don't call them. I'm not a child. I'm handling it."

"You're not handling it; he's still there!"

"He's there because they don't believe me. And they wouldn't believe you either. When you explain the story to someone, it sounds crazy. And you don't know how he comes across—like Mr. Perfect. He has ID and Jay's credit cards. He sounds calm, in control, rational, and really... nice. I sound like a nut case, because I'm so upset, so scared."

My mother whimpered softly. "Please don't say that."

"It's the truth. Are you sure you didn't tell anyone? Maybe someone overheard you? If you were talking about my accident, and you said something about me still needing them once in a while?"

"No. I wouldn't do that. I didn't do that. I'm sure of it."

"Okay."

"This whole situation is out of control. I'm so worried about you. I think you should come home. What good is it doing for you to be there? You're not helping them look for him."

"I'm not leaving Jay." I crossed my ankles. The sun felt hot on my feet, but the rest of my legs were shaded by the canvas covering. I longed for something to drink—a cocktail—but no servers were nearby.

"It's so dangerous. If you insist on staying, you need to get him out of your room."

"I told you, I can't. They don't believe me. And there aren't any other rooms. I'm stuck."

"This is unacceptable."

"I know that, Mom. But right now, there's nothing I can do. And I'm not leaving this room. It's my room. Besides, he has Jay's credit cards, so he must know something. Right?"

"Maybe. Unless he found them."

"He knows. He just won't tell me. For whatever reason, he wants to pretend he's my husband. I don't get it."

"It's dangerous. Anything could happen in that room. It's the resort's job to protect you."

I knew this, intellectually. But I also knew what they were thinking. The man in my room was a gracious, well-spoken, very good-looking guy. He was calm and gentle toward me. He had ID telling them he was the man who had registered for that room and the man who had just celebrated his wedding here. I was a woman with a story that sounded absolutely insane, like something out of slapstick film. Every time I spoke, my voice was shrill, and I came across as impatient, snappish, and delusional.

"They don't think I need protecting from anyone. They think I've lost my mind."

"I really wish you would come home, Chelsea. This man could murder you in your sleep."

"I bought a knife."

She laughed, with a sound that ended in a snort. "How is a knife going to help you if you're sound asleep?"

"I don't think that's what he's doing. He would have done that the first night, when I didn't even know he was there."

"You're being gullible. It's so unsafe."

"But he must know something."

"How are you going to make him tell you? Can you remember anything unusual Jay said after you arrived in Hawaii that this man might be involved with? If you're not finding out anything from him, if he's just playing some fantasy game with you, what good is it doing you to stay there?"

"I wasn't going to tell you this. I'm not sure… He left me a note, telling me not to worry. That's he's okay and he's going to explain everything."

"What? Who?"

"Jay. He left a note outside my room."

"Why would he leave a note? If he was outside your room, why wouldn't he come back? That doesn't make any sense!"

"I don't know! But I know it was from him. He must have had it delivered by someone on the staff. It sounded like him."

"How can you know that?"

"I just do!"

She sighed.

"I know it's from him! I can't abandon him. I love him. I'm not going to do that to him."

She heaved another sigh, louder this time. "Please be safe. And I'm not sure the knife is a good idea. He could use it against you."

"That's not going to happen."

"Promise me you'll text me every hour."

"Mom..." I laughed. "I can't do that. But thanks for making me laugh. And I will keep in touch."

When I hung up, I felt as if I'd lied to her. I didn't feel as safe as I'd made it sound. I didn't feel safe at all.

TWENTY-THREE

CHELSEA

The sun had crept up my legs by the time I finished talking to my mother, making me aware I hadn't put on sunscreen, assuming I was protected by the canvas tent. I bent my knees, holding my phone against my thighs, staring at the dark screen as if a message might appear, telling me what to do.

It was hard to listen to the worry in my mother's voice. Hearing her plead with me to come back home made me sad. I felt so helpless. She was right that I'd accomplished nothing. Talking to that man was like talking to a concrete wall. He never changed the expression on his face for even a single moment, letting me see behind the mask of pretense. He never lost patience or slipped in any way to give me a glimpse of the real person behind his playacting at being Jay.

Talking to my mother had cleared my head, though. I remembered Jay's out-of-place phone call at our wedding reception. I'd talked to him after, but he'd said it was nothing. Because I'd woken up to a stranger in my bed, it had slipped out of my head.

Was it possible that phone call had something to do with his disappearance?

If this guy was so good at pretending he was Jay, did he know something about that phone call? Jay had said it was an upset father, which was something he dealt with on a regular basis. I shouldn't have let it slide so easily. Calling a teacher on his wedding day was beyond the norm even for these over-involved, micromanaging parents. Was this someone who was unstable and threatening, going to extremes in his obsession over his child's future?

It seemed absurd, but Jay had told me some wild stories, and there had been that college entrance cheating scandal that made national news and was turned into a documentary a few years ago in which parents with money resorted to bribery and fraud to get their kids admitted to top-rated schools. Anything was possible. Parents went crazy over their little darlings. I grabbed my bag and returned to my room.

To my surprise, the man was still on the balcony. He was leaning against the rail, his back to the view, his attention focused on the door as if he'd been waiting all that time for me to return, not moving from that spot so that he didn't miss the opening of the door.

"I have a question for you." I dropped my bag on the end table and took off my sunglasses. "What did that parent want who called you at our reception? What was so important that he had to interrupt our wedding?"

His answer was smooth, as if it had been rehearsed. "It was nothing. You know how those parents are. Every week. Almost every day, sometimes."

"But you were really tense. More than usual. You almost ran out of the reception."

He gave me a slow, eager smile. He thought he had me. He thought I was yielding to his story. He could smile all he wanted. I just needed to know about that phone call.

"His kid wanted to be captain of the golf team. He had already put it on his college applications, but he didn't have the

GPA required. You remember. I told you about it a few weeks ago."

I nodded. I did remember now, but it had seemed like all the other complaining parents. Jay had told the guy he would have to follow up with the colleges to make the correction. The high school policy wasn't changing. The parent had gone to the principal, who had backed up Jay. The parent was furious, but the policy stood.

It seemed strange he would be calling now. At our wedding. "Did something change?"

"Of course not, it's always the same. The parents think their child is special, the rules don't apply. They try to make threats."

The story felt slightly off, but at the same time, I'd heard enough of those stories. They were all the same. Almost identical in some ways. I went into the bedroom, changed into shorts and a summery top, grabbed my purse and phone, and left for the business center.

The man called after me to ask where I was going, but I didn't reply.

In the business center, I went to the website for Jay's school. I dug through the golf pictures, looking for photos of the boy who wanted to be captain. It wasn't hard. The school was small —only fifty boys in each year. I found the golf team photos labeled with each boy's name.

From there, I found pictures of tournaments and located one of the tournaments that boy had won, and a proud father-son photo. I printed it out and went to the reception desk where Kim was on duty again.

I gave her a calm, easy smile to show her I wasn't hysterical or delusional. I placed the printout on the counter.

"Hi, Kim. Remember me? Chels—"

"Yes, I remember." She glanced over her shoulder, then back at me.

I pointed to the father's face. "Can you tell me if this man is a guest at the resort?"

She looked up at me, her eyes wide. Without looking down, she pushed the paper toward me, but my fingers were firmly on the page, and it bent rather than sliding toward me. She glanced over her shoulder again, keeping her head turned.

"Is he staying here?"

She looked at me, but her eyes were vacant, as if she was looking at someone standing behind me. I turned, but no one was there.

TWENTY-FOUR
CHELSEA

Pulling her hand away from the paper, Kim took a step back from the counter. "Our privacy policy states I can't tell you who is a guest here."

"But I just need to know..." My voice trailed off. I didn't have an argument for her. I picked up the photograph and turned away.

"Sorry!" she called after me.

I kept walking, wondering if she'd seen him or not. The resort was huge. There were four high-rise towers and the smaller two-story buildings with suites like the one Jay and I had chosen. There were hundreds of people staying there. Chances were, even if he was a guest, she might not know. But the other guests might. And I wasn't going to give up that easily.

The parents at the school where Jay taught could be vicious. They were winners in life, and they would do everything in their power to ensure their children were as well. In the case of this boy, his future was now in danger. If he was caught lying, he could lose all chance at attending any of the colleges on his list.

I started in the first bar, making my way along the few people seated on stools, asking the guests sipping tropical cocktails and beer if they'd seen the man in the photograph. No one had. From there, I made my way among the tables where people were enjoying appetizers and drinks. The responses to my question were the same. Some of them hardly glanced at it, but the printer was a good quality with sharp colors so I kept my fingers crossed that a quick glance would tell them if they needed to study it more closely.

I went to a table near the door where a young couple was sipping white wine. "Excuse me."

The woman flipped her hair over her shoulder and turned so her back was toward me.

"I just have a quick question." I placed the sheet of paper on the table. "Have you seen this man around the resort?"

"We're celebrating our anniversary," the woman said. "Will you please leave us alone?"

"Just take a look. It will only take a second."

She flicked the paper with her pointed, pearl-colored fingernail. The paper sailed off the table and landed on the floor. I bent down to pick it up.

The man laughed. "Come on, Tiffany."

Tiffany put her hand with her dagger fingernails on the back of the man's neck. She pulled him toward her and gave him a long, deep kiss.

I waited for the kiss to end, but as it continued, I realized she wasn't going to look, even when it did.

I left the bar and went out to the pool area, making my way from lounge chair to lounge chair, and then past all the cabanas. I was headed toward the pool bar, when I saw Shep walking toward me. I turned and made a sharp right around a large hibiscus plant with its luscious red blossoms.

Shep followed. "Chelsea. I'd like to speak to you for a moment."

I kept going, following the curving path to the area where steps led into the water at the side of the bar.

"Chelsea! Mrs. Davis. Please wait."

I couldn't step into the water, and I slowed, wondering how I was going to get the attention of the people drinking at the bar in the pool.

Now, Shep was beside me. "I understand you're bothering the guests."

"I'm not bothering anyone. I—"

"Interrupting people trying to enjoy their vacation by asking them to identify another guest."

"I just need to know if this man is staying here."

"Kim already told you that's a violation of our privacy policy."

"For you, not for the guests."

"It's the same. People are here trying to relax. They want to enjoy their privacy. You have no right to play detective, or what-ever it is you're trying to do. What *are* you trying to do?"

"This man was harassing my husband, and I need to know if he's here."

"Your husband seems fine."

"Not that man impersonating my husband. My missing husband who everyone refuses to look for. Who could be hurt, or in danger, or—" A sob choked off the rest of my words.

"Okay. Let's calm down." He put his hand on my shoulder.

Now, I wanted to cry even harder, because once again, he thought I was deranged. Hysterical. He was looking at me as if I'd escaped from a mental hospital and was wandering around in my standard-issue gown, with disheveled hair, my eyes wild and unfocused, babbling nonsense.

"You can't bother the other guests, or you'll be asked to check out. Is that clear?"

I glared at him.

"Is that clear, Mrs. Davis? We had a complaint."

I wondered what Tiffany would have done if she woke up with a strange man in her bed. She probably would have stabbed him with her pointed fingernails.

"Will you please return to your room. And give me the photograph." He held out his hand.

"It's mine."

"Then put it away. I don't want to see it or hear about it again."

I stepped around him and walked back in the direction I'd come, past the end of the pool. I knew it was my imagination, but it felt as if everyone in the water and all the guests lying around the sides of the pool were staring at me, wondering what was wrong with me. Maybe they hoped I would bother them again so they could have me kicked out of the resort.

When I reached my room, a white envelope was lying under the mat, half of it sticking out. My heart began pounding so hard I could feel it in my ears. I grabbed the envelope. My name was written on the front in the same neat cursive as it had been before.

TWENTY-FIVE
CHELSEA

I tore open the envelope, slicing my finger with an invisible, but immediately painful cut from the shimmery white paper. The pearlized color and texture reminded me of Tiffany's nail polish. I pulled out the card.

Chelz—

I know you must be sick with worry, but please trust me. Don't give up on me. I need you to be patient. If you're thinking of going home, thinking of ending the trip we planned together, I'm begging you not to.

I love you forever.

J.

All my frustration dissolved as I read his words. I read them again. Hope pricked my heart then blossomed inside me. everything would be okay. I wasn't losing my mind. Something terrible was going on with Jay, but he would explain it. And I wouldn't make the same mistake again. The man waiting behind the door to my room would not have a chance to destroy this note. Wanting to keep it close to my heart, I stuffed it inside my shirt. I pressed my hands over my face as the tears began to spill out of my eyes.

Jay was alive. That was all that mattered. Whether it was that manic golf father, or someone far worse, Jay was alive. He was able to think and write clearly. I was at the center of his thoughts. He was worried about me. He knew I was scared. He knew me so well, he understood that my mother might be pushing me to go home. Because I'd met him when I was still recovering from my accident, he'd known how she looked out for me, how concerned she was for my well-being, and he'd guessed I might be thinking about going home, that my mother would want that.

As I thought about his words, I leaned against the building. Why hadn't he told me what was going on? The last note said he would explain things soon. But this one said nothing.

I was supposed to trust him. How long would this go on? It was wearing me down. Even though it had only been two days, it felt like an eternity. I felt as if this stranger had been lurking in my room, watching my every move, pretending to be my husband for weeks. I felt like I'd been questioning my thoughts and my sanity for longer than I could remember. In some ways, I had been. In the days and weeks following my accident, my dreams and waking hours, my medicated state, made everything a blur. Reality felt like a dream, and my dreams felt so real, I talked to my parents about them as if the events that occurred when I was asleep had actually happened. This felt very much the same.

When was Jay going to tell me what was going on? Why was he staying away? These notes made it sound as if he was free to do as he pleased, that he'd left our room, our bed, our honeymoon by his own choice. Did he know about this man who had taken his place? He hadn't mentioned it, but he must know his credit cards were gone. He must know something.

Even though the notes made me feel incredible relief because I knew he was alive, they made me feel worse because I felt like he could end this and tell me what was happening, but for whatever reason, he wasn't doing that.

I was trapped in this surreal nightmare, and he wouldn't tell me why. I just had to trust him. But if he could write me notes, why couldn't he call me?

When I thought of it that way, a flicker of anger began to burn inside me. I didn't deserve this. I pressed my forehead against the doorframe, pushing hard so the wood made a dent in my skin, enjoying the pressure of it driving into my bone, feeling as if it were cleaving my brain, helping me think, easing the growing anger.

As I moved away from the door, I realized it had cleared my thoughts. One reason Jay might not be able to call me was that his phone was still locked up in the hotel safe where he'd put it after mine had been destroyed. They'd refused to give it to me, but if the entire staff believed the man behind this door was Jay Davis, they would give it to him. Why hadn't I thought of that before?

I yanked the key card out of my pocket and stabbed it into the slot.

The man was on the balcony, drinking what looked like a gin and tonic based on the tiny bottle from the minibar that sat on the table beside him.

"Hey," I called. "I need you to go to the front desk and ask for Jay's phone."

He turned slowly. "Will you come out here."

It wasn't a question, or even a request.

"No. I need you to get his phone. I don't know why I didn't

think of it earlier. I need it right now. You can pretend you're Jay. You can act like you're Jay right now, I don't care. I'll even say it as if you are. Please go get your phone, Jay." I gave him a mocking smile.

He stood, swallowed the last of his drink, and stepped into the room. "The manager called. He said you were harassing the guests."

"I wasn't harassing anyone. I showed a photograph to some of the guests."

"That's a little obnoxious, don't you realize that? You need to be careful. We don't want them kicking you out of here." He smiled in a way that made me feel as if he might be threatening to make that happen himself.

"It's not obnoxious when my husband is missing and no one is looking for him."

"You're seriously at risk of being asked to leave the resort."

"I don't think they can do that."

"Yes, they can. And I don't think you want that, do you?"

"I need you to get the phone. Now."

"I can do that, but you need to be careful. If you do something like that again, I might have to take you to a clinic for a psychiatric evaluation."

I laughed. "Is there even such a thing? At an urgent care clinic? I don't think so."

"Just be careful. Please."

"Go get the phone."

He came toward me. He grabbed my wrist, pulling it toward him. "I know you don't believe this, but I'm looking out for your interests."

"Good to know. Now go get the phone." I yanked my arm to get away from him. At first, he didn't let go. Then, he released me. I went into the bedroom. I didn't relax until I heard the door close.

I wasn't sure what I would do once I had Jay's phone. I

didn't know his passcode. All I was likely to see would be missed calls and text messages from friends. I collapsed onto the bed, defeated. It had seemed so important when I'd first thought of it. Now, I realized it was another dead end.

TWENTY-SIX

ANONYMOUS

Everyone knows that it's not healthy to nurture old wounds. Constantly reliving deeply painful experiences keeps them fresh in your mind. It makes them feel as if they happened just yesterday. If you imagine them enough and think about them with enough vivid detail, it can seem like they're happening all over again. It damages your soul, if you believe in such things. But even if you don't, it destroys your mental health and your day-to-day well-being.

I know that.

It's not as if I've fed on my pain twenty-four hours a day, brooding over it until I looked like a bent and twisted creature who had crawled out of the sewer.

I filled my life with other, fabulous things. I lived it to the fullest. I built an incredible career. I acquired more than enough friends. I've enjoyed plenty of satisfying lovers, some of them for many years. I traveled all over the world. I saw the pyramids and spent time visiting India. I've enjoyed my life immensely.

I didn't let the sickness fester.

But the pain was always part of me. It became as solid as my bones, holding me up and helping me move through life with strength and purpose.

When someone cuts your heart out with a knife, cleanly severing it from your arteries, all that remains is an empty cavity. And that hole has to be filled with something.

What filled the hole was watching. Waiting. Making plans. Planning is a satisfying pursuit. It can take the place of your heart. It's almost like having a dream.

TWENTY-SEVEN

CHELSEA

While the man was out of the room, I hid Jay's note inside the Bible in the nightstand. If he went through my clothes or my suitcases, he might find it, but I didn't think he would flip through a hotel Bible.

I stepped outside onto the balcony and leaned on the railing. The sun was moving toward the horizon, casting a million diamond-like sparkles across the surface of the ocean. The glitter made my eyes ache, but it was so beautiful I didn't want to dim it by putting on sunglasses. I put my hand to my brow to block the rays and let the sparkles dance in front of me.

Tears pricked at the backs of my eyes as I thought about what it would have been like to drink in this view with my husband beside me, looking forward to a delicious evening meal, a few glasses of chilled white wine, a moonlight walk on the beach, and a romantic evening in our suite, with the sound of the waves and the wind through the palms as the only music.

I heard the door open and turned.

The man stepped into the room, holding Jay's phone out to me like some kind of peace offering.

When I took it out of his hand, the screen was filled with so many missed calls and messages, they were layered on top of each other, so I really couldn't see much. The last few calls were from Sean. I could see a text from his mother. That was it.

I swept up and tried tapping in a few codes, hoping he'd used something simple, like his birthday or, if I flattered myself, my birthday, our wedding date. None of them worked. I tucked the phone into my pocket, defeated. It felt like a blow that put me back to the starting point. The police wouldn't help, and I was on my own until Jay chose to, or was able to, get in touch with me again. This guy staring at me knew something, but I was completely helpless in getting him to give me even a whisper of information.

The man sat down, then crossed his legs, resting an ankle on the opposite knee. "I think it would be better if you didn't go out of the room unless I'm with you."

I pulled Jay's phone out of my pocket again. I held it up to the man's face, then quickly turned it toward me. The screen was still locked as I knew it would be. "It's interesting that you claim to be Jay Davis, but your face didn't unlock his phone screen."

He shrugged. His expression was neutral. He looked utterly disinterested, and unconcerned. He didn't even bother trying to explain why the phone wouldn't unlock.

"Are you ever planning to tell me what's going on here?" I asked.

He was quiet for a long time. His gaze wouldn't meet mine. Finally, he said, "We should go out to dinner. Do you want to stay here, or try one of the—"

"I don't want to go out. I want you to tell me where my husband is. I want you to tell me what you're doing in my room. I want you to tell me why you're acting like this and why you think I'm so mentally deficient I'll believe that you're my husband. This is my husband's phone and you can't open it." I held out the phone. "Use the passcode."

He didn't take the phone. Instead, he stood and moved toward the door. "You have to eat something."

"Order room service. And a bottle of wine. Two bottles."

"You got it." He went to the phone on the credenza under the TV as if he was eager to make my stay as pleasant as possible. He opened the top drawer and pulled out the room service menu. "Do you want to have a look at this?"

"Order whatever you want. You must know what I like." I went into the bedroom and closed the doors. I sat on the floor with my back against the bed. I opened my phone and began searching again for reports of accidents or any strange stories that might suggest something that would tell me where Jay was. He couldn't have just vanished off the island.

His ID was gone, so it was possible he could have taken a flight somewhere. But then, how would he have left the handwritten notes? I pulled his phone out of my pocket. I tried our wedding date as a passcode. I tried my birthday. I tried random numbers that were lined up in a single row which I knew some people did to make their passcode easier to enter. Nothing worked.

I heard the man's voice on the phone ordering dinner. As I'd asked, he added two bottles of white wine to the order. The idea of getting drunk was very appealing right now. I thought about calling Bella, but she would tell me to come home. I could text her, but it would be the same. And the same for my mother. Maybe I would call Katherine later. Sometimes, on the rare occasions when my mother reverted to seeing me as her tiny baby girl needing protection and caretaking, Katherine was a fabulous mentor, someone who pushed me to do more and be stronger. I hadn't been in touch with any of my other friends yet. Trying to explain my situation was exhausting. The gasps of disbelief, the questions, the admonitions to leave were all too much.

Closing my eyes, I let the phone drop onto my crossed

ankles. I leaned my head back and rested it against the bed. It felt like this would never end. Would Jay keep sending cryptic notes, teasing me for days? Possibly longer? Would this man keep pretending he was my husband, insisting I couldn't leave the resort, and now, not even my room?

I laughed out loud, a slightly manic shriek filling my room. I clenched my jaw to stop myself from losing control.

After a while, I heard the man talking again. The food must have arrived, but it seemed like too much effort to rise to my feet and join him for dinner. I wasn't even sure I was hungry, although a glass of wine sounded really good. It was the only thing I wanted, the only thing that would stop my thoughts from spinning in wild endless circles, clawing for answers that weren't there.

He knocked on the door. "Our dinner is here."

Calling it *our* dinner made my skin crawl. But not enough to forego a few glasses of wine. I put both phones on the dresser and went into the other room. The meal had been arranged on the balcony table. There were indeed two wine bottles, both in chillers, sitting on the smaller table off to the side.

He'd ordered scampi with pasta for both of us. It wasn't a dish that said he knew me inside and out, but it wasn't far off. I definitely chose it once in a while when I ate out. I tried to ignore the chill that ran down my spine.

Was that the game? Had he gotten rid of Jay and he was hoping that this constant drip of so-called proof that he knew quite a lot about me and what I liked, and the things that had made Jay and I bond as a couple, would soften me over time? Did he believe that would make me fall for him? But why would he even want that? I was a total stranger. Maybe he was after my family's money.

Was that what this was about? Some elaborate scam to pretend he was my husband so he could weasel his way into our finances? Or maybe he did mean to kill me, it was just a long game. He needed some way to prove a legal marriage first. I shivered again, more violently this time.

"Can I get you a hoodie?" he asked.

"I'm fine. The food will warm me up." I picked up the already full glass of wine and took a generous sip.

We sat down. He raised his glass. "To us."

I cut a piece of shrimp and ate it.

He took a sip of his wine, looking disappointed but willing to follow my lead.

After a few minutes of silent eating, when I was already into my second glass of wine, he began talking. "I know you were upset that I mentioned your meds from the accident. It's okay if you still need to take them. You shouldn't feel that makes you weak, if that's what you're thinking. I don't mean to assume I know all your feelings." He twirled some pasta around his fork and ate it.

He continued, "The damage to your body was horrific. All those broken bones, torn ligaments. It's understandable that you're still going to have residual pain. And even if you don't, the fear of having pain can be powerful. So having them with you just in case, as an extra reassurance, makes sense."

"You don't know anything about my accident." My voice sounded rough, breaking and squeaking slightly as I spoke because it was a lie. It sounded like he knew quite a lot about my accident. Again, the thought pounded against my skull— how did he know, how did he know, how did he *know*? There was so much. It felt as if he'd crawled inside my head and down-loaded my memories like you can download data off a computer.

"I know opioids are dangerous. I'd hate for you to forget and take them when you're drinking. Or forget you'd taken them and take more, since you're sleeping alone. It's important to have someone else aware. It would be terrible if you overdosed."

His words were chilling, despite his attempt at a comforting smile. I continued drinking wine, and he continued trying to discuss my accident, telling me I didn't talk about it enough. He said it was good that I'd had so much physical therapy, but it would have been helpful if I'd had therapy to help me process the emotional trauma. No one had thought to address the fear I'd felt. He wondered why that aspect of my healing had slipped through the cracks.

He wasn't judging me, or my parents, or even the doctors, he said. He was just making an observation. He supposed it was because the damage to my body was so extensive, the impact on my mind had taken a back seat. It was invisible. It was forgotten, as mental and emotional injuries often are.

We were halfway into the second bottle before he stopped. He suggested we sit on the lounge chairs and look at the darkening sky and emerging stars while we finished the wine.

I was terrified and I wanted to drown my fear in another glass of wine. Had this man hacked my medical records? What was he *after?*

Later, when I stumbled to bed, I placed a chair in front of the plantation doors and closed the blinds across the doors to the balcony so I would hear him no matter which way he attempted to enter my room. Even with that, I slept with my fist curled around the handle of my knife. I still didn't sleep well, despite the wine.

TWENTY-EIGHT
CHELSEA

They were drinking too much, driving the boat too fast, but Brent wouldn't listen to me. He never really listened to me and maybe that should have been a red flag.

The four of us had been having a fabulous summer afternoon on Lake Berryessa, but things turned dark once Brent and Troy passed the seven beers mark. I knew what Brent was like after six—fun and full of laughs and good times. He was goofy and had his hands all over me. But seven was an entirely different story. He'd promised he wouldn't. He'd promised only a six-pack each, which was still way too much for driving a high-powered speedboat around a lake.

The dares had started after four beers.

Wanting Jillian and me to take off our bikini tops. Diving off the boat while it was moving. Standing on the front while it was speeding.

But this was horrific. Brent had pushed it to the top speed and was driving straight toward the concrete support of the bridge that spanned the lake, sixty feet above us. I was screaming at him to slow down, to turn the boat. Jillian was crying and screaming incoherently. Troy was laughing. "You're crazy, dude. Three hundred bucks if you keep going."

Brent kept going.

Then, everything went black. I heard the crying and the laughing and the screaming. I felt the boat racing across the water. I saw the concrete turning from a bridge support into a wall. My mind felt as if it was breaking into pieces, disconnecting from my skull. Was he really going to keep going? It didn't seem real. He wouldn't. He wouldn't slam the boat into that wall going fifty miles an hour across a lake. He wasn't stupid. He didn't have a death wish.

But he did have seven beers pumping through his body.

He believed he was superhuman, that he could turn at the last possible moment.

And then everything shattered.

I don't remember what happened, only what I was told. We were all in the water. I was pulled out unconscious. Brent and Troy were groaning and crying, gulping water. They were lucky they lived. Jillian fared the best because she saw it coming and made a clean dive off the boat. She was the one who swam to shore and made her way to the boat launch area where they called for rescue services.

At one point while I was in the water, I regained consciousness for a while. I clung to a single piece of fiberglass, shivering and terrified that I was going to die. My right arm was drifting in the water, useless. I couldn't seem to move my legs at all. I felt myself sliding off the thing keeping me afloat. The pain filled my whole body, but I didn't have the strength to scream. I felt I was screaming, but I knew my mouth wouldn't open. Then I lost consciousness again.

I was in the hospital for three weeks. Both legs were broken, my collarbone was fractured, and my left arm was broken in two places. When I was released, I found someone to take over my half of the apartment I was sharing with a classmate from law school and moved home with my parents. That way, my mother could drive me to physical therapy, cook for me, and in the beginning, help me shower and dress.

Without law school, without my roommate, communicating with my friends mostly by text—friends who were working in demanding jobs, going places on the weekends—I soon became bored. As the pain became manageable and physical therapy a routine that wasn't as torturous, I found myself antsy sitting around my parents' house. I couldn't drive because I was still taking a low dose of pain meds.

After hours of reading, binging a few shows a day, and some time on social media, I needed more. Obviously, Brent, serving only eighteen months in jail for a first offense, was out of my life with a text message. Bella didn't think he deserved even that.

I signed up for online dating. Maybe it was a rebound. Absolutely it was a rebound. But I wanted something to look forward to every day besides the next book on my tablet or my physical therapist cheering me on by telling me I was exceeding her expectations.

Jay and I clicked immediately over our love of noir films. What drew me to his profile was he had used a moody black and white photo. He noted in his profile that he used it because he loved noir. How could I not nibble on that bait? My parents had introduced me to those old films when I was only eleven years old. Every Friday night, we ate popcorn and watched a classic film. I have no doubt that buttery popcorn, and the comfort of my parents beside me made those stories and sultry images sink deep into my psyche.

It wasn't long before Jay and I were chatting every day.

My mother didn't think it was safe. "You should meet someone the normal way."

"And how would I do that?"

"You'll be up and about soon."

"Not that soon. Besides, this is how a lot of people meet now."

She rolled her eyes. "That's no fun. And you have no idea who these people are. It could be anyone. They could be prisoners. Con men. They could be married. You don't even know if he's a man. Or an adult."

"So could someone I meet at law school."

"It's far less likely."

"Is it?"

She was especially worried that someone *tech savvy* had *somehow* figured out that our family was wealthy. Jay wasn't interested in me at all. In fact, his fascination with noir films was pretense. He was doing it to lure me in. He was making himself into a person I would trust and then he would worm his way into my life and take me for everything I had. She reminded me of a documentary we'd watched right after I was released from the hospital.

I got off the window seat where I was propped up with five or six pillows. I walked to the bedroom door and held out my arm. "You can leave now." I said it with a smile, I said it in a gentle tone, but it worked.

She sighed, and she left me alone. But she didn't stop talking about it in the weeks that followed.

It made me think she didn't have a very high opinion of me as a future attorney if she thought I was so gullible that I would be taken in by someone that easily.

TWENTY-NINE

CHELSEA

I woke with a headache which was to be expected. It would have been from all that wine under normal circumstances, but this time, I truly believed it was from feeling my brain swell and press against my skull as that man talked about my boating accident as if he'd stood on the bridge and watched the entire episode. He acted as if he'd seen the X-rays, discussed my prognosis with the orthopedic surgeon, and received regular updates from my physical therapist.

It made me ill thinking about the intimate details he'd managed to acquire about my life. At the rate he was going, I wouldn't have been surprised if our next conversation might involve him telling me about the details of my sex life with Jay. For that reason, and a hundred others, I didn't want there to be a next conversation. But I felt so cut off from the rest of the world. Talking to him had felt inevitable. Who else was there? And he'd been there, watching me, smiling at me, following me around, telling me what to do, probing my life every minute since I'd woken to find him in my bed.

I couldn't escape him.

It was starting to feel as if we were actually married. The

thought disgusted me to the core of my being. Or, was he telling the truth? Maybe there was something going on in my brain that I didn't understand. Maybe I should have had therapy after my accident. Maybe something had broken deep inside my psyche that I didn't understand, and the excitement of meeting and starting a relationship with Jay, planning a wedding, and the wedding itself had caused me to lose touch with reality.

Was it possible this man was my husband and there was something horribly wrong with me that made me think he wasn't?

I took a cool shower, hoping it would ease my headache, along with the painkillers and a liter of water. The pain had moved to the back of my head and had been reduced to a minor annoyance by the time I left the room.

When I saw him, I was jolted back to reality. He wasn't Jay. He couldn't be. Nothing about my senses felt distorted. Did it? He was drinking coffee and eating bacon, eggs, and toast from the breakfast for two he'd ordered. He looked nice enough, but he wasn't Jay, no matter how much he knew, no matter how kind he was or how gently he smiled.

I walked out the door of my suite carrying a slice of buttered toast, without jam. I didn't want sticky fingers when I went to the business center.

Using my phone for all the work I planned to do would have worked just fine, but I needed to get away from him. And I wanted to be sure my emails were clear. And I needed to look up names and addresses. A desktop computer was a more efficient choice.

I bought a cup of coffee from a kiosk in the lobby and settled at one of the computers in the business center. I went to the list of instructors for the high school where Jay taught. I copied and pasted the email addresses of everyone I'd heard him mention, as well as the address of the school principal, into a notes document.

First, I called his mother. I reached her voicemail. The message informed me that she and her husband had gone to a meditation retreat that included a detox from technology. They would return in two weeks. I left a message for her to call me, but didn't tell her why. I allowed myself a wild hope that Jay would be back in my arms and everything would be fine well before the two-week mark.

After several false starts, I composed a brief email to Jay's colleagues, telling them Jay had gone missing. I didn't mention the crazy parts of the story. I asked if they'd heard from him, or anything about him, to let me know right away. It sounded pathetic, asking strangers if they'd heard from my husband, as if I, his new wife, was the last to know. I didn't tell them about the strange notes left outside my door. The less said, the better.

I sent the emails individually so it would seem more personal, and they wouldn't think they could more easily ignore me since there were plenty of others to respond. Within minutes, there were a few replies, including the principal. All of them said they hadn't heard anything.

One or two said they'd searched for reports of missing people in Hawaii and hadn't seen any news articles. They wanted to know why. I was forced to write back that the story had some *complicated details* and hadn't yet been reported. I knew that would generate more questions, but I figured I could ignore them. I didn't know these people. All I wanted was information. I didn't care if they thought I was rude to ignore their follow-up questions. I needed to find Jay. That was the only thing I cared about.

My email traffic quieted down after the first five or six replies from the types who were always checking email. I closed the window and logged off.

Even though it was still early, the area around the pool was crowded, all the cabanas occupied, and the lounge chairs taken.

I kicked off my flip-flops and sat on the edge of the pool, putting my feet into the water and resting them on the first step.

Within minutes, I started to feel out of place among the happy couples and families. I stood and went to the path leading toward the beach. It was less crowded out there. I found a lounge chair with an umbrella beside it and was immediately offered a towel and a complimentary tube of sunscreen.

I propped up the back of the chair, put sunscreen on my legs, spreading it up beneath the hem of my cutoffs, and settled back, my knees bent, my upper body in the shade of the perfectly angled umbrella. Before I could close my eyes, a server was beside me asking what I wanted to drink. I ordered water and a Bloody Mary.

After gazing at the calming rhythm of the surf, sipping my drink, and letting the warm sun bathe my legs, I felt relaxed, almost as if I were on vacation. For a moment, I forgot about everything.

"Mind if we join you?" The voice was melodic.

I opened my eyes. Two women stood at the foot of my lounge chair looking at the two vacant chairs beside me. Both women had light brown hair. The one standing closest to my chair had hers clipped in a pixie. She wore oversized pink sunglasses and a matching pink bikini with a sheer white cover-up. Her friend had on a black tank suit cut up over her hip bones. Her hair hung almost to her waist and the frames of her glasses were white. They looked like they could be just under forty. They also looked like they could be close to fifty. I wasn't sure. I also wondered why I was assessing their ages.

They held up their drinks. "Bloody Marys also. It's destiny," said the one in pink who had spoken the first time.

Any other time in my life I would have laughed and agreed. This time, everything had changed. And because of that, something entirely unexpected happened. I burst into tears.

"Oh, no," said the one in pink. "I'm so sorry. I didn't mean...

we were just…" She backed away. "I'm really sorry. We didn't mean to intrude."

I shook my head. I reached into my bag for a tissue and slid it under my glasses, patting my eyes. I pulled it out and wiped my nose. Now, I laughed. "I didn't mean to do that. I'm on the edge." I laughed again. "You have no idea."

"It looks like you need another drink." The one in black and white gestured toward a server at the cabana beside us.

A moment later, they were on the lounge chairs and three more Bloody Marys were on their way to us, along with an order of chips and hummus.

"If you feel like talking," the one in pink said, "I'm Lori and this is Kendall. But if you'd rather just drink, we're always good with that, right?" She clicked her nearly empty glass against Kendall's.

"I'm Chelsea, and I've never needed to talk more in my life. But you might think I'm a lunatic when I'm finished," I said.

"Never." Kendall raised her glasses off her face, pushing her hair back. "We have crazy stories to match anything you have to say. I promise."

"Nothing like this."

After our drinks and hummus arrived, I told them what had happened. When I finished, they stared at me without speaking. Their mouths were partially opened, their drinks in their hands, straws untouched, the sides of the glasses growing slick in the warm air.

"That's…" Kendall said.

"It's scary," Lori whispered. "How did he get in?"

"I wonder where your husband could *be*?" Kendall said.

"You believe me?" I asked.

They stared at me. "Why wouldn't we believe you?" They spoke at the same time, their words echoing each other.

"Of course, we believe you!" Kendall asked.

"The police officer doesn't. He believes this guy's ID. That's it. Same with Shep."

"Who's Shep?"

"The resort manager."

"What are you going to do?" Lori asked.

"I've done everything I can think of. After the notes, I'm sure he's going to get in touch with me. In person. Call me, or something."

"Why is it always that way? Like waiting for some guy to text or call after the first date." Kendall stuck the straw between her lips and sucked up so much spicy tomato juice mix and vodka, I could see the level of the liquid sliding down in her glass.

"I don't know what else I can do."

"Hire a private investigator?" Kendall asked.

"Maybe. I hadn't thought of that."

"How would you even find one, or know if they're any good when you don't have anyone to give you a recommendation?" Lori asked. "It's not like the resort will have a list."

"I feel better knowing he's at least alive. And that he's not kidnapped and tied up or something like that. He's not uncon-scious or in a hospital somewhere, without anyone knowing who he is."

They both nodded, straws in their mouths.

"It just sounds so dangerous, having a total stranger sleeping in your room," Lori said.

"I lock my doors. Even the bathroom door."

They nodded again, but Lori looked suspicious. "I wouldn't be able to sleep at all. Every time there was a sound, I would think he was trying to break down the door."

"I have a knife," I said. "Under my pillow."

"Is that enough?" she asked.

"I hope so."

"He must know more than he's saying. He didn't just

randomly show up at your room, with your husband's credit cards. And he already had ID in his name. How long did he have to be planning that? It's really fishy."

I sipped my drink and gazed at the ocean. It was such a beautiful, soft blue, the foam on the breaking waves so white it looked like the clouds. I sensed someone behind me and turned to look, but no one was there. It was my nerves—jumpy and on edge. I sipped my drink.

"Why would he keep pretending he's your husband when he knows you don't believe him? Even when other people aren't around? It doesn't make any sense," Kendall said. "It's like he's demented. Maybe he's been stalking you. Maybe he got rid of Jay so he could have you."

I shivered. "But Jay sent me notes."

"Did he?" Kendall asked.

"If he was stalking me, and wanted to get rid of Jay, why would he send me notes?"

"Hmm," Kendall murmured.

"It just sounds so dangerous. I think you should move into our room," Lori said.

"You're in the same room?"

"Oh, yeah," Lori said. "This is our divorce-a-versary. Six months for both of us." She laughed and clicked her glass against Kendall's. "So that's why we know *all* about men and their games. You definitely should stay in our room. It's not safe where you are."

"Yes," Kendall agreed. "This isn't about your husband. It's about you. I'm sure of it."

THIRTY

CHELSEA

Lori's words hung in the air. Her second comment sounded almost threatening. Why was she so sure this was about me?

It would feel safe in their room, but I had to believe Jay would get in touch with me again. If I left our room, how would he reach me, since he didn't have his phone? Right now, our only connection was his handwritten notes.

When they stood to go, Lori nudged my chair with her shin. "Think about it. You'll be safe in our room. Our door is always open. We're here for five more days."

"I'll think about it." Maybe Kendall was on to something. Had this man been stalking me before I even came to Hawaii, planning to hurt Jay and slowly gaslight, then brainwash me into believing he was my husband? That didn't sound any crazier than anything else I'd considered.

"Please think seriously about it." Kendall placed her hand on my knee. "We want to help."

She took her hand away and I swung my legs over the side of the lounge chair. "Thank you so much for listening. And for believing me. You have no idea what it means to me." I stood and we hugged each other, our fingers, wet from our drinks, were clammy on each other's backs.

"Let's exchange numbers," Lori said. "We're in room 735. In the north tower."

I gave them my room and cell numbers. I turned to the table near my lounge chair. "Did you see my phone?"

"Nope," Lori said.

"Where was it?" Kendall asked.

"On this table."

"I've been holding my drink, I didn't notice," Kendall said.

"Did they knock it off when they moved the umbrella?" Lori asked.

"Maybe." I walked around the pathway that ran along the edge of the sand where the lounge chairs were set up, nicely spaced with plenty of room for people to pass between them on their way closer to the water. I kicked at the sand close to the pathway to see if my phone had been partially buried by foot traffic.

Unless someone had dug a hole and nestled it into wet sand, covering it up again, it wasn't there.

"I can't believe it's gone. Two phones in less than a week?!"

"Maybe Pele wants a sacrifice," Kendall said.

"Who?"

"The Hawaiian goddess of the volcano," she said. "Pele."

I laughed. "That's cute, but I'm really upset. I had to go to Kailua-Kona to get a new phone, get all my data transferred when mine fell into the koi pond at my wedding reception. I'm lost without it." My voice caught. I wasn't going to cry again in front of these women. I'd already introduced myself by sobbing. I took a long, slow breath. "I wonder if he took it."

"Who?"

"The man in my room."

"I didn't see him," Kendall said.

"Me neither."

I hadn't seen him, but we'd been talking, facing the ocean, lost in our conversation. We'd hardly even noticed the person who delivered our drinks. Anyone could have grabbed my phone off the table while we were captivated by my bizarre experiences. But who here needed to steal a phone? And there was one person determined to keep me on the resort and in my room.

Maybe he also wanted to cut me off from everyone I knew.

THIRTY-ONE
CHELSEA

After saying goodbye to Lori and Kendall with flamboyant hugs and promises to keep in touch once I located my phone or at least calling each other from the landlines in our rooms, I trudged back along the path from the beach to the pool.

My pace slowed as I approached the lobby area. Reporting my phone missing was necessary, but I could imagine the look on the face of anyone I encountered. By now, they all knew who I was—the woman who didn't believe the man in her suite was her husband. The hysterical woman with wild stories of a missing husband. The woman who *harassed* other resort guests.

Now, they would imagine I'd misplaced my phone, dropped it into the ocean while I was walking in the surf, or let it fall into a drift of sand as I downed a cocktail in the middle of the morning.

At the reception counter, I faced a middle-aged man with a shaved head and a jet-black goatee. He smiled at me as if he'd been waiting all day to greet me. Maybe he didn't know who I was. My dark mood shifted slightly. I returned his smile.

"How can I help you, miss?"

"I feel a little uncomfortable saying this, because I don't like to make accusations, but I think someone stole my phone."

His smile flattened, but he nodded as if he couldn't wait to hear more.

"I was sitting in one of the lounge chairs on the beach, talking to some other people, having snacks and drinks, and my phone was on the table. When I got up to leave, it was gone."

"It could have fallen off."

"I checked the area."

"If it's turned in, we'll contact you."

"But I think someone took it."

He smiled sympathetically. "I don't know why they would. Phones are locked. But if they did, I don't think there's anything we can do."

"You can't take a report? In case it turns up?"

"If someone stole it, why would it turn up?"

I gave him a defeated shrug. I realized how my logical thinking had deteriorated over the past few days. Maybe this was why they treated me like I was unstable. I sounded that way to myself, replaying my words in my head right now.

"Phones aren't a typical theft problem. At a resort, there's nothing someone can do with a stranger's phone. Only pros can unlock them."

"I guess that's true."

He smiled. "You know that's true. Have you ever tried to unlock a friend's phone? Your partner's phone?"

Now, I felt like he was patronizing me. "Will you still make a record of it? Just in case?"

He sighed, almost imperceptibly, but it was there. He asked me for the brand and color of my phone and what the lock-screen photo was. Then he asked my name and room number. When I told him, his smile stiffened, and his eyes narrowed. "You've had a difficult stay with us, Mrs. Davis. I'm sorry to hear that. I hope you can enjoy the Hawaiian spirit for the rest of your time here."

"You'll let the rest of the staff—"

"I'll take care of it. As I said, phones are not a typical theft problem, but I understand you're upset, and I'll make a note."

When I turned away, I knew I would never see the phone again. There was a very good chance it hadn't been stolen by a passerby at all. It had been taken by the man in my room. He'd walked behind us, unnoticed, heard bits of my story as I'd poured out my heart to the first people who believed me outside of my parents and my best friend, and grabbed the phone to cut me off from everyone once again.

I wasn't entirely sure my family and Bella believed me either. The miles of ocean between us and my choice to let this stranger remain in my room didn't feel real to them. I heard it in their voices and read it in their messages to me.

I even questioned myself. Was I really as trapped as I felt? It was a sensation I couldn't describe. I did feel trapped. And for some reason, despite his sneaking into my room and trying to take over my husband's identity, and even though I felt I needed to sleep clutching a knife, there was no visceral fear deep inside. It was part of what made me feel constantly confused and disoriented. This was the reason I kept wondering if I was hallucinating. I hated it. I wanted to escape. But maybe what I wanted to escape was my own mind.

Climbing the stairs to my suite, I felt as if my feet were encased in concrete. Whether or not the man had taken my phone, the outcome was the same. I would never see it again. The thought of returning to the phone store for yet another purchase and data migration exhausted me. But without a phone, I was more isolated. The business center became the only slender, easily broken thread tying me to the people I loved, the people who cared about me.

I was still fifteen feet from the door to my suite when I saw the envelope. My heart began thudding and I felt a burst of joy. As much as I'd imagined the peace and relief of moving into the room with my newfound friends, I'd been right to stay where I was. It was the other lifeline I had. The only lifeline to Jay, and right now, it was the lifeline that mattered more than my phone.

Breaking into a jog, I raced along the corridor and grabbed the envelope off the mat before the man could open the door and come out, once again trying to drag me back inside the room in his mistaken belief that I was only *safe* inside those walls with him by my side.

I tore open the envelope and read the words on the card.

Chelsea—

Don't cancel the boating trip tomorrow. I know you won't want to go alone. It was supposed to be a romantic trip for the two of us, but I still need you to go alone.

When the boat stops at Kiholo Bay, make an excuse to leave the group. There's a small waterfall past the waterhole that everyone else will be exploring. Follow the trail until it forks to the right. Follow that to the waterfall. I'll meet you there.

Don't tell anyone. This is serious. No one!

Love forever.

J.

The words blurred and washed away as tears filled my eyes and poured down my cheeks. Finally, this was over. I would see Jay. In less than twenty-four hours, he would take me in his arms. We would hold each other closer than we ever had. It was over! My captivity, my torment. The gaslighting and all the people who thought I was crazy and delusional.

Jay would explain everything. Why he'd left me and where he'd been all this time. I didn't know what he would tell me about that man in my room, but once I had Jay back in my arms, nothing else mattered.

THIRTY-TWO
CHELSEA

With the note tucked safely in my bag, I scurried away from the door to my suite, anxious to get far away before the man came out looking for me. I ran down the stairs. On the last step, I tripped, tearing the strap on my flip-flop.

I walked barefoot through the lobby to the shopping wing. I bought a new pair of flip-flops, sturdier ones this time. I also bought a pair of water shoes since I wasn't sure what the area would be like around the waterfall where I was meeting Jay. I smiled as I handed over my credit card, thinking about standing alone in a lush garden, the sound of splashing water behind us, while Jay and I kissed and clung to each other like the newly-weds we were. This time, my face would be wet with tears of happiness. After this ordeal, our marriage would be stronger than I'd ever dreamed.

With one new pair of shoes on my feet and the other in a bag, I went to the business center and emailed my mother, Bella, and Katherine. I told my mother and Bella that Jay was alive. I assumed my mother had told Katherine what was happening, but I caught her up on the details and how I was feeling. I told them about meeting Lori and Kendall, the missing phone, and my plans for the following day.

Each stroke of my fingers on the keyboard made me feel better. A smile spread across my face, and I wondered if the other worried-looking woman at the computer across from me thought I was slightly demented, grinning at a computer screen, typing emails.

What I was telling them was far from pleasant, but knowing I could pour out my heart caused the involuntary smile. I told them about my stolen phone and my plans to meet Jay. I tried to describe the incredible relief I felt, knowing I would see him soon, hold him soon. I felt a thousand times better knowing he would answer all my questions, maybe even explain the presence of this stranger in our room, in our bed when I'd woken that first morning.

It was difficult to believe Jay was involved in that. I couldn't imagine him putting me through something so horrible, or allowing another man into our honeymoon suite, but I knew there was an explanation. I knew he was in some horrible situation beyond his control.

One of the great things about the way our relationship had developed was that instead of starting out with an intense physical relationship like a lot of couples do, we'd spent all our time talking. For months, we'd done nothing but tell the stories of our lives. We knew each other inside and out. That had allowed us to develop a deep level of trust. It meant I knew how he thought and how he reacted to life.

There were a few more messages from Jay's co-workers. No one had heard from him, but I no longer cared. Of course they hadn't. He was only communicating with his wife. Why would he be in touch with them? I was the most important person in his life, the center of his world.

Hoping that I'd hear back soon from my mother or Bella or Katherine, I went to a coffee kiosk between the opening to the lobby and the garden area leading to the pool. I sat at a small table, took out the notecard, and reread Jay's message while I waited for my coffee to cool.

Putting the card away, I sipped my coffee, and turned my attention to the garden. I watched people walking by, letting my mind relax. The coffee was strong and good. The tropical air soothed my skin, and the anticipation of seeing Jay filled me with hope.

I shifted in my chair and saw a bench partially hidden by several small potted palm trees. Sitting with his legs crossed, the deck shoes I'd become familiar with, was the man who had taken possession of half my suite. He was leaning back so only his legs were visible, but as I watched he leaned forward slightly, possibly to get a look at me, confirming it was him.

He was *following* me? Had he watched me in the business center? I clutched my cardboard coffee cup, almost bending it with the pressure of my grip. Was it possible he'd stood behind me and read the emails I'd typed? I'd been so caught up in the thrill of what I was writing, I hadn't been aware of anyone else but the woman across from me.

I picked up my cup and took several large swallows. I stood and carried the cup to a nearby trash can, dropped it in, and hurried away from the garden.

Maybe I had it wrong. Maybe Jay knew nothing about this guy, and he was using me to get to Jay. Maybe he thought I knew where Jay was. After he'd seen that first note and destroyed it, he hoped that Jay would write again, that I would lead him to Jay.

But none of this could have anything to do with a parent at Jay's high school. No parent would go this far because he was upset about his son's college application. This line of thinking felt more sinister. It seemed like criminal-level behavior. Was Jay in far more serious trouble? Maybe he'd lied to me about who that phone call was from because he didn't want to scare me. Why hadn't I considered that until now?

Turning away from the trash can, I scanned the garden area. The man was still on the bench. He'd moved to the end so more of the palm branches obscured him from my view, but because I knew he was there, his attempt at concealing his presence no longer worked. I stepped behind the coffee kiosk and cut across the lobby. I walked into the shopping wing and hurried down the wide hallway. At the end, I turned down a hallway that curved back toward the resort offices, the medical facility, and the business center.

I didn't see the man anywhere in my range of vision ahead and I'd continued to look over my shoulder as I'd passed the stores. I slipped into the business center and chose a computer facing the door.

Three new emails were waiting for me.

I opened Katherine's first because I wanted a fresh perspective.

Chelsea—

Your mom told me about your nightmare. I'm really happy you got in touch. I knew, thanks to me, your phone was dead. Please call me if you need to talk. You know I'm always here. I can't imagine what you're going through. It's too horrible, but you're a tough girl. I know you'll figure out the right thing. But if you need me, I'm here. Call. Any hour of the day or night. Hugs.

Even though Katherine didn't say anything new, her message made me feel better. Elated, almost. She'd always had that effect. I almost felt as if I could see her face, feel her confidence in me. Maybe I would call her. There was something about her, maybe because she was older, but she didn't worry about me like my parents did. She respected me in the same way they did, but she never slipped back into seeing me as a child.

When I read the emails from my mom and Bella, I was crushed. I felt as if both of them were vigorously rubbing and fraying the thin threads that connected me to the people I loved.

Their messages echoed each other so closely, it almost felt as if they'd talked on the phone before responding. They told me it sounded as if my situation was growing *more dangerous*. They were very upset about the stolen phone, both of them *absolutely certain* the man in my room had taken it.

Worst of all, neither one of them wanted me to follow Jay's directions to meet him.

They said it sounded *dangerous*. They said I had no idea what kind of trouble he might be in, *what kind of people* he was *mixed up with*. My mother, especially, insisted that I hardly knew Jay at all.

You don't know anything about his life before he met you. Not really. Only what he chose to tell you, and that might have all been lies. He left your room on his own, Chelsea. He's the one who let that man in, and Jay is probably the one who told him so much about you. I'm begging you, please don't do this.

I'd never read so few words dripping with so much distrust for the man I was in love with, the man I'd married.

Both of their emails ended with identical words: *Please come home.*

THIRTY-THREE
ANONYMOUS

I know what it feels like to have hope. It's a crippling, chronic affliction. It's something that can keep you alive and filled with energy and positive feelings for a very long time.

Hope can shape you into a good person. A kind and generous human being. It can drive you to become a productive member of society. It makes you strong and resourceful. Hope makes your skin glow and shines in your eyes. When it's solid enough, it makes your heart sing.

I know the hope of loving another human being, knowing that soon, your relationship will grow into something long-lasting, something deep and satisfying and permanent. It's a divinely beautiful, transformative feeling.

Losing that hope is like plunging off a fifty-foot cliff.

Soon, Chelsea will find out what that loss of hope feels like. Her meeting with Jay will not go as she imagines.

The hope that's blooming in her heart is about to be shattered into a million fragments.

THIRTY-FOUR
CHELSEA

The boat that was taking us on our day trip was a small yacht. Not that I knew the designation of boats or could definitively say when a motorboat became a yacht, but that's what it looked like to me. It comfortably held the twenty people who had booked the tour to visit a black sand beach as well as our first stop at a beach that was well-known for a secluded cove where sea turtles often came ashore to rest. The first stop also featured a watering hole and lava tubes that the more adventurous among us were free to explore.

I planned to do none of those things. All my energy would first be spent trying to keep the memories of my boating accident under control. I needed to stay calm. I needed to keep the man from finding out I was terrified. He might know all the details of my accident and recovery, but he didn't know what was inside my heart. He didn't know my fears.

Letting anxiety take over my facial expression or my behavior would make it more difficult to slip away from him, and the rest of the group, so I could walk to the waterfall where I was supposed to meet Jay. They needed to see that I was having fun on the boat. They needed to think I couldn't wait to explore the watering hole and lava tubes, so that wandering off, hurrying ahead of the group, seemed natural and didn't raise questions.

It was unlikely most of the others would pay any attention to me. The area wasn't large, and before we boarded, the crew handed us leaflets that showed the various trails leading to the features we might want to explore. They offered to go with us or allow us to walk or hike on our own.

The man kept trying to grab my hand, as if we were a real couple and we would be walking together to the secluded part of the beach where the regal, tranquil sea turtles were sunning themselves.

I had a plan for how I would leave the man behind me. If he could act as if we were a honeymoon couple, I could just as easily do the same. As we stood on the dock, bags over our shoulders, waiting for the preliminary arrangements to finish, I scoped out a couple who looked to be about my age. I would befriend them with gushing stories of our wedding, a glowing introduction of the stranger tagging along beside me, and cling to their sides during the boat ride.

By the time we arrived at Kiholo Bay and the Keanalele Waterhole, I would have done my best to make sure the other couple had wound their sticky web around the man's legs and arms, making it more difficult for him to follow me when I slipped out of sight while they talked and enjoyed the sights.

The moment I'd seen them at the railing, looking across the water, I knew they were perfect for entrapping the man who was holding me captive in my room. I grabbed the man's wrist, the first time I'd touched him, and dragged him across the pier. "Those people look like they know a lot about the bay. We should talk to them."

"How do you know that?"

"He was pointing in the right direction. Not very many people can do that."

The man followed and I dropped his wrist, trusting he was behind me.

The desire to meet Jay, the thrill of leaving this man behind and starting my honeymoon over made me bold to the point of aggressive friendliness.

"Hi," I said. "I'm Chelsea. This is Jay. We're on our honeymoon." I grinned as if the man I loved with all my heart was standing beside me. I knew I should grab his hand or cuddle up to him. Did I have that in me? I took his hand, trying not to think. I pulled him toward me in the hope of shocking my body into obeying what my mind was telling it to do.

"Tara and Luke," the woman said. "We're celebrating our one-year anniversary! We got married here." She wound her dark, nearly black, waist-long ponytail around her hand and flung her hair over her shoulder. She wore a pink visor with the resort's logo on it. Her husband's visor was dark blue.

"We were married at Hibiscus Garden Waterfalls," I said. "Our reception was here also. How perfect. When I saw you, I knew we should introduce ourselves, right?" I looked up at the man, grinned, then turned back to them. "Have you taken this trip before?"

"We did it on our honeymoon," Luke said. "The lava tubes were incredible."

"And the sea turtles." Tara clasped her hands and held them close to her throat. "I love them." She held out her arm and showed me a silver bracelet with tiny turtles formed into a chain.

"What's the best place to start?" I asked. "We'd love it if you could show us around. If we're not crashing your anniversary."

I felt the man tense beside me.

"Not at all," Tara said.

"As long as we're not crashing your honeymoon," Luke said.

"I don't—"

I interrupted the man. "Sounds perfect. It's so much more

fun with new friends, experienced friends who know all the ins and outs."

They basked in my compliment as the man beside me moved closer, shifting around, trying to edge between us, clearly not happy with the situation. It was too late. I kept talking, refusing to let him speak or change the plan I was weaving, attaching myself to them as securely as I could, preparing to leave the man in their eager hands.

As we boarded the boat, the man hung back. "I need to talk to you."

"About what?"

"These people. And—"

"Aren't they great? What are the chances of meeting a couple that was married only a year ago? It's like it was meant to be."

"It wasn't meant to be." His tone was sharp.

I walked along the side of the boat, finding a place by the rail, hoping the presence of Tara and Luke would distract me from the visceral memories of a racing boat crashing into concrete. It was also possible the size of the boat would make this experience feel different from the speed and careening sensation I'd had two years ago on the powerboat when it flung me into the air and sent me spinning into the dark water, pummeled by debris.

As the boat motored slowly away from the pier, the man tried to nudge me away from Tara and Luke. He knew better than to try taking my hand or putting his arm around my waist. But his body language was clear. He didn't want to be with these people. I wanted to laugh. Except for the few moments with Lori and Kendall, I hadn't laughed in days. The feeling was very welcome. Now, it was his turn to feel trapped and helpless.

We pulled out of the harbor and the boat picked up speed. I gripped the rail. My knuckles were white, but the thick bar felt good beneath my palms. I felt secure and the textured deck made my feet feel firmly planted. The boat rocked gently, but it wasn't bouncing and jumping over the waves as the speedboat had done. I didn't have the same sensation that our speed was out of control, even though we were moving fairly quickly across the water, the sprawling resort growing smaller behind us.

In an effort to distract myself from my memories, I pestered Tara with questions about their wedding, the resort, and Kiholo Bay. She was willing to answer, eager to talk, and it helped. I listened to her and even though I felt a whispering unease in the pit of my stomach, a tremor of fear at the base of my skull, I was able to smile and listen.

The flow of Tara's words swelled higher than the water, filling my ears, then my head. They blotted out the past. They blotted out the growing agitation of the man who had been my constant shadow for nearly a week.

And then, we were pulling into the bay. They dropped an anchor and loaded large inflatable boats into the water near a low deck at the back. We were told to climb down a short ladder to the platform and step into the boats, four passengers and a crew member for each.

The inflatable boats had outboard motors, and the boats bounced over the surf, but the water was relatively calm. The tide was out, making for easy access to the shore. I was reassured, knowing that within five or ten yards, my feet would be able to touch the sandy bottom of the bay. But I didn't feel completely calm until I was on the beach, walking through soft, damp sand.

I'd mentioned to Tara I was eager to see the sea turtles first, so we headed immediately in that direction. The man had calmed himself somewhat, resigned to his fate, possibly in the same way I'd temporarily resigned myself to my dreadful circumstances.

We spent about half an hour admiring the enormous turtles, studying their beautiful shells, watching them occasionally lift their heads to gaze back at us with wise, ancient-looking eyes. It almost felt as if they wondered about us, that they were curious about why we were so interested in their sunbathing. The longer I watched them, the calmer I felt. It seemed as if they communicated their calm directly into my heart. I wanted to ask if Tara felt the same, but it wasn't a question I wanted to discuss with the man, so I kept my thoughts to myself.

As we turned away and began following the trail to the watering hole, I watched for the break in the trail Jay had described. Following that would take me away from the others, through a narrow space and out into a grotto with a lagoon where the waterfall splashed from an outcropping of rocks about fifteen feet above. The lagoon was moss-covered and too slippery for swimming, so it was rarely visited. Everyone went to the waterhole and the lava tubes.

I positioned myself beside Luke and gave him the history of Jay's high school, telling him all about the golf team, Jay's students, and the classes he taught. Then I moved to the side and nudged the man forward.

"Tell him about last season's championship. I can't capture the excitement as well as you can." My voice sounded fake and giddy in my ears, but since Tara and Luke didn't know me, I hoped they assumed that's the kind of person I was. The man didn't know me at all either, despite the download of data he'd received from somewhere.

Once again, I walked more slowly, letting the others pull ahead, listening to the man stumble through stories about high school golf. Finally, I realized he didn't know as much as he'd pretended to. He'd clearly read a lot about the school and the golf team, but the details were off.

I saw the turnoff and stopped walking. They pulled farther ahead, and I made a sudden turn, walking as fast as I could along the narrow trail. Once they noticed I'd left the group, they would look for me. I needed to be as far out of sight as possible. There had been several branches off the path, so I could hope they might not immediately choose this route.

Once the path turned, I took off my flip-flops and started running. It was packed dirt, damp from showers the night before last, but not muddy. I willed my feet to remain steady, my toes digging into the earth. I was going to see Jay! I wouldn't fall; I wouldn't stumble. I would get there as fast as I could. This nightmare was about to end.

Even if he didn't have any ID with him, Jay could eventually unlock his phone and prove who he was. Even if he couldn't immediately, or wasn't believed, I would have my husband with me, and that was all that mattered. It was everything.

I saw a small sign indicating the waterfall was one hundred feet ahead. I'd already heard the splash of falling water. The pleasant sound increased as I drew closer, a soothing melody like rain. A moment later I was standing a few feet from the lagoon.

The waterfall looked like something out of a fairy tale. It cascaded over the rocks at the top, falling free like silken strands before splashing into the lagoon. The water was deep blue, and the pool appeared to be almost bottomless. Near the shore, it was so still, the three or four small clouds were reflected in the water.

I looked around at the lush plants, searching for Jay.

He had to be here. He'd told me to meet him. Where was he? Once again, my gaze traveled around the clearing and the edge of the water.

A few feet from the waterfall there was a large pile of rocks that formed an outcrop between where I stood and where the waterfall splashed into the lagoon. Protruding from the rocks was the lower half of a man's leg.

THIRTY-FIVE
CHELSEA

I screamed, the sound filling my lungs, my body, my head. It carried across the water and up the waterfall. It seemed to fill the sky as I ran to the rocks.

Dropping my flip-flops, I raced around the edge of the lagoon. I stepped into the water and immediately skidded as my foot made contact with the slick moss on the solid rock hidden below the dark surface of the water. My eyes filling with tears as I looked at the leg, the bare foot, the hem of his shorts, and now, the tips of his fingers that had floated to the surface, I crouched down, trying to see into the water, looking for a safe place to step.

I tried again, easing my feet onto the slippery rocks. I moved carefully, but after three steps, I skidded again. My feet lost their grip, and I splashed down hard. The rock hit my tailbone, sending a painful jolt up my spine. I crawled back to the shore, crying harder now.

I had to get him out. Was it him? Through tear-filled eyes, I scanned the clearing, but I was still alone, the only sound my rasping sobs.

After three more tries to get into the water, I stood and

shimmied out of my shorts and top. I'd worn a bathing suit under my clothes, packing a change of clothes in the bag that I'd left on the boat. I'd never expected to go swimming. Meeting Jay was the only thing on my mind, but I'd needed the man to believe I was out for a pleasure cruise.

The moment I was ready to dive into the water, I realized it was too shallow around the boulders. I couldn't walk in without falling, but diving risked cracking my skull. I sat down and tried sliding across the rocks toward the man's leg. Finally, I reached him, but as I closed my eyes, feeling sick with fear and desperate to know if this was the nightmare I'd imagined coming to life, I grabbed his ankle. I pulled, but he didn't move.

I eased myself back to shore and went around the outcrop. The bottom was slightly less slippery on that side, but as I slowly made my way into the lagoon, the waterfall began splashing over me as if there were five shower heads all running at once.

Crying, my face slick with tears and water, I stepped back out. I returned to my clothes, tugged them on over my wet bathing suit, grabbed my flip-flops, and began running blindly back along the trail to get help.

At the juncture for the two trails, I ran into the man. Literally. He'd left Tara and Luke behind to come looking for me.

"Where were you?"

"I need help! There's a man's body. Jay. I'm scared it's Jay. He—"

"I'm—"

"Don't. I need help." I shoved past him and began running back to the beach where the boat was anchored. When I came to the beach, I slowed, not wanting to fall or twist my ankle on the soft sand.

"Help! I need help!"

People scattered across the beach turned to look as they heard my screams. Two crew members stood in the shallow water. I rushed toward them, gasping out the story of what I'd found. One of them called someone on the boat, and in less than two minutes, another rubber boat was headed to shore with a third crew member. She climbed out, carrying rope and a backpack with emergency supplies and tools.

Because they knew the area, the crew members led the way, with me following, and the man trailing behind me. When we reached the lagoon, they went to work. They were so efficient and practiced at extracting the man's body from where it was wedged in the rocks, it seemed as if they'd done this before, but I couldn't imagine anything like this had ever happened.

I sat on the thick moss covering the shore, hugging my knees, crying softly, knowing in my heart the body was Jay's. He'd said he would meet me here and he hadn't. I knew now that someone else had written those notes.

Some monster had filled me with hope, lured me here, and then destroyed my heart once and for all.

As the body was pulled toward the shore, held by the crew members, I recognized one of Jay's shirts. I knew by the shape of his legs, the distinctive form of his feet, it was him.

I sobbed as if my whole body was breaking into a thousand, a million pieces.

This was what I'd feared from the moment I'd woken with that man in my bed. And this was what I'd hoped with all my heart would not happen.

"It's my husband!"

The man sat beside me. He placed his hand on my shoulder. I shook it off and moved away from him. "Do not touch me ever again."

"He's not—"

"Don't speak to me."

I watched the slow procession. The drumbeat played in my head—it's Jay, it's Jay. My husband is dead. My husband is dead. My husband is dead.

Then, I saw his face, and I knew I'd hoped the drumbeat had been wrong, that it was only a rhythm of fear. A sound came out of me that seemed to originate from a place I hadn't known existed inside me. A shriek so inhuman, I wondered if the others recognized it. I wondered if they would cover their ears.

I saw something that made me turn and spill the contents of my stomach all over the ground. Because of the exotic fish that called the lagoon their home, his face was unrecognizable.

THIRTY-SIX

CHELSEA

Once Jay's body was on the shore of the lagoon, the police and coroner were called. Two of the rescuers left to meet them at the beach, ready to lead them to the waterfall. They suggested I return to the boat, but I refused. I wasn't leaving my husband's side. Just as I'd refused to leave the island without him, I was not leaving him alone now.

The man tried to assure me the body belonged to a stranger. "You don't know him. You're having a traumatic, hysterical reaction to finding a corpse, that's all. We should leave so you can get these horrific images out of your head."

Every time he spoke, I turned so my back faced him, but he refused to give up. He continued to reposition himself, trying to lean in, looking me in the eye. He was eager to comfort me, eager to tell me the body lying a few feet away from me wasn't Jay. He wanted to pull me away from my husband's side. He wanted me to turn my back on him.

"It's not healthy to look at a deceased person. And having a shirt that's similar to one that belongs to someone you know means nothing."

"It's not *someone* I know. It's my husband."

"I'm your husband, Chelsea. Let me help you. Let's go back to the boat. We can sit on the deck and have a glass of wine. It will calm your nerves. We can look at the water and relax. This isn't good for you, for us."

I shoved him away from me. I hit him hard, but he remained solid, his body only moving a few inches as he absorbed the impact. He tried to put his arm around me, but I walked away from him. After a few more attempts, he left me alone.

It seemed to take forever, but finally a detective, two police officers, a forensics person, and the coroner arrived. All but the detective got busy collecting evidence and tending to Jay's body. The detective came immediately to where I was sitting.

"Detective Morr. Are you Mrs. Davis?"

I nodded. "Can we talk over there?" He gestured toward a few rocks that seemed designed to serve as stools.

When we were settled, he asked for my name, contact details for where I was staying, then wanted me to describe how I'd found the body. I hated that he kept calling Jay, the body. It sounded cold and final. It almost sounded as if he'd never been a person at all.

He asked if the man who had been standing beside me a moment earlier was my husband. I told him the story of how I'd woken up a few days ago. I told him about Jay going missing and my attempt to speak to the police. As I repeated the series of events, he grew quieter, asking fewer questions, looking more disbelieving as I went.

When I was finished, he said, "I see." Then he asked me to tell him again how I'd come upon *the body*. When I was finished, he stood and gestured for the man to join us.

As I expected, when the detective asked for his name and contact information, the man provided Jay's.

"Mrs. Davis has just reported the deceased as Jay Davis at that address."

The man gave him a patient, calm smile. He pulled out his

fake ID and handed it to the detective. The detective looked at the photo, studied the man's face, glanced at me, then handed it back. "I see."

I pointed to Jay's body. "I know that man is my husband." The words came out strangled and raw. I pulled Jay's note out of my bag and handed it to the detective. "He asked me to meet him here."

The detective gave me a strange look, puzzled that my husband would be sending a note, arranging to meet at a secluded waterfall far from our resort. He glanced at the note, then gave it to a technician for bagging.

"Thank you for that, but it's impossible to identify the body at this point," he said. "We'll need to use dental records."

"What about his wedding ring? It's engraved." I pushed away from the two men and started to where they were enclosing my husband in a zippered bag. "Wait!"

One of the police officers stepped in front of me. "It's not a good idea to come closer. He's—"

"Can you check his wedding ring? For identification?"

"He's not wearing a wedding ring."

"He must be. We were just married a few days ago. I know he'd never take it off."

"If this man was wearing a ring, it might have come off in the water. But in any case, he isn't wearing a ring now."

I heard the loud zip of the bag as it closed, like a tearing sound in the fabric of the universe.

THIRTY-SEVEN

CHELSEA

The boat ride back to the resort was relentless torture. I stood alone at the stern, as if I was saying goodbye to Jay, watching the place where his life had ended fade into the horizon as we moved farther away. I gripped the railing with every ounce of strength I possessed. All the anxiety I'd kept squashed down earlier, rose to the surface like a sea monster reaching its tentacles over the side of the boat, trying to attach its suction cups to my arms, my legs, my brain, my heart.

This time, I didn't have the chatter of Tara to distract me, nor did I want it. I didn't have people standing around me. I wanted to be alone, and because everyone on the boat knew what had happened, they left me to myself. The man wanted to stay with me, but I'd told him I didn't want to see his face.

As I spoke those words, they stuck in my throat like thorns.

The moment I was off the boat, I walked as quickly as I could back along the path that ran parallel to the grassy strip behind the beach. I opened the gate into the pool area and went up to my suite. I could feel the man close behind me. It felt as if he was chasing me, his strides long and aggressive. The hot afternoon breeze made me imagine I could feel his breath on my neck.

Inside, I locked the bathroom door and took a long, hot shower, scrubbing off the moss from the bottom of the lagoon and the dirt from running barefoot. I scrubbed my entire body with strawberry wash and shampooed my hair until I felt like I'd removed all the sweat and salt air. I cried the entire time.

I put on a dress and sandals and ordered an Uber.

When I went out, the man started to follow me.

I turned to face him. "Stop following me. Stop pretending you're someone who's now *dead*! Get out of my face, get out of my life." I pulled the door closed and hurried down the stairs.

The police had told me it would be several days before they had the dental records to confirm the body I'd discovered was Jay Davis, so now I was faced with more waiting and despair. The detective had said it as if waiting were as easy as waiting for a dental appointment of my own. "You'll just have to be patient. These things take time."

I took the Uber to the mobile phone store and purchased my second new phone, waiting numbly while they transferred my data from the cloud and set up my plan.

With another beautiful new phone in my hand, from which I took no pleasure, I texted Lori.

> I have a new phone. Can we meet for a drink?
> Things have happened.

It felt too awful telling her in a text message that Jay was dead. I stared at the screen, waiting. There was no response. I supposed they could have been out for the day, just as easily as I'd been. They might be snorkeling. They might be dozing in the sun.

I rode back to the resort with my hand on the phone, longing for a reply. I was so lonely for someone to believe me, to comfort me over my husband's death. I knew I should tell my parents. And Bella. Katherine. My other friends. But I couldn't, in fact, I probably should not tell Jay's family and friends, not until it was confirmed. Which meant maybe I shouldn't tell anyone.

Did those thoughts mean that my instinct was telling me I wasn't sure the body was his after all? I knew that shirt. I knew his legs and feet, didn't I? The man's hands had been distorted by water, so it was more difficult to say, but even though his feet and legs were swollen, I was sure I recognized them. Seeing them like that made me cry, but I recognized them. Or had I made that assumption because of the shirt, because I'd expected to meet Jay at that spot?

The car arrived at the resort, and I climbed out. I went into the lobby and walked through to the main garden. I scanned the pool area, but I didn't see Lori or Kendall. Of course, they could be anywhere. There was the pool bar, two smaller pools, three restaurants, several bars... the list went on. The resort covered several acres and was filled with pathways and lush gardens. I couldn't just give it a quick glance and expect to see them.

I didn't feel like going back to my suite. The thought of seeing that man, of even knowing he was nearby if I sat on the balcony, was unbearable.

Finally, my phone vibrated. Lori:

A drink sounds great. The Golden Rim? We need to talk to you—we saw a man wearing the hat you told us about—with your husband's school logo. Maybe it's him?

THIRTY-EIGHT
ANONYMOUS

Waiting so long to take revenge had caused it to change shape. Plans appeared in my thoughts and were later discarded. Sometimes I thought I was ready, but it turned out the timing was off. If I wasn't such a patient person, I might have become overwhelmed with frustration.

All it took was a threatening phone call to lure him out of the honeymoon suite. And then everything began to unfold as I'd imagined it would.

Holding on to a secret like mine takes extraordinary self-control. Most people don't have that level of self-discipline. But that's the kind of discipline required to complete the plan I'd finally developed. It was going to take time, and there were a lot of details to consider.

I never doubted I could do it.

That secret burned inside me like the eternal flame of life, keeping me focused and alive.

THIRTY-NINE

CHELSEA

My fingers turned numb as I read Lori's text message. The phone wobbled in my hand, and I almost dropped it. I fumbled and grabbed it before it crashed to the ground.

No. That couldn't be real. She hadn't seen Jay. Someone else must have his hat. He'd lost it. That was probably what I'd seen before. It was nothing but grief and delusional hope that made me think I'd ever seen Jay. He'd probably worn the hat when he'd gone out that night and had lost it. Maybe running from his killer before he ever reached Kiholo Bay. It fell off at the resort and someone picked it up.

Why had I assumed it was him? If he'd been wandering around the resort, of course he would have returned to our suite. It showed how out of touch I'd been with the rational side of my mind that I'd believed for even half a second the man wearing that hat was Jay. My cheeks grew warm, thinking about how I'd told Lori and Kendall about it. Had they laughed behind my back? Were they laughing now? Teasing me with hope by telling me they'd seen a man wearing it?

I closed my eyes. It had felt so good to have someone listen to me, laugh with me, believe me. I took a long, deep breath and opened my eyes. No. It wasn't that. They were trying to help. When you were filled with hope, it was logical to believe what you saw. There was nothing wrong with being optimistic.

Feeling only slightly anxious, I started walking toward the Golden Rim bar. Lori and Kendall were already seated at a small table near a raised pool of water with several gently burbling fountains. The chair they'd saved for me was pulled out from the table, waiting for my arrival. I offered them a tentative smile.

They both stood and gave me warm, tight hugs before we took our seats. We ordered drinks. As if we'd been talking for half an hour already, Lori began speaking mid-thought, "So, we were sitting on our balcony and he was walking toward the beach. Kendall saw him."

"You never saw two girls run so fast when they weren't in a marathon," Kendall said.

"But we got out there, and he was gone." Lori gazed at me with such sorrowful eyes, I thought she might cry. She looked as if she felt personally responsible for losing sight of a stranger wearing a hat that used to belong to my husband.

Unless the man in the lagoon wasn't my husband and my husband had amnesia, or something. I laughed, incredulous at my desire to fabricate stories to offer myself a thin strip of hope in the face of absolutely no hope at all.

Our drinks came and we clinked our glasses together, but no one offered a toast. When they heard what I had to tell them, they would be glad they hadn't even said cheers.

I took a few generous sips of my drink, then told them about the final note from Jay. I began describing the lagoon, the waterfall, and the discovery of his body, or *the body*, trapped among the rocks.

As I talked, their drinks remained untouched on the table. Their eyes seemed not to blink, and their lips slowly parted in shock.

"How awful," Kendall said.

"It sounds horrifying," Lori whispered.

I told them about the crew removing his body and calling the police.

"Oh my god." Lori put her hands over her face. Kendall looked slightly ill. "I can't even," Lori said.

Kendall shook her head, picked up her drink, and slurped loudly, pulling it through the straw as quickly as she could, not stopping until she put it down hard on the table, pressing her fingertips to her temples.

"What are you doing to do?" Lori asked.

"There's nothing I can do. I haven't even told anyone." I felt the tears filling my eyes again. The entire time I'd been talking, I sounded, and felt, detached, numb. Now, the tears flowed down my cheeks. "I keep hoping maybe it's not him. But I know it is. If I tell my family and friends, and definitely if I tell his family, it's real. And I don't want it to be real. And maybe it's not him, right? What if I'm wrong? They told me to wait for the dental records for identification. But I have no idea how long that takes."

"Wow," Kendall said.

"I know. I just want it to be someone else. But it looked like him. Even though..." I slurped my drink as loudly as Kendall had.

They both put their straws in their mouths and slurped.

They laughed. I laughed through my tears.

"This definitely calls for a lot of alcohol." Kendall put her hand over mine. "That's what the doctor ordered. So, you have to follow the protocol."

I smiled.

We immediately ordered another round.

"It's so creepy how you found his body in the water," Lori said.

"If it's him," Kendall said.

I put my straw between my lips, sucking in the fruity drink, letting the icy liquid pour into my body, hoping for the brain freeze I normally dreaded, wanting to numb myself in any way possible. I wanted my thoughts to stop. I wanted the questions and the uncertainty to stop. I wanted to know where Jay was. I wanted to rewind my life to the day of my wedding when I didn't think I could ever be any happier.

"If it was him," Kendall said, "then he probably didn't send the note telling you to meet him. Unless he sent it and then someone killed him." She pushed her straw to the side of her glass and took several gulps without it. "He must have been there for... a while."

I nodded.

"The killer sent the note," Lori whispered. She stared at me. "He knows where your room is. What if he's *in* your room?"

No one spoke. It was the thing my mother feared. It was the thing Bella had warned me about without speaking the words. It was the thing that made me buy the knife. And yet everything about that man had been kind and polite and respectful. Wasn't that what they said about a lot of serial killers? They were always polite.

"He wanted you to go there," Kendall said. "He wanted you to find your husband's body. If it's him."

I knew it was him. Why else had I received that note telling me to meet him at that waterfall? And I knew. My heart knew, my body knew. It didn't matter that his ring was gone, that they hadn't confirmed his identity. I knew. All the thoughts contradicting that fact were flimsy hopes, desperately clawing for life because I didn't want him to be dead. I didn't want this to be happening. But I *knew*.

"Are you okay?" Kendall put her hand on mine. "Drink some water." She picked up my glass and held it out to me. I took it from her and pacified her with a small sip. Then I returned to my cocktail. I wanted to get drunk. I wanted to see their faces, their concern, their belief in my story through a haze. I wanted to forget everything. I didn't want to go back to my suite. I didn't want to go home. I didn't want to think about dental records or the police or try to figure out what that man was doing in my room.

I turned my attention to my drink, sipping steadily, watching them watch me with pity and horror. Was that what their expressions said? I wasn't sure. They were strangers. It's difficult to read the expression of someone close to you, how can you ever think you're reading the expression of someone you've only recently met? It's possible you never even correctly read the expression of someone you've known for decades.

We talked about other things for a while. Rather, they did, I sat numbly, letting their words drift past me. Kendall ordered a third round of drinks. When they came, I sucked at mine greedily.

We talked more, but my brain was growing foggy. I was having trouble focusing on the thread of our conversation. More about Jay and how awful the situation was. More speculation about the man and whether or not he was a killer. Their eyes bore into mine. Their expressions shifted, from pity to concern. From certainty to disapproval.

I should have *demanded* the resort find me a room. It was a clear case of men believing men over women. It was unjust. It was unsafe. I hadn't pushed back hard enough.

Everything felt blurry. I felt as if I'd had five drinks. Maybe six. Had they put something in my cocktail? Their eyes were huge, staring at me. Smirking. Maybe they didn't believe me at all. Maybe I was just someone to entertain them because they were bored.

Why was everything spinning? I felt someone's hand around my wrist, twisting, pulling at my skin. I whimpered.

"Shh. Don't make a scene."

FORTY

CHELSEA

The first thing I noticed was that I had to pee. I wasn't sitting in the bar. I was lying on a sofa, a pillow under my head. I tried to open my eyes, but they felt glued shut. I squeezed them gently, then eased them open. The room was dimly lit. I smelled gardenia, but that wasn't unusual in Hawaii, I smelled it often.

Where was I? I tried to remember what had happened.

I was having drinks.

Lori and Kendall were with me. We'd decided to get drunk. I guess we had. But I'd never been so drunk I passed out. Why was I lying on a sofa? Why did I feel so strange? Where was my purse? My phone? My shoes? I realized my feet were bare. Who had taken my sandals? Or maybe I'd lost them somewhere. That didn't seem possible. I should sit up.

I was so thirsty. Incredibly thirsty. But I also had to pee, I remembered that now.

I tried to sit up, but I realized someone's hand was on my ankle, holding me down. Not hard, not restraining me really, but making it hard for me to sit up, impossible to move my legs.

"What's going on? I need to—"

"Shh. Try to get some rest. You've had a lot of trauma."

I recognized her voice. Kendall. I think. Yes. My new friend. But why wouldn't she let me sit up? Was she my friend? I'd thought she was, but now, I wasn't sure. I remembered them looking at me, their concerned faces turning to pity then condemnation. Or something. "Where am I?"

"In our room."

I tried to sit up. Her hand on my lower leg tightened, like a vice with the crank turning ever so slightly. "I need to use the bathroom."

"Just rest."

"Now."

She sighed. "You're very drowsy. I don't want you to fall. Can't it wait a few minutes?"

"No." I struggled to move my legs. She still wouldn't let go. I twisted, kicking at her thigh.

"Don't do that."

"Let go of my legs." I now realized she had a grip on both ankles. My feet had lost their feeling. I wasn't sure I would be able to walk once she did let go. She was right about risking a fall once I tried to stand.

"You need to sleep. Don't fight it."

"I'm not sleepy. I need to check my messages, and I need to—"

"You need to what? There won't be any more messages from Jay coming to your room. And the police won't have any information yet. It's better if you rest. Lori and I want you to stay with us. It's not safe in your room."

"All my things are there."

"Nothing you need right now."

For some irrational reason, maybe just the history of fear from my accident that had embedded itself in my memory, I thought of my pain medication. I didn't need it. I hadn't taken it for months. But that was the one thing in my room that I didn't want left unattended, that I didn't want to be without.

Besides, these women were strangers. I was no longer sure they were my friends. Why were they so eager to help? I tried to remember how I'd met them. Was it as casual as it seemed, or had they been waiting for me? I couldn't remember. And as much as I hated that man, as much as I despised his gaslighting and loathed his refusal to tell me what he knew about what had happened to Jay, he was my only connection to the truth. I wasn't going to cut that off. Not that I'd extracted a single molecule of truth from him so far.

"I have to pee. Right now. Let go of me."

She eased her grip. "Okay. But don't do anything crazy."

"Like what?"

"Like trying to leave. I'm serious. That man probably killed your husband, and you know it. You just don't want to admit it. Everything points to it. He had the key to your room and a fake ID saying he's your husband. He set this up and you're acting like you're perfectly safe because you have a knife under your pillow. You're way out of your league. He has the entire resort staff and the police believing his story. Not yours. We're trying to help you, Chelsea."

"I have to pee!"

She let go of my ankles and took my hand, helping me sit up. She showed me where the bathroom was.

When I returned, my eyes had cleared. I scanned the room, looking for my purse and sandals. There were two queen beds, a dresser and small desk, a TV mounted to the wall, and the doors to the balcony. A quick glance around the tidy space suggested they'd put my things where I couldn't easily find them. "Where are my things? I need my phone."

"Just rest," Kendall said. "Sit down."

"Where's Lori?"

"She went to get us something to eat."

"Why didn't you call room service?"

Kendall shrugged.

"Where's my purse? I need my phone."

"Why?"

"I haven't talked to anyone at home since I found Jay. I..." Why was I explaining this to her? I'd asked for my purse. She had no right to hide it from me. What was going on here? A wave of lightheadedness came over me, the room tilting slightly, the edges of my vision turning blurry, then dark. I sat down quickly, bending forward to put my head close to my knees.

"You got up too fast. And now you're upsetting yourself. Let me get you some water." She took a small bottle out of the fridge, twisted the cap as if I were an invalid, incapable of opening my own water bottle, and handed it to me. "Don't drink it too fast."

I gulped the water. I didn't say anything until the entire six-ounce bottle was empty. I stood. "Where's my purse."

"Let's wait until Lori comes back with some food. You had a lot of alcohol."

I felt the wave of dizziness, followed by some nausea. I wanted to sit, but I didn't want to prove her right. I was starting to wonder if I'd had more than three drinks, which was what I remembered. "What time is it?"

"Eleven fifteen."

"And she's just now getting dinner?"

She laughed. "No, silly. It's eleven-fifteen in the morning. She's getting breakfast."

I'd been passed out for over twelve hours! They must have dropped something into my drink. But wouldn't I have noticed? We'd been seated at a small table. How would I have missed that? But I had no recollection of finishing my third drink, leaving the bar, or coming to their room.

"I need to get back."

"You do not need to get back to anything. Or anyone, that's for sure. It's not safe. Open your eyes." She came toward me, standing between the sofa and the coffee table, blocking my way. "You don't look well. Please sit down. Lori will be back any minute."

She was right. I didn't feel well. I was having trouble remaining on my feet. The thought of taking the elevator down from their tower room, crossing the resort to my building, and climbing the stairs made me feel as if I might be sick.

I collapsed onto the sofa. Kendall brought me another bottle of water. Lori returned with the food—lunch, not breakfast after all. I nibbled my way through half a turkey sandwich, listening to them remind me over and over how unsafe it was to return to my room, listening to them outline the *proof* that the man in my suite was Jay's killer, and he was now making plans to kill and dismember me.

After I'd eaten, and consumed several more bottles of water, I felt more stable. I stood and went to the dresser. "I'd like my purse and shoes. I need to get back to my room. Right now."

"Haven't you listened to anything we said?" Lori asked.

"I did. And I appreciate your concern. I'm really grateful you let me stay here. But that man knows something about what happened to Jay, and even though I've gotten nowhere finding out what it is, I'm not giving up. It's all I have."

"He could kill you!"

"He hasn't. If he wanted to, wouldn't he have done that?"

"He's a psychopath. You don't know what he's thinking or what he plans to do." Lori's voice rose, shrill and trembling with her own fear.

"I need to know what happened to my husband. I need to know why that man was in my room and how he got in there. Most of all, I need to find out how he knows so many things about my life. I don't feel unsafe. I honestly don't. It's my choice and I want my things. You can't kidnap me."

Kendall laughed. "We're not *kidnapping* you."

"It feels like you are. If you don't get my things right now, I'll start opening your drawers. Or I'll call security."

Kendall heaved a dramatic sigh. Lori started crying softly. "We want to help you," Lori said.

"I really do appreciate it. And I hope I can call you if I need help. But right now, I need to find out who killed my husband. And I don't think it was that man. He literally hasn't left my side since I woke up four days ago."

"Maybe he—"

"I want my purse."

Finally, Kendall took my purse out of the nightstand and handed it to me. They got my sandals out of their closet, and I left. Lori was still teary-eyed. Kendall looked at me as if I were the psychopath.

FORTY-ONE

CHELSEA

As the door to my suite came into view, I found my eyes drawn to the doormat. It shocked me that after only three notes, my thoughts were attuned to looking for a note from Jay. The overwhelming sense of disappointment followed by a wave of grief was like a punch to my solar plexus. I bent over slightly, gasping for air.

After a moment, my breathing returned to normal. I straightened and continued on. I unlocked the door and went inside, steeling myself for an encounter with the man. I had decided that despite all my previous failures, I would try once again to get him to tell me what he knew about Jay's disappearance, and now his murder. I would ask him to tell me how he knew so much about me. Because his intimate knowledge had been so unsettling each time he revealed a piece of it, I wasn't sure I'd ever directly asked him that question.

Inside, the room was so bright, I couldn't immediately make out where the man was sitting. I went to the doors leading to my bedroom, turning to look back at the room from that angle. I saw then that he was standing at the far corner of the balcony, looking toward the building from which I'd just come.

In a flash, he was at the door, sliding it open, stepping into the room. "Where have you been? I've been so worried about you."

"With some friends." I touched the handle of the bedroom door. I wasn't sure if now was the right time to ask him my questions or if I should wait until he calmed down. Maybe now was best *because* he was wound up, showing a crack in his façade. It might be easier to get him to expose his thoughts. His agitated state might cause him to say something he normally wouldn't.

"When are you going to tell me how you know so much about my life? About my relationship with Jay?"

"You were gone all night," he said. "I told you it wasn't safe for you to leave the room without me. Why aren't you taking me seriously? This isn't a game."

"Why should I take you seriously? You won't tell me anything about what's going on."

"Can't you trust me?"

"There's zero reason for me to trust you."

"Have I done anything to hurt you?"

"You've lied to me every minute of every day," I said.

"Why didn't you come home last night?"

"I don't have to explain anything to you."

"I'm relieved that you're safe, but you have no idea how worried I was." He came toward me, then stopped.

"Unless you're going to tell me how you know so much about me and Jay, and unless you're going to tell me how you got into my room and why you're here, there's nothing for us to talk about. And I prefer that we stay far away from each other from now on."

"Why can't you accept me as your husband?"

I laughed. "Because you're not. And if you think I would believe that for one second, it's beyond insulting. It says you think I'm borderline stupid, or that I've lost my mind."

He looked like he wanted to say more, so much more. It was

clear that he could answer all my questions. It was obvious he knew everything that was going on, but for whatever reason he was refusing to tell me. The rage that filled me was indescribable. I wanted to rush at him and shove him to the ground, sit on his knees, and punch him in the face until it was a bloody pulp, unrecognizable, just like Jay's.

I pressed down on the door handle, felt the door swing open behind me, and stumbled into the dark room. I slammed the door and locked it. I pulled my phone out of my purse, dropped my purse on the floor, and collapsed onto the bed. I lay on my back and tapped my mom's number to call her.

The phone rang and went to voicemail. I left a message telling her to call me as soon as she could. I sent her a text message telling her the same. I called my father next. That call also went to voicemail where I left a message followed by a text. When the same thing happened with Bella and then Katherine, I threw my phone at the pillows. I turned onto my stomach, pressing my face into the crook of my arm, sobbing with all the energy that remained in my body. A moment later, I heard the man knocking on the plantation doors, rattling them in their frame, speaking my name.

With Jay dead and my family unreachable, it felt as if everyone I loved had disappeared from my life. I felt as if I was doomed to spend the rest of my days with a stranger who knew everything about me but refused to tell me a single thing about what was happening in my own life. He was controlling me as if I were a puppet, preparing to use me for something I knew nothing about.

FORTY-TWO

CHELSEA

After a while, my tears subsided. I turned onto my back, staring up at the ceiling fan, watching its slow rotation. I let the movement mesmerize me until I lost track of time. I dozed for a while, then I woke and checked my phone. There were no text messages. No returned phone calls.

I got off the bed, locked the bathroom door into the living room, showered, and changed my clothes. I checked my phone again, with the same results. My legs felt twitchy. My mind wouldn't stop running in circles. I couldn't stay in the room for another second.

Tearing off my clothes again, I slipped on a swimsuit, a cover-up, and grabbed my beach supplies. I checked my phone in the pathetic hope that somebody would have responded to me by now. It had been over an hour since I'd called and texted. I couldn't believe, knowing what they did about what was happening with me, that nobody was responding.

The moment I burst out of the bedroom door, the man stood up from his place on the sofa. "Where are you going?"

"Out." I headed toward the door.

"I'll go with you."

"No."

I flung open the door, lunged out of the room, and started walking as quickly as I could. When I heard him behind me, I stopped and turned. "Don't follow me."

"I've already explained— "

"I told you not to follow me. I need you to back off, now."

Almost running, I hurried down the stairs, past the pool, and out to the beach. As I turned to close the gate behind me, I saw him.

I walked past the rows of cabanas and found an empty one that was situated between two that were occupied. I spread out my towel, placed my bag on the table beside me, and settled down. I put my large sun hat over my face so that if the man walked by, he wouldn't be able to disturb my tranquility by making eye contact or standing in my range of vision.

I knew I should put on sunscreen to protect myself from the intensity of the tropical sun, but for now I just needed peace and quiet, and to settle my racing heart. Once I felt at ease, I would check to see where he was, and then I could settle in more completely.

After several minutes, my heart rate returned to a normal pace. I felt my shoulders and arms relax. My breathing began to steady itself. I focused my mind on the sound of the waves and let my mind drift. It wasn't long before everything faded into the background, and I found myself slipping into sleep.

When I woke, I could feel my skin starting to burn. I removed my hat and sat up. The man was nowhere in view. First, I checked my phone. The screen was dark. There were still no messages or returned calls. Frustrated, I tucked it back into my bag. I put on sunscreen, then signaled a server who was passing by. I ordered a bottle of water, a strawberry margarita, and a bowl of pita chips with hummus. I adjusted the back of my lounge chair and took my paperback novel out of my bag.

I read two paragraphs, then gazed out at the ocean. It

should have calmed me, but it didn't. I looked at my book again and read the same two paragraphs. My drink arrived and I took several sips. I drank half the bottle of water. I read the same two paragraphs in my book for the third time. I had no idea what I had just read. I placed the book beside me. I drank my cocktail too fast, then ordered another. I finished the bottle of water while I drank my second cocktail. I checked my phone multiple times, but there were still no messages.

I continued sipping my drink and nibbling my snack. I sent a second round of messages to everyone. None of them responded, not even with an emoji. I took a few pictures of the ocean and sent them to Bella. No response.

Finally, I'd had enough. I packed up my things and returned to my suite. I stood on the balcony and called Detective Morr. The call went to voicemail. I asked him if he had any news about the dental records for identifying Jay's body. When I ended the call, I saw that I had somehow missed a call from my father.

I called him back and was shocked to hear his voice. He sounded as if he'd been punched in the throat, his words sounding rough and raw.

"Hi, sweetheart," he said. "I'm so sorry we didn't pick up when you called. I have to tell you something." He paused for a moment. "I hope you'll forgive us for hiding something from you. But we wanted you to have the best time of your life for your wedding. We never expected all of this to happen. We expected you to be enjoying your honeymoon right now, lost in everything Hawaii has to offer, in each other..." His voice trailed off.

"What are you talking about?" I asked. "You're scaring me."

"I'm so sorry. I don't mean to. We did what we thought was best. I hope you understand. What I'm trying to get to is, they found a lump in your mother's breast two weeks before your wedding. It was cancerous. She had surgery this morning."

"Oh my God! Why didn't you tell me? How is she? Let me talk to her!"

"I explained why not. We thought it was the best thing. I'm sorry. And she's fine. Really. She's doing great. They removed all of it. And it hadn't spread."

"Please let me talk to her. I can't believe this is happening. I feel so awful. Why didn't you *tell* me?"

"It seemed like the right thing. We didn't want to spoil your wedding."

"Mom is more important than my wedding!"

"She wanted you to enjoy your day. She'll be fine. It wouldn't have changed anything if you'd known."

"I feel terrible."

"Please don't. We love you. We wanted you to be happy."

I didn't say anything else. Look what had happened now. I couldn't talk about my happiness. I wondered if I would ever be happy again. It was best to let it go, for now. They'd made their decision. There was no point in arguing about it. I needed to focus on giving her positive energy for her healing. And continuing to find out what happened to Jay. That was all that mattered. Still... I swallowed. I tried not to feel betrayed, or left out, like a tiny child with the adults whispering around me.

"Can I talk to her?"

"She's sleeping right now. I'll have her call you as soon as she's awake."

"Okay."

"We love you, Chelsea."

"I love you, Dad. Tell Mom I love her."

"I will."

I hung up before he could ask about Jay. Neither one of them needed that right now. Then, I gripped the balcony railing with both hands and let the tears flow.

FORTY-THREE

RACHEL

Waking up the morning of my wedding, I felt as if the sunshine streaming in my window was a good omen for the rest of my life. Andrew was the perfect man for me. I'd known it from the day I first met him. We'd met in our college library, and he'd been interested in the art history book I was reading. He wasn't interested in the way that some guys were, pretending to care so that he could flirt with me. He asked meaningful questions that let me know he was interested in what I thought.

At our engagement dinner, Andrew had given the final toast of the evening. He raised his glass, looked around the table at our family and friends, and said, "Every time Rachel's face comes into my mind, I smile." He looked down at me. "The best thing I can say about you, Rachel, is that you tamed my wild ways." As he raised his glass and took a drink, everyone laughed. A few people shouted, *Hear! Hear!*

It was an unconventional toast, but it charmed me. It told me I'd changed his life as much as he'd changed mine.

A month earlier, I'd moved out of the house I'd been sharing with three friends. Now I was sleeping in the bedroom I'd grown up in. It was the last morning I would wake up alone in bed. The last time I would eat breakfast with my family as a single woman.

After I was showered and dressed, my hair still loose, ready to be styled for my wedding gown, I went downstairs for breakfast. My mother had made my favorite—homemade scones with raspberry jam and butter. The aroma of coffee filled the room. The rest of my family was already there.

Our wedding would be a lavish, formal event, because that's what Andrew's family wanted. It wasn't as if they'd run over my wishes, I was consulted on every detail, but they wanted a spectacular show. They'd insisted on paying for all of it.

Andrew's family had a lot of money. It wasn't entirely clear to me how they'd made it. They didn't discuss it, and asking felt crude. I knew his father had a lot of investments. I knew his father before him had also had money. His father traveled all over the world, and he was always busy with meetings, phone calls, and working in his home office, but no one ever explained what those trips involved or what those phone calls entailed. He was just always very, very busy.

Andrew was getting his MBA because his primary role in his father's various business activities would be to manage their investments and ensure the growth of their family's wealth. Beyond that, I didn't ask a lot of questions. He had his world, and I had mine. I was getting a degree in art and had been working in a gallery as an assistant.

I'd been apprehensive, knowing how much money they had, wondering if they would be very different from my family because we came from such different backgrounds. But they were so down to earth, so easygoing. I'd connected right away with his mother. His father was a little sterner and more standoffish, as were his siblings, but I could tell his father liked me, and I knew that over time, we might become close.

Since we've been engaged, I'd adapted to Andrew's life-style. I knew this was what my future would look like, and I'd come to terms with living a different kind of life. It wasn't going to stop me from building a career of my own, and it wasn't going to change me into a person who felt entitled or superior. I was confident that we would build our own kind of life where we would use the money we had to do good things in the world.

As we finished with breakfast, and I began to think about putting on my make-up, having my hair done, and finally, stepping into my beautiful wedding gown, my sister left the room. She returned a few minutes later with the mail. She placed a pale blue envelope addressed to me on the table.

I broke the seal eagerly, expecting a greeting card congratulating me on our marriage. Inside, was a plain, pale blue card with my name written on the front in elegant script.

I opened the card and read the note.

Andrew doesn't belong to you. I will be watching you today. I will be watching you every day for the rest of your life.

People need to pay for what they've done. Never forget it.

I stared at the words in disbelief. I was too shocked to cry. Too hurt to say anything.

Why would someone ruin my wedding day like this? What kind of person would send me a letter like this? I had no idea what I'd done to deserve it. I'd tried to live a good life. I *had* lived a good life. I'd been kind and generous to everyone I knew.

"What is it?" my sister asked.

"What's wrong?" my mother looked close to tears as she read the expression on my face.

I couldn't tell them. I didn't want to hurt them like I was hurting. They wanted to see me happy, blissfully married to the man I adored. "Just a congratulations card."

"You look upset," my mother said.

"You look like you're going to cry," my sister said.

"I'm too emotional." I gave them a watery smile as I folded the note twice and pressed it into my palm, closing my fingers around it so that my hand formed a fist. I refused to let this interfere with my happiness. I wasn't going to tell Andrew about it either. I wasn't going to tell anyone. If I didn't talk about it, those ugly words would fade to the back of my mind.

I left the table and went upstairs. I tore up the note and flushed the tiny pieces of card down the toilet.

As I got caught up in the wedding preparations, the force of my willpower pushed those cruel words to the back of my mind, and they began to fade. It wasn't until I was sitting at the reception, gazing at our friends and family, sipping champagne, that I began to study the faces looking back at me. Maybe Andrew's family wasn't as welcoming as I'd assumed.

FORTY-FOUR
CHELSEA

My tears stopped, and I settled on one of the balcony chairs, turning it slightly, so I was facing the ocean. The sun was moving closer to the horizon. There were a few scattered clouds in the sky that were turning a soft pink. It wouldn't be one of those dramatic Hawaiian sunsets, the kind you see and photographs that take your breath away with fiery orange streaks exploding like something magical and surreal, but it was always satisfying and calming watching the sun go down over the ocean at the end of the day, especially here.

Even when I've been caught up in fear and despair over the past week, I'd enjoyed every single sunset.

I tried to drink in the beauty of what I was looking at, breathing in the soft air, the aroma of gardenias that seemed to permeate everything. Part of me wanted to stay here forever, because the thought of going home without Jay was too horrible to contemplate. But now that I knew my mother was fighting cancer, even if it was gone from her body, I wanted to be with her. I felt torn in two.

I heard the door open and sensed the presence of the man behind me. "Do you want to go out to dinner?" he asked.

I kept my attention on the sunset. I was desperately hungry. Maybe eating dinner with him wouldn't be too terrible. I was no longer sure I trusted my new friends, as much as they claimed to want to help me. I didn't like being held captive by anyone. Knowing they'd drugged me made me wonder whether they'd had something else in mind and I'd woken too soon. The support I had felt from them had dissolved into a feeling of uncertainty, bordering on fear.

If I went out to eat by myself, I would be left simmering in my uncontrolled thoughts. If I stayed in the room and ordered food, I would still spend the evening, staring at him, watching him watch me.

"I wouldn't mind going out to eat, "I said.

"Really?"

He sounded thrilled, as if we were in junior high school, and I'd agreed to go to the dance with him. He stood. "Which restaurant do you prefer?"

"You choose."

When the man came out, he was dressed in slacks and a dark blue collared shirt. His hair was still wet and combed neatly. He'd even shaved and put on cologne. He held the door open for me, and we went out.

He'd made reservations at the seafood restaurant which had an ocean view. Somehow, despite his last-minute call, he'd managed to snag a window table. We ordered our food, and he ordered a bottle of red wine after asking me what I liked.

We tentatively shared an appetizer of calamari rings. After eating one and taking a small sip of wine, he leaned back in his chair.

"What were you up to last night? I'm just curious."

"I spent the night with some women I met." The lie rolled off my tongue as easily as the calamari slid down my throat.

"Where did you meet them?"

"On the beach."

"How do you know it was safe to stay in their room?"

"It's not less safe than my own room."

"Have I done anything to make you feel afraid?"

"Yes."

"Like what?"

I stared at him, not believing the question. Did he really not get it? I decided not to answer. If he didn't get it, I wasn't going to explain.

"It just seems a little trusting to spend the night with two people you know nothing about."

"No worse than spending over a week with one person I know nothing about."

He didn't say anything more. We finished the calamari and when our meals were served, we ate in silence for several minutes. I sipped my wine, taking small bites in between. The man did the same. In the silence, my thoughts turned to my mother. I was still upset that my parents hadn't told me about her cancer. I understood why, but I felt as if they'd treated me like a child. Hadn't they believed that I had the emotional maturity to handle her health problems and still enjoy my wedding? It felt as if they thought I was emotionally unstable, that they believed my accident had made me incapable of coping with life.

I thought about what my mother had gone through over the past few months. I hadn't been available to support her at all. How had she felt at my wedding? Overall, she was an optimistic person. It was possible she managed to put it out of her thoughts. But I would never know because she would never tell me. Had they told her it was small and likely contained? Maybe she'd gone into her surgery with confidence, knowing they would take it all with one cut and that would be it. My father hadn't mentioned anything about chemotherapy, so I had no idea if she was facing that or not. Maybe that was a decision yet to be made.

"You're quiet," the man said.

Before I realized what I was doing, I started talking about my mother. The words tumbled out of my mouth as if I'd tripped over a jar of pebbles, knocking them all over the floor, watching them scatter across the tile.

"She has cancer. She didn't even tell me. She had it at my wedding, and I didn't know. She had surgery today. I couldn't reach anybody. I called and left messages, even my best friend wasn't responding to me. I had no idea what was going on." I paused and put a fork full of black rice into my mouth, chewing vigorously, feeling the sticky dense stuff in my teeth, glad that I had something that felt so solid. "I'm still in shock. It seems like it's not real. It's so hard being here, knowing she's back there lying in a hospital, unsure about what's going to happen. They got the tumor, and it hadn't spread, so that's good, but no one said whether she's having chemo or anything, so I don't really know what's going to happen."

The man placed his fork on his plate. He leaned forward and reached his hand out, resting his fingers gently on the back of my hand. I felt myself recoil, but then I relaxed and let his fingers remain there for a moment.

"I'm so, so sorry, Chelsea. How terrible for you. I can't imagine what that must feel like."

"Thank you." I slowly moved my hand away from his fingertips.

I was surprised by what he'd said. His words were sensitive and gentle, and without any suggestion that he was trying to tell me how I should feel or trying to give me false reassurance.

Again, we ate in silence for a few minutes. After that, we talked casually about the food, the resort, and the diners seated around us. When we returned to the room, I felt genuinely relaxed, looking forward to a good night's sleep.

I thanked the man for dinner, went into my bedroom, and locked the doors. I checked my phone and saw that I had a missed call from my mother. Before calling her back, I listened to her voicemail.

"*Hi sweetie. I'm dreading this call, but I have something disturbing to tell you.*"

I tapped to return her call immediately. "Isn't cancer disturbing enough? What else could be wrong?" I could hear the panic in my voice as I tried to keep fear from taking control.

"This is worse."

FORTY-FIVE
ANONYMOUS

I love writing letters. In a letter, it's easy to hide who I am. Digital everything has destroyed all the romance, the mystery, and the secrecy. The whole world knows who you are, what time you sent a message, and the precise coordinates of the location it came from. You can't hide anything.

I also enjoy writing letters because there's something intimate about them. Typing out individual letters of the alphabet on a keyboard, or worse, tapping tiny marks on a phone is robotic. It doesn't come from the heart. Handwritten script feels as if it's flowing right out of my heart through my blood vessels and muscles and bones into the pen, bleeding into the ink and out onto the page.

The ironic thing about all of this is that nowadays, you can conceal your identity in a handwritten letter more easily than you can with an electronic device because no one recognizes your handwriting. Most people have never seen it.

FORTY-SIX

CHELSEA

My mother's words stunned me. How could anything she had to tell me be worse than the fact that she'd just had surgery for cancer? I heard the strain in her voice, weakened by the operation and the anesthesia she was still recovering from. It was clear she was forcing herself to speak in a louder voice, trying to sound firm and clear when she didn't have the strength to do so.

"How can anything be worse than cancer?" I asked.

"Maybe worse is the wrong word," she said.

"All I want to know is how you're doing," I said. "I feel terrible that I didn't know what was going on. Are they sure they got everything? Are you going to have chemo? How long have you known?"

"That's not important right now. We'll discuss it later," she said. "I'm worried about you."

"It's absolutely important. Will you have chemo?"

"Yes. But that's fine, I can handle it. It's part of the process."

"I want to be there for that. How are you feeling right now?"

"I need to tell you this other thing," she said. "It's really important. It's scaring me."

"*Cancer* is scaring me! I'm still really upset that you didn't tell me. I understand why, but I feel terrible that you didn't trust me to handle it."

"I really need to talk to you about this, Chelsea. My surgery went well. They got everything. My prognosis is good. This other thing is really important."

"Okay. What is it?"

"It's something I never told you. I've had this person, a stalker, for lack of a better word, for over thirty years. I didn't tell you because they never did anything to really hurt me or seriously threaten me. But they've sent me disturbing letters over the years."

"Okay. That does sound awful. Why didn't you ever mention it, and why are you telling me now?"

"I didn't want to upset you. In some ways, it didn't seem important. It was so infrequent that I received these letters and cards that sometimes I forgot about them for years at a time."

"How many did you get? And why are you telling me now? Is someone *threatening* you?"

"I only received about five or six over the years. They started when I became engaged to your father. So, you can see how long it's been. The reason I'm so scared, and the reason I'm telling you now is because I just received another letter."

"What did it say? Read it to me."

"I just really want you to come home, Chelsea. It's not safe there. You know I've thought that from the first day. The moment that man showed up in your room. And Jay disappeared. Let the police do their job. There's nothing you can do to help. Please, please come home."

"Tell me what the letter said."

"It's like the other letters and cards, basically telling me I don't deserve to be happy. I don't really understand it. I never could figure out who was sending them or why somebody felt that way about me. And I have no idea what it has to do with you, but this is what scares me. The letter is postmarked from Hawaii. That's why you need you to come home."

I didn't say anything for a few seconds. It was terrifying to think about somebody in Hawaii threatening my mother. What did it even mean? Telling my mother she didn't *deserve* to be happy? What did that have to do with me? Was it implying that something was going to happen to me in order to punish my mother? It was the strangest thing I've ever heard.

I wasn't sure what to say to her, but I couldn't go home. If I left, the police would do nothing. They already seemed to be taking forever. How long did it take to get dental records?

Reluctantly, I told her about finding the body I knew was Jay's. I hated to burden her when she already carrying so much, but I was used to letting her into my life. And this wasn't something I could hide. It wasn't something I wanted to keep from her, even now.

"Oh, Chelsea. I—"

"You can see why I'm not coming home, Mom. I need to find out what happened to Jay. Right now, I'm not even 100 percent sure that the body I found is his. But I can't leave here, not knowing. Because then I might never know. And I need to find out who this man is who showed up in my room. Do you understand that?"

"Of course I understand. But I'm scared for you. A man was murdered! What if this person who has been stalking me is after you? The letter was postmarked from Hawaii!"

"I know. You told me that. But it doesn't say anything about me, does it?"

"No. The threat is more subtle. He knew I would see the postmark. That man in your room. Don't you realize that?"

"I don't think so. He doesn't seem... I know he knows things, and I know what he's done is really creepy, but he doesn't seem like a killer."

"How on earth can you tell if a man is a killer? You have no idea. You need to come home."

"I know you're scared, Mom. And after what you've been through, what you're going through now, it probably feels worse. But I can't come home right now. I just can't."

"Then I'm going to ask Katherine to come stay with you."

"I don't need Katherine to babysit me."

"If you don't want Katherine, then I'll ask Bella, or one of your other friends. Or maybe your father— "

"I don't need anyone to come take care of me. I can handle this myself. Bella just started a new job. And Dad needs to be there taking care of you."

"I'm just so scared for you, Chelsea."

"You said yourself, you've only had a few letters, and nothing ever happened. It's probably nothing. Just some creep who's jealous of you."

"This person is *in* Hawaii!"

"Okay. But that's how creeps scare you. With constant fear. You said they've never done anything."

I wasn't sure I believed this. The fact that it was postmarked from Hawaii was terrifying. But I wasn't going to tell my mother that. She needed to heal her body. And having one of her friends, or one of my friends, was not going to help anything. It might give me support and strength, but at the same time, I might be putting someone else in danger. And I didn't want to do that either.

What I needed, was for the police to do their job. They need to identify Jay's body. And they need to find out who the killer was. I needed to put more pressure on them.

FORTY-SEVEN
CHELSEA

Knowing that the letter to my mother had been postmarked from Hawaii did make me afraid. At the same time, it proved to me that whatever happened to Jay was not a random murder. Someone had planned very carefully to end his life and to try to make mine as miserable as they possibly could. Now, it looked like they also wanted to make my mother suffer. Who hated us that deeply to go to so much trouble?

First thing in the morning, I would call that detective and demand to know what they were doing to identify Jay's body. I would ask what they had done to find out who had killed that man, whether or not he was my husband. If he wasn't, they needed to find him!

I had a hard time falling asleep after talking to my mother. When I finally did, I slept fitfully. I woke as the sky was growing light. It was just past five thirty in the morning. I doubted the detective would be there and willing to talk to me at this hour.

To work off my nervous energy, I took a quick shower, changed into a tank suit, slipped out of the room without waking the man, and went down to the pool. I tossed my towel on a lounge chair, and dove into the deep end without pausing to check the temperature.

The pool was deliciously warm. I began swimming, feeling the water flow across my skin like silk. I swam quickly and smoothly, almost racing from one end to the other. After a few laps, I lost count of how many times I've gone back and forth. I lost track of time and I stopped thinking. The only thing in my mind was the movement of my arms, the kicking of my legs, and the rhythm of my turning head as I drew air into my lungs.

After swimming, I ate a large breakfast of bacon, eggs, toast, and fruit. I drank two cups of coffee, then headed to the business center.

I pulled out Detective Morr's card and called his number. To my surprise, he answered.

"Hi, this is Chelsea Davis. I'm calling to find out if you received the dental records for the man whose body I found in the lagoon at Kiholo Bay."

"Yes, Mrs. Davis. We received them yesterday. We should have the results in a few days."

"A few days! Why so long?"

"That's how long it takes," he said.

"But why?"

"Because it does."

"What does *a few days* mean? Two days? Three? Longer?"

"I can't give you a precise answer. That's why I said a few days."

"Do you have any information about who he was with? Or when he died?"

"The investigation is ongoing."

"What does that mean?"

"It means we're investigating."

"What kind of information do you have so far?"

"I can't share that with you, I'm sorry."

"Why not?"

"First of all, because we don't know your relationship with the victim. Second of all, because we don't share the details of our investigations."

"But I'm his wife."

"That's yet to be determined. And even if that's proven, we don't hand out all the pieces of our investigation to everyone who asks. I think you can understand why that isn't a good idea."

"I don't understand that at all."

"It's to avoid leaks."

"I'm not going to tell anybody anything. Who would I even tell?"

"That's not how we operate."

"So, you're not going to tell me anything at all?"

"When we identify the body, if the man is Jay Davis, we'll notify you," he said.

"That's it?"

"For now, yes. Do you have any other questions?"

"I asked you my questions, and you refused to answer them. It's a bit of a farce to ask me if I have more questions, don't you think?"

"Is that all, Mrs. Davis?"

"Please call me when you've made an identification." I hung up the phone without saying goodbye. Maybe I was sabotaging myself by doing that. Maybe he would think I was rude and go out of his way to avoid speaking to me again. But he was refusing to give me any information, so what difference did it make?

To get my mind off the non-action of the police, and the fears my mother had stirred up, I decided I needed to escape the resort for the day. A list of daily activities in the lobby included a snorkeling trip at eleven that morning. Now that I'd faced my fear of boating and prevailed, I felt as if spending time in the water might give me the escape I craved. It was better than a day spent drinking, or probing my mind for evidence of hallucinations, asking the same questions—was the dead man my husband? Was the man in my room my husband and I was living in a delusional state? Were those women going to attempt to *rescue* me again, or were they my friends? The questions never stopped.

I packed my beach bag, then went outside and settled on the balcony until it was time to go.

When the man asked what I was planning for the day, I told him I would be spending it alone. He looked hugely disappointed. I turned my head away from him and focused my attention on my phone. I spent the next hour texting Bella, even though I had to wait ten minutes between each message for her to reply. When she did respond, her messages seemed cool and slightly distant, as if she didn't have time for me. Was I imagining that too? My hands still felt cold, and my fingers trembled as I tried to tap out messages to her, feeling less and less sure of myself, more and more cut off.

The snorkeling trip was everything that I had wanted it to be. I met a few interesting people and told them nothing about what had happened to me. All I said was that I was on my honeymoon and my husband wasn't feeling well, so I'd come snorkeling by myself. I saw some amazing tropical fish and reveled in the beauty of being underwater hearing nothing but the thrumming of my own blood in my ears, which had the effect of drowning my thoughts.

That evening after a light dinner in my suite, seated far away from the man on the sofa, watching a movie, I took my glass of wine out to the balcony. I stood looking at the stars, and the gently moving palm trees.

As I turned slightly, I saw the glint of moonlight off two perfectly round discs coming from a second-floor balcony on the opposite side of the pool.

It looked as if someone was aiming a pair of binoculars directly at my balcony, watching me drink my wine.

FORTY-EIGHT

CHELSEA

As softly as I could, I slid open the door from the balcony into the main room. The man had fallen asleep on the sofa, the TV tuned to a hockey game. It was a strange choice for a sporting event while in Hawaii, but maybe it had come on while he was sleeping.

I crossed the room as quietly as I could, slipped out the door, and raced along the corridor. I hurried down the stairs, taking them two at a time. I ran around the edge of the pool and cut across the soft grass. I stopped a few yards away from the two-story building that faced mine and looked up at the balcony where I'd seen the moonlight reflecting off the binoculars.

Scanning the rooms on the second floor, I no longer saw the binoculars. There didn't appear to be anybody out on the balconies. Starting at one end of the building, I walked slowly past the rooms, staring up, peering into the darkness, trying to see if I saw anyone in the shadows close to the side of the building who hadn't been obvious at first glance. No one was there.

I turned and began walking back. When I reached the third room, I saw a couple sitting on their patio on the first floor who I hadn't noticed during my first pass. They were close together, holding hands and whispering to each other. As I stood there, the man turned and began kissing the woman. He put his hand on the side of her face, pulling her closer, cradling her head gently. Their kiss deepened. I felt like a voyeur. I'd missed my opportunity to ask whether they knew anyone on the second floor. It was probably a ridiculous question. I didn't know anyone else in my building, why would they? At the same time, lots of couples held destination weddings at this resort. It was possible they had other family and friends still staying here. I had to ask. I had to know.

Taking a few steps closer, I cleared my throat softly. They continued kissing. The man moved his hand down to her neck, then along the top of her shoulder, and down her arm. A moment later, he was stroking her breast. Now, I felt like a bona fide creep. But it wasn't going to deter me.

I coughed again. If they heard me, they must have assumed it was just a neighbor on their patio. Someone enjoying the evening who couldn't see them and had nothing to do with them.

"Excuse me," I said.

They continued kissing. The man was now massaging her breast. He moved his hand, his fingers beginning to probe inside her shirt.

I raised my voice. "Hello, I'm sorry to interrupt you, but I just wanted to ask you a quick question."

They continued kissing with more passion and intensity now. Were they ignoring me? I wasn't sure. I moved closer to the edge of their patio. All that stood between me and them was a narrow strip of dirt filled with waist-high flowering plants.

"Hi, I'm so, so sorry, I just need to ask you a question."

"Get lost," the man said in a rough voice.

"It's really important," I said.

"Leave us alone!"

This wasn't working. I needed to get to the point. "I was just wondering if you know anyone on the second floor of your building. Someone was watching my suite through binoculars and I'm trying to find out who it was. I think they were in the room diagonally up from you to the right. Is there any chance you know—"

"I said, get lost!"

"Do you? Know anyone on the second floor?"

The woman broke away from the man. "Are you hard of hearing? Go away. Now. This is supposed to be our private area. Do you want us to call security?"

"All I wanted—"

"Now!"

I took a few steps away from their patio. Tears burned in my eyes. I blinked them away. It had been foolish to ask. The chances they knew anyone on the floor above them were almost nonexistent. I turned and began walking toward the lobby.

Even as I moved purposefully in that direction, I knew that my next question would also go unanswered. I would be smacked down by rules and regulations. But once again, I was compelled to try. Somewhere, at some point, there had to be someone with a thread of sympathy who would bend or break a rule to help me.

I wove my way through the garden area, past comfortable wicker chairs arranged in groups, where people were enjoying cocktails and coffees, tea and desserts. They were talking and laughing, without a care in the world. Or at least that's how they appeared. Melodic Hawaiian music played in the background. Every so often, a burst of laughter punctuated the evening air.

There were only two clerks on duty because no one was checking in at this hour. One of them was Kim. I wasn't sure if she would be helpful because she'd been inclined in that direction when she first met me, or if she would shy away from me, remembering the baggage I carried. Because she was a familiar face, I decided to approach her. Impatient, I decided not to waste any time with niceties.

"Hi," I said. "There was a man in the building that faces mine, in the suite three rooms from the end on the ocean side. He was using binoculars to watch me on my balcony. Can you tell me his name?"

She stared at me as if I'd lost my mind. Or perhaps, as if she hadn't understood the question. Maybe I'd given her too much information at once.

"I can't give out guests' names," she said. "I think you know that." She gave me a firm, polite smile.

"He was watching me on my balcony," I said. "Don't I have a right to know who he is?"

"I doubt he was watching you. He was probably enjoying the view. It's really difficult to tell where someone is aiming a pair of binoculars." She gave me another firm smile. "Is there anything else I can help you with?"

"I really need to know—"

"We don't give out the names of our guests."

"But I—"

"I think you've been told, Mrs. Davis, you need to stop bothering the other guests. If you don't, the resort will be forced to ask you to check out." She gave me a friendlier, more sympathetic smile. But then, she turned aside to her computer and didn't make eye contact again.

Slowly, I started back across the lobby. As I reached the edge where it opened into the garden, I glanced to the side and saw a man headed toward the main swimming pool. A pair of binoculars hung around his neck. I stopped with a soft gasp, then began following him.

FORTY-NINE

RACHEL

Before Chelsea said goodbye, I knew what I was going to do. I couldn't understand why she was being so cavalier about the situation she was in. She was allowing that strange man, that monster who might have murdered her husband, to stay in her room and acting as if she was completely safe! Her life was in danger, every moment of the day and all through the night.

It was making me sick. I hadn't wanted to put the burden of my surgery on her, I've never wanted to put the problem in my life on my daughter. That's why I never told her about the person who had stalked me intermittently through the years. But knowing that man was in her room, and knowing that her husband had gone missing and was now surely dead, was making me far sicker and far more scared than I had felt for a single instant in all the time I'd known I had cancer.

I was angry with myself for letting this situation go on as long as it had. Just because my daughter was a thirty-two-year-old woman, it didn't mean I didn't have the same feelings I'd had when she was a helpless little baby. Mothers push those feelings away as our children get older. We pretend they aren't there. We bury them deep. But they simmer like molten lava far below the surface.

Right now, Chelsea had become my precious, sweet, darling, baby daughter once again. And as intelligent and educated and savvy as she was, she was making a terrible, life-threatening mistake. It's one thing to let your children make mistakes that might cost them financially, or force them into course corrections that they'll have to pay for in damage to their career or friendships or romantic relationships. But this was different. This mistake was in a class by itself.

I wasn't going to sit by and let her spend one more moment with a man who might be a cold-blooded killer.

The moment my call with Chelsea ended, I called Katherine.

"Hi, how are you feeling?" she asked.

"Better. Just in a holding pattern until the chemo starts. Andrew's been amazing."

"I'm really glad to hear that," Katherine said. "He always is. You don't have a lot of pain or anything?"

"Nothing that Tylenol doesn't take care of," I said. "I called to ask you a favor. It's kind of a big one. A really big one."

"Aww, there's no favor too big for you."

"This is a lot," I said. "I'm hoping you can manage to rearrange your schedule and take some time to go back to Hawaii."

"Are things worse?" Katherine asked.

"Yes," I said. "I can't take it anymore."

"Oh, Rachel. You don't need this. You really don't. I'm so sorry."

"It's not about me. It really isn't. And yes, it's worse. It's not that I can't take it anymore, Something else happened. Remember that stalker I've had on and off?"

"Yes. What happened? I thought this was about Chelsea? And that man. And Jay. What's going on?"

"I received another letter. It's nothing terrible, about the same as the others. Except for one thing. It's..."

"What? What's wrong?"

"It's postmarked from Hawaii."

"Oh my God! Oh my God, Rachel. How scary! Do you want me to come over?"

"No. It's not me. It's Chelsea."

"Right, yes. Of course. I can go. Absolutely. Does she—"

"No." I laughed. "No, I know what you were going to ask. She doesn't want you there. But it doesn't matter. She needs you. And I need you to be there. She doesn't know what she needs. She's not thinking clearly. I don't know what's wrong with her. Maybe it's grief. Maybe fear. Maybe... I don't know. She said he was pretending he was her husband, maybe he's more clever and manipulative than I realize. Do you think she actually believes him? On some level?"

Katherine didn't respond immediately. When she did, her voice was quiet and careful. "I can't believe she would. She's smarter than that. No matter how smooth he is."

"I don't understand it. I don't understand why she's letting him stay in her room. It doesn't make any sense. That why I really need you to—"

"You don't need to say anything else. Maybe the way it happened, waking up like that. She might be having some kind of trauma. Do you think?"

"Maybe." I found myself nodding even though we weren't having a video call. "I don't know. I don't understand and I can't explain it. I just want it to stop. I want someone there with her. And obviously I can't go. And she's being so stubborn about it. She needs help."

"Yes. She does. It must have been awful, waking up with a stranger in your bed. Someone in your room would be terrifying enough, but sleeping in your bed? God. It makes me shudder every time I think about it."

"Thank you," I whispered. "Thank you so much. I feel so helpless."

"Don't. You're not helpless. You're fighting a battle. Concentrate on that. Okay?"

I smiled, feeling the warmth of her words come through the phone.

When she said goodbye, I felt as if I could unclench my jaw for the first time in a week. I felt as if, finally, Chelsea would have the comfort that only comes from the physical presence of someone who loves you. But I was still scared. And I worried whether Katherine would get there in time.

FIFTY

CHELSEA

The man with the binoculars didn't appear to notice me following. He stopped by the edge of the pool, appearing uncertain about where he wanted to go next. After a moment, he turned and left the pool area. He walked more quickly now, headed in the direction of my building. As I watched from the end of the building, he turned into the corridor behind the suites on the bottom floor, he stopped at one of the rooms, took out his key card, and went in.

I turned away, defeated.

When I opened the door to my own suite, the first thing I saw was the man standing on the balcony. He was talking on the hotel phone. The cord was stretched across the room to reach the balcony. As the door opened, his voice was loud, but I couldn't catch what he'd said. He was turned slightly with his eye on the door, and he stopped talking the moment he saw me.

Whoever was on the other end, continued talking. He nodded as if they could see him. Then he shook his head violently. He opened his mouth as if he wanted to say something, but his attention was on me.

"No. No. I can't. That's not going to happen."

I let the door fall closed behind me. He turned so he was facing me fully, watching me as well.

"I need to hang up. No. I need to go." He replaced the receiver. He carried the phone back into the room and set it on the coffee table. He gave me a welcoming smile. "Where have you been?"

"I went out for a walk," I said.

"A walk to where?"

"It's none of your business."

"I've told you, you shouldn't go out without me. It's not safe. Especially at night."

I decided not to dignify that with an answer. He still refused to explain what was so unsafe about this five-star resort that I couldn't go walking around by myself. I understood that Jay had been murdered. But it wasn't at the resort. And when the man said things like that, for some reason, it sounded like he was the one who was more of a danger. And then I began to wonder if my parents and the women I've met were right to warn me about him.

"Who were you talking to on the phone?" I asked.

"It's not important."

"It is to me. Who were you talking to?"

"Should we go out to dinner?" he asked.

"I'm not hungry."

"You have to eat something."

"Do I?"

"Yes. If you don't want to go out, I'll order room service. What would you like"

"A sandwich is fine."

"What kind of sandwich?"

He was making this too difficult. I truly wasn't that hungry. I wanted to know who the man with the binoculars was. I wanted to know who this guy had been talking to. I wanted to know why he'd been so upset, almost angry. But I knew he wasn't going to tell me. "Turkey. With some avocado and tomato."

"Anything else?"

"Some white wine."

When the sandwiches came, along with a bottle of wine, we ate them on the balcony in silence. He poured a glass of wine. He sipped his slowly, but I downed mine in a few gulps.

After a while, the silence got to him. He cleaned up the remains of our dinner, left the bottle of wine on the table beside me, and went into the room. I sat there for a long time, my eyes glued to the balcony across from me, drinking wine, and willing that man to come back outside with his binoculars. He never did.

Even when the wine was gone, I continued to sit there. I considered what Kim had said. I wondered if the guest across from my room had been simply looking at the view. It seemed unlikely because it had already been dark when I'd seen him. It was difficult to believe that someone was watching for whales at that hour of the night. Maybe he was looking at the stars or searching for planets, but binoculars weren't ideal for that kind of activity.

It was after midnight when the man came outside again.

"Are you ever going to bed?" he asked.

"Eventually. "

"Is something wrong?"

I shrugged.

"I overheard your phone call earlier. I assumed it was with your mother. It sounded like she wants you to go home."

"I don't appreciate you listening to my phone calls."

"That might be the best thing."

"What might be the best thing? Having you eavesdrop on my calls?"

"Going home is probably a good idea. It might be safer for you. It *would* be safer for you."

"Despite your pretense, you don't know anything about me," I said. "So you don't know what would be safer for me."

"I do know it would be safer for you at home. And I do know that you can't do anything here to find out who killed that man."

"Do you mean my *husband*? Jay Davis?"

"I know you're worried about your mother. It seems like the best place for you is at home with her. Why don't we look into booking flights and plan to leave the day after tomorrow?"

I stared at him in disbelief. He was planning to carry this all the way to the end. It was incredible to me that he thought I would eventually go along with him. Or maybe he didn't. Maybe he'd never believed that. Maybe it was some other kind of game for him. I had no idea, and I didn't care.

"I'm not flying back to my home with you. You're not my husband."

He gave me a look that I couldn't read. I left him standing there and went into my bedroom, locking the doors behind me as always.

I picked up my phone off the bed. A missed call and voicemail from Katherine. I listened to her message.

"Call me. It's important. It's not your mom, she's doing fine. It doesn't matter how late, just call."

It was only nine thirty in California. When I called, she answered on the second ring. "What's going on?" I asked.

"I talked to your mom. I know you know. And I'm coming back to see you. No discussion allowed. Got it?" She laughed, her usual raucous, it's all good, no matter if I sounded too blunt, you know I love you, laugh.

"No. I told her I—"

"Chelsea. This is important. Your mom needs peace of mind. And you need some support. I know you're not a kid. But this is a weird situation and you need someone with you. Okay?

It's not a big deal. Let's just admit this is the most bizarre thing that's ever happened to anyone we know. Right?"

She was right. I couldn't argue with anything she'd said. I never could. And the thing that swayed me was my mom. I didn't need her worrying.

"It's all good," Katherine said.

When I hung up, I thought about sitting on the beach with Katherine, drinking cocktails. Maybe it *was* all good.

FIFTY-ONE

RACHEL

Thirty-two years ago

My sister had covered our front door with an enormous sheet of white paper decorated with tiny pink stars. Over that she placed a large pink ribbon with an enormous pink bow in the center. A card dangled from the bow. It read, *Welcome home, Chelsea!*

Andrew opened the car door and I stepped out onto the pavement. He opened the back door of the car and unbuckled the car seat. I reached inside and carefully lifted out our tiny baby girl. We stood there for a moment, gazing at her perfect face.

Together, we walked up the front path. Andrew unlocked the door, and we went inside.

We moved from the entryway into the living room. On the coffee table was a lavish flower arrangement of pink and white roses.

"Who are they from?" I asked.

"They're from me," he said. "For the beautiful mother of my beautiful baby girl."

My eyes blurred with tears. "Thank you," I said softly. "We're so lucky to have you."

"I'm lucky to have the two of you," he said. "My life is perfect now. There's nothing else I need." He went into the dining room and came back with the basket where Chelsea would sleep for the first month or two and placed it on a cart that had come with it so we would be able to keep her beside us when we sat on the sofa.

"I don't want to put her in there right now," I said. "I just want to hold her."

He took Chelsea from me while I arranged myself into a comfortable position. When I was holding her once again, he sat down and put his arm around me. We remained there for over an hour, holding her, touching her face, gazing into her eyes, talking about how precious she was. We talked about our dreams for her. We imagined all the things we would teach her about the world, the places we would take her, and the experiences we would share as a family.

When she became fussy, Andrew changed her, I fed her, and we finally relinquished her to the bassinet.

While she slept, I took a nap on the sofa beside her. Andrew unloaded our things from the car. Our friends and family had brought all kinds of food to help us through the first week at home. He took one of the meals out of the refrigerator and began preparing it.

After dinner, we cooed and fussed over Chelsea some more. We changed her and fed her again then put her to sleep in our bedroom. While I'd been napping, Andrew had gone through the mail. Now, he placed a stack of cards on the coffee table, and we began opening them together.

All of them wished us well with our new baby girl. Some of them contained checks or gift cards. The second to last card was in a pink envelope. Andrew handed it to me as it was my turn to open the card.

As the other cards did, the words on the card carried a poetic sentiment about the wonder of new life. Tucked inside was a smaller envelope that was also sealed. I broke the seal and opened it, pulling out a small white card.

The message on the card read: *Don't think I've forgotten what you did!*

FIFTY-TWO

CHELSEA

The next morning I was still wondering who the man had been talking to when I walked into the room and heard his voice raised. Why had he been talking on the hotel phone instead of his cell phone? What had he been so angry about and why had he ended the call as soon as I arrived?

I left the room, headed toward the beachside restaurant for breakfast. The man followed me, talking to me as he walked behind me. Even though he'd been sensitive about my mother's cancer, it didn't mean I suddenly felt connected to him or wanted to strike up a friendship. He seemed to think our conversation that night had been an open door, giving him permission to move deeply into my life. He seemed to think I was softening toward him, that I was going to start accepting his charade that we were a married couple, that I might be softening to the idea that he was Jay and I'd been deluded to think otherwise.

When I arrived at the restaurant, I asked for a table for one. The man entered, standing close behind me.

"Do you mind if I join you?" he asked.

"Yes."

He moved into my range of vision and gave me a weak, understanding smile. The hostess looked confused for a moment, then recovered and led me to a table. I took the chair facing the ocean. In addition to the peaceful view, I wouldn't have to watch the man watching me while I ate.

After breakfast, I went to the lobby and approached the registration desk.

Everyone on duty was new. I felt relieved that I could have a fresh start. Hopefully this would be an innocuous conversation, and I could get out of it with my dignity intact.

I gave them my room number and asked if they could tell me about any calls that had come into my room from outside of the resort or calls that had been placed from the phone in my room to outside numbers.

"Absolutely." The clerk tapped her keyboard. She studied the screen for a moment, tapped a few more times, then looked at me. "There haven't been any incoming or outgoing calls for your room."

"Are you sure?"

She looked at me, her gaze hardening slightly. "Yes, I'm sure."

"Is there any way to tell if there have been calls from other rooms at the resort?"

"No, that information isn't available."

"Are you sure?"

Her gaze turned to a glare. "I'm absolutely sure," she said. "Is there anything else I can help you with? "

"No thank you." I turned away. Everything I asked for ended up at a dead end.

I crossed the lobby and sat in one of the armchairs. I closed my eyes for a moment, trying to think. When I opened my eyes, I saw the man across the room. He was sitting at a small table, drinking a cup of coffee. He was looking at his phone, pretending he wasn't watching me.

I took my own phone out of my purse, looked through my recent calls, and tapped the number to call the detective.

To my surprise, he answered the phone. It was the one thing that seemed to fall in my favor. But maybe that suggested he wasn't very busy, that he wasn't working very hard on trying to identify my husband's body, to find out who had murdered him.

When I asked him if they had results from the dental records, there was a brief silence.

Finally, he spoke. "Unfortunately, the digital files we received were corrupted. We're currently waiting for a second set."

"Corrupted?! How does that even happen?"

"It happens. It's an image file. The files are very large. I'm not a technical expert, but sometimes the mail server, or the email tool, or something, doesn't accept it."

"You *email* them?"

"How else would you do it?"

"You don't have a tool to upload files?"

"I said I'm not a technical expert. Some of our tools are old. This isn't the Silicon Valley. This is a small town on an island. This isn't even Honolulu. I don't know what to tell you. The files were corrupted. We're waiting for a second set. You need to be patient. You also have to realize, we're an out-of-state police agency, and this isn't the top priority for the dental office."

"In the meantime, what are you doing to look for the person who murdered my husband?"

"The investigation is moving forward, but I need to remind you that right now, we have no evidence this man is your husband."

"I told you he's my husband. Why isn't my word good enough?"

"We need evidence, Mrs. Davis."

"So, you don't do anything to look for the killer until you've identified the body? That doesn't make any sense. You should be working to find out who did this. You should be questioning everybody who had any interaction with my husband from the time he arrived in Hawaii. You should be talking to his friends and family. You should be finding out what was going on in his life."

He heaved a deep sigh. "As I've explained, we don't know that this man is your husband. The man who was with you showed us valid ID stating that he's Jay Davis. Until we get that resolved, we won't be notifying his family, or contacting his place of employment, stirring up unnecessary trouble. Surely, you understand that."

"What I don't understand, is why you distrust me so completely. How do you know that man wasn't showing you fake ID?"

"Until we identify the body, I don't know anything. I'm not distrusting you, I'm dealing with what I can verify. That's how this works. Is there anything else?"

"Yes. I hope you'll get busy investigating this murder, whoever it is." I hung up the phone without waiting for him to say anything else.

I wanted to hurl my phone across the lobby. Then I laughed at my instinct. After purchasing two new phones, the worst thing I could do would be to destroy this one. Instead, I called Bella.

She answered right away.

"Can you talk?" I asked.

"Yes," she said. "I'm sorry I've been unavailable. I'm really sorry about your mom. And of course, everything with Jay. It's such a strange story. Unbelievable."

"It's not a story," I said.

Her laughter sounded uncomfortable, going on longer than it should have. "It's just that... what's going on? Have you gotten rid of that creep in your room?"

"No, he's still there. Some really weird things are happening, and I can't figure anything out. It seems like somebody here is watching me. The guy in my room follows me everywhere I go, and now he's telling me it's not safe to leave my room, but he won't say why. He's still pretending he's my husband, which is so ridiculous, I want to laugh, but it's not funny! Not at all funny. And I don't know if he thinks I'm utterly stupid, or if it's some sick game, or if he thinks this is some weird version of Stockholm syndrome, and I'm eventually going to start believing he's my husband. I don't know. The police don't seem like they're going to do anything until they prove the dead man is Jay. And the dental files got corrupted..." My voice started to sound strangled. I couldn't say any more.

"You sound a little... Are you okay?"

"I sound, what?"

"Like you're losing it, to be honest."

"I am!"

"You should come home."

"I can't."

"You absolutely can! You shouldn't be letting him stay with you."

"There's nothing I can do about it! And he's my only connection to Jay!"

"You need to get him out of there, Chelsea. After all this time, if he's still playing that game, still trying to gaslight you, and you haven't learned anything, you know you never will. He's not going to help you find out what happened to Jay. There's a very good chance he's going to kill you."

"I honestly don't think that's what this is about. If he was going to kill me, he would have by now."

"What else could it be? He murdered your husband!" Her voice was so loud, I wondered if people sitting around me could hear her. It blasted out of the phone as if I had it on speakerphone. I move the phone away from my ear. Her voice was so sharp and so shrill it made my eardrum ache.

"Please don't shout at me."

"I'm sorry. But you don't sound well. I'm scared for you."

"There's nothing wrong with me."

"You're being naïve."

"This is hard enough, without you making it sound like it's my fault."

"That's not what I'm saying. Like I said, I'm scared for you. I can't keep getting these emails and calls and text messages that you don't know what to do and you don't know what's happening."

"I can't leave until I find out what happened to Jay."

"If you say so," she said.

There was a long silence.

"I need to go. I hope you'll come home instead of calling everyone with the same confusing story that, honestly, makes no sense."

She hung up without saying goodbye. I felt as if she didn't believe me. She seemed tired of listening to me. Why didn't she believe me? It wasn't my fault the things that were happening sounded crazy! They were!

I placed the phone in my lap. There was nothing I could do but wait for the police. It seemed like that might take forever. How did I know the new set of files wouldn't get corrupted? They would also be sent by email, so it made sense that they would have the same issue as the previous set of files. I wondered if they were ever going to investigate Jay's murder.

I shoved my phone into my purse and stood. When I turned, I saw the man had moved to a chair directly behind me. Had he listened to my conversation? He must have. I tried to remember everything I'd said. I knew for sure that I'd said confidently that I didn't think he was going to kill me.

I felt an icy chill run down my arms.

Everyone was telling me to go home. When I returned home, I would tell Jay's family he was missing. I would tell them everything that had happened. Maybe they would be able to force the police to put more resources into their investigation. From home, without this man pretending to be my husband, flashing around his fake ID, the people I knew would be able to take better control of the situation. Maybe staying here was causing the problem. While I was here, everyone believed the man with the fake ID, the calm and gentle persona, the nice smile, the good looks, and the caring demeanor toward me.

I went into my bedroom and took the knife out of my beach bag. I placed it under my pillow. I took a quick shower and changed into shorts and a T-shirt. I opened the closet and pulled out my suitcase where I'd hidden my wallet when I'd gone to the beach, taking only my phone and the room key card with me.

My credit card and driver's license information were stored with the airline, but if I needed to book with another airline because I was trying to find a last-minute flight, I needed a credit card and my license handy. I absolutely needed my license to fly home.

I shoved my hand into the pocket where I'd put my wallet. It wasn't there. I lifted my suitcase up and placed it on the bed, unzipping all the flaps, feeling around for my wallet. I was sure I'd put it in the same enclosure where I stored my medication. It wasn't there. The bottle of painkillers was still there, but no wallet.

I should have been the one with a sublime smile on my face.

Everything they had should have been mine. I never had a moment of doubt that I was right. My life, and the love I deserved, had been ripped away from me. I was tossed into the gutter like a piece of trash. It was so unfair, so degrading.

I was there first. I'd done everything right and I didn't understand why things had turned out this way. It wasn't how things were supposed to work and it wasn't what everyone told me when I was growing up. My heart was shattered forever.

Now, I'll never be whole, I'll never heal. Not ever. All that's left is revenge. Savory, mouth-watering revenge.

FIFTY-FOUR

RACHEL

Twenty-five years ago

The card in the mail looked like the others I'd received. I should've recognized it right away, but of course I'd been lulled into a false sense of security as the years went by. Just as I'd been in the years between my wedding and the day Chelsea was born. It was easy to forget my tormenter. I *wanted* to forget them. I wanted them to die. I wanted them to fall into a pit so deep that no one would ever hear them scream.

When so many years go by, bad things fade to the back of your mind. I wanted to believe they'd gone away, that they'd forgotten all about me. I wanted to believe that it was just a cruel prank, someone who wanted to hurt me for a moment or two, but had finally grown up and gotten over it.

So, when the card came in a pale pink envelope, a beautiful high-quality piece of stationary, it didn't register with me that it was similar to the other envelopes I'd received. I thought it was a greeting card, even though it wasn't my birthday or any other special occasion.

I opened it with innocent hope, as foolish as ever.

Inside was a pink card with daisies on the cover. There were no words. I opened the card. The beautiful script belied the words written there in tight, tiny penmanship, filling the entire space inside and on the back.

I saw your little girl at the park the other day. It would be so easy for someone to snatch her. All you have to do is turn your head for a minute and she'd be gone.

I watch you when you carry her into the house at night after you've been out, I see her draped over your husband's shoulder, her tiny head nestled against his neck, so safe and secure with her daddy's body protecting her from every danger.

I hope you're keeping a close eye on that precious baby girl of yours. I hope you hold her tight every night. I hope you kiss her and tell her that you love her.

It would be terrible if a tragic accident happened to her. It would devastate all of your lives. I don't know if you'd ever recover from something like that.

I tore the card in the envelope into as many tiny bits as I could. I took them into the kitchen and placed them in a foil pan. I struck a match, set them on fire, and watched them burn. Then, I dumped everything into the trash.

But I couldn't burn the words out of my mind. They etched themselves into my memory, where they would remain for decades.

FIFTY-FIVE
CHELSEA

I closed my suitcase and put it back in the closet. I stood in the center of the bedroom, looking around the room. Was it possible I had put my wallet someplace else and forgotten? It wasn't as if I was thinking clearly. I yanked open the desk drawers and searched every one of them. It wasn't there. I looked in the nightstand and dresser drawers. It wasn't in any of them. I went into the bathroom and searched the cabinets, knowing as I did that it wouldn't be there.

In the main room, I tore through everything, opening drawers, looking in cabinets, searching under the sofa. I even opened the man's suitcase and dug through the pockets. It wasn't there.

He must've taken it. Had he done this before I'd even gone out to the beach? I couldn't be absolutely certain I'd put it in my suitcase before I went to spend the day lying in the cabana.

I tried to remember the things I'd said to Bella. I didn't recall telling her I had even considered returning home. That's what she wanted me to do, but I hadn't agreed with her. So, it wasn't as if he'd taken my wallet to prevent me from booking a flight. Besides, he'd *wanted* me to go home. In his fantasy, we were going back to my home together.

Despite knowing what the response would be, I called the front desk. I told them my wallet had been stolen from my room. I was told they would make a record of my report. They asked if anything else was missing. I told them not that I was aware of, but that I hadn't made a complete search yet. They thanked me for calling. They told me if it turned up, they would be sure to let me know. I hung up the phone and collapsed onto my bed, knowing I would never hear from them.

Once again, I felt utterly and completely alone. If I texted my mother or Bella to tell them what had happened, all they would tell me was how dangerous the man was. There was no one who would listen to me without telling me what to do or criticizing me for my choices so far.

When the man returned, I stormed out of the bedroom, standing by the plantation doors with my arms folded across my chest.

"Where's my wallet?"

"I don't know."

"It was in my suitcase, inside an interior pocket. And now it's gone."

"That's disturbing," he said.

"That's all you have to say?"

"What do you want me to say?"

"I want you to tell me where it is. You must've taken it."

"I didn't."

"Then who did?"

"I don't know," he said. "You must have misplaced it."

"I didn't misplace it; I put it in my suitcase."

"You've been under a lot of stress. Maybe you've forgotten what you did with it."

"I don't like your attitude," I said. "I know exactly what I did with it. And it has nothing to do with stress. I know what I do with my things."

"Maybe it fell out of your purse when you were on the

phone in the lobby. You seemed very distressed. I heard you raise your voice."

"You were listening to me?"

"You were very... loud. Quite a few people heard your conversation, I imagine."

"That's not true."

He gave me a sympathetic look. "Did you have any dinner?"

"Right now, I'm concerned about my wallet."

"Did you report it missing?"

"Yes. So, you haven't seen it?"

He shook his head. "Maybe you should have something to eat and get some rest. If it's not in the room, the best thing to do is put it out of your mind for now."

"I can't fly home without it. Do you understand that?"

"I'm just saying, if it's missing right now, the best thing to do is get some rest. Maybe we'll figure out a solution tomorrow."

"The only solution is finding my wallet. I need my ID and my credit cards."

"I'll help you look for it and see what else can be done. Tomorrow."

"Where were you? When I was on the beach?" I asked.

"I was in the Golden Rim having a drink. I was trying to give you some space. Since it seemed like that's what you needed."

"Did you take my wallet so I can't leave the island?"

"Why would I do that? It was my suggestion that we go home."

I ignored his implication. I was exhausted from trying to argue with his delusion, his game, whatever it was. Right now, all I needed was my wallet.

"Let's get something to eat," he said.

"I'm not hungry." I grabbed my phone and key and went down to the lobby, headed to the Golden Rim bar. Before stepping inside, I found a quiet spot in the lobby and went through the process of reporting my credit cards stolen.

Although it was seven in the evening, the bar was surprisingly empty. Four or five people were sitting at the bar, and a few more at the tables that formed the perimeter between the bar and the garden. I went up to the bar and waited until the bartender was finished making a cocktail. I signaled for him. I decided not to complicate things with an explanation of my situation.

"I'm looking for my husband. Was there a man in here about fifteen or twenty minutes ago?" I described the man and what he was wearing. "He had a drink. He either used a credit card with the name Jay Davis, or he charged it to room 322."

The bartender shook his head. "I don't need to know his name. There haven't been any guys in here solo all evening."

"Thanks." I left the bar. So, he'd lied about that too. I had no doubt he was also lying about taking my wallet. No one had broken into our room. It hadn't fallen out of my purse in the lobby when I was talking to Bella. I hadn't raised my voice at all when I was speaking to her earlier that day. He'd heard me because he'd moved close to where I was seated.

He was lying about everything, as he had been from the moment I woke beside him in bed that morning. I didn't need to prove it to myself at all.

My phone buzzed in my hand. I looked to see a text from Katherine.

> I'll be there the day after tomorrow. I know your mom is eager, and I'm sorry to leave you alone still, but I had to get some things tied off here. I hope you understand.

I stared at the message, filled with disappointment. I hadn't wanted her to come at all, but now, I felt oddly abandoned and more isolated than ever, knowing it would be two more days.

I put a thumbs up on her message. It was all I could manage.

The next morning, I was shocked to wake and find the sun streaming into my room through the shutters, which I had only closed partially when I went to bed. It was nine thirty. I hadn't slept that late since the days when I was recovering from my accident. I felt as if I were wearing a heavy coat of exhaustion on my back, but until now, that constant awareness hadn't done anything to help me sleep at night. Most nights, I tossed and turned, having trouble falling asleep. When I did sleep, I had fitful dreams, waking often, staring at the ceiling, my mind spinning wildly.

Because swimming had made me feel so much better a few days earlier, I put on a swimsuit and left the room without speaking to the man. I let his questions follow me out the door unanswered and went down to the pool. People were already lying on the lounge chairs, but the pool was empty.

I dove into the water and swam ten laps as quickly as I could. I climbed out, toweled myself dry, and returned to my room.

After I showered and dressed, I called my mother. She asked if I'd spoken to Katherine, and worried out loud that

Katherine hadn't hopped on a plane the moment my mother had asked her to. I didn't tell her about my missing wallet. She would only worry more.

I dodged her questions and remained silent in the face of her worries, as she ran through the list a second time, then a third. At every opportunity, I tried to change the conversation back to her health status. Her chemotherapy was due to start on the upcoming Monday. I had a sick feeling in my stomach, knowing I probably wouldn't be there for it.

As I thought about the future for the first time since my wedding, I realized that my reservation at the resort was due to end in a few days, so maybe I would be going home soon. I wouldn't be able to get another room. If Shep was to be believed, the resort was fully booked for weeks.

When I left to get breakfast, the man didn't ask where I was going, but he trailed behind me. He wasn't even pretending anymore that he was letting me go freely, or wasn't trying to make himself unobtrusive. He walked behind me like an unwanted, unnecessary bodyguard. Or perhaps, a more appropriate description, was that he followed me like a stalker.

As I nibbled the last of my bacon and sipped my coffee, my phone vibrated with an incoming call. Detective Morr's name filled the screen. I picked up the phone. "This is Chelsea."

"We have some information on the deceased man you claim is your husband. The cause of death was drowning. However, he was struck on the back of the head first, which caused him to lose consciousness. We expect he was then pushed or dragged into the water where he drowned."

"So, he was murdered."

"Yes."

"And you've identified him as my husband, Jay Davis?"

"We've run into some difficulties with that."

"How can you run into—"

"We received the updated dental records, but there was also

damage to his gums and lips. The damage to the gum area, especially, caused some of his teeth to fall out. They were lost in the bottom of the lagoon. We haven't yet recovered them. This makes it impossible to make a definitive identification."

"Are you serious?"

"Yes. So—"

"I don't understand why you—"

"I'm giving you the facts. We can't make a positive identification."

"Well do you *think* it's him? If it's not a positive identification, do you suspect it's him?"

"That's not how this works. We don't make partial identifications."

"I know it's my husband! He was wearing Jay's clothes. Even though his wedding ring was missing, I know it's him! Everything else about his body looked like him! Don't you usually ask someone's spouse to identify them? Why are you doing this? It seems like you don't want to know who he is. How are you ever going to find his killer if it's taking so long just to prove that it's him? When are you going to interview the man who has a fake ID in my husband's name?"

"We ask a relative to identify the body when there isn't so much damage. We need to be sure about who he is before we proceed. We can't make accusations against someone until we're sure. If you want us to find the person who killed this individual and build a case that will stand up in court, we need to follow the proper procedure. And the first thing we need to do is make a positive identification. I've explained that to you repeatedly."

"What are you going to do now?"

"We're bringing in someone with more expertise with this type of situation. This individual has experience identifying bodies that have been deceased for a period of time. We should have a positive identification once they've reviewed the dental charts and the body."

I pushed my plate away from me. I felt ill. I wondered if I was going to lose my breakfast all over the table. I'd asked the questions, and he'd answered them, but it was sickening to think about what he was saying. I tried to wipe the words out of my head and focus on my next question. "How long is that going to take?"

"It shouldn't be more than a week or two."

"A week or *two*?! I don't have a *week*, or *two* weeks! I need to check out of my room in a few days. The resort is fully booked. I'm not sure I can find another place to stay. What am I supposed to do?"

"Your presence isn't really necessary here, Mrs. Davis. Why don't you return home? We can communicate with you by phone. That's what we're doing now. You'll probably be more comfortable at home."

"That's not true! I want to take my husband's body home."

"That won't be immediately possible. And it's premature, very premature to be discussing that. I think it's best if you return home."

I felt tears pooling in my eyes. I signed the check for my meal and hurried back to my suite. I went out to the balcony, feeling lost and adrift.

I couldn't stay here. There was no place to go. I also couldn't return home. I had no idea how I would get that man to give me my wallet. After all this time, he hadn't once broken his façade. I felt like one of those people left to wander around an airport, lacking a passport, unable to return to her own country, but unable to gain entry to any other country on the planet. I was in a state of limbo from which I couldn't escape.

I pulled my legs up close to me, hugging them, crying softly, not wanting anyone on the neighboring balconies to hear me.

After a while, my tears stopped flowing, but the ache inside remained sharp.

I stood and went to the railing. I turned my attention to the bar in the swimming pool. It was only partially visible from my balcony, but the section I could see was unobstructed by trees. The man was standing so that I could see his profile. He was talking to Lori and Kendall. They all had drinks in their hands. They were laughing and chatting like old friends.

FIFTY-SEVEN

RACHEL

Looking at my daughter lying in the hospital bed, she seemed like a little girl again. A broken little girl, her body almost drained of life. Her breathing was shallow and seemed infrequent. Sometimes, I moved close to her, placing my ear next to her lips to see if she truly was breathing.

Andrew told me to stop. He said I was infecting her with my fear. I needed to be strong for her. We needed to fill her hospital room with positive energy. He was right, but I was so scared. Her eyelids were almost translucent. I could see every flicker of her eyeballs. Watching them quiver made me anxious. I feared she was being tormented with terrifying dreams.

She had so many broken bones. Right now, she was in an induced coma until the swelling in her brain went down.

Knowing they had done that to her made me wonder what they weren't telling us. Was there something wrong with her mind?

What did it mean to be put into a coma? The doctor had explained it to us, more than once, but his words flowed through my own brain like vapor. I couldn't make sense of them. What if she never woke up? Was her brain deteriorating while we stood there helplessly watching her?

She looked peaceful. Sometimes, if I narrowed my eyes, and let the room grow blurry around me, I could imagine that she was sleeping. I could send myself back to when she was a child, watching her nap, gazing at her sweet, precious face.

Now, her face was anything but flawless. It was bruised and scratched, swollen and so distorted she didn't even look like herself.

"What's going to happen to her?"

"She's slowly going to heal," Andrew said.

"How do you know?" I asked.

"Because that's what the doctor told us."

"What if he's lying to us?" I asked.

"Why would he lie?" Andrew asked.

I shrugged. Maybe he didn't know the answers to our questions. Maybe he just told us what we wanted to hear. Maybe they didn't know how she was doing, and they were giving us positive news because they didn't want to see us upset.

For all I knew, maybe they thought we would grow discouraged over time, and when the truth came out, we would accept it more easily because we'd grown defeated sitting there day after day, watching her slowly turn into a vegetable.

What was an induced coma? Why couldn't I understand when they explained it? It was scary, knowing they could control her brain like that. Maybe she had hardly any brain function at all. She never moved. Her arms and legs were perfectly still. She never turned her head. She never spoke, of course.

I stood and went to the bed. I placed my ear close to her lips. Was she breathing? Did she sense my presence?

I sat on the edge of the bed and slipped my hand into hers. It was limp and lifeless, her skin cool. I leaned my ear close to her lips again, telling myself I wouldn't move until I felt her breath on the side of my cheek.

It must have been ten minutes that I remained in that position, my neck and back aching from the strain of leaning over. One moment I thought I felt her breath. The next, I wasn't sure.

It wasn't that I wouldn't love my daughter in whatever state she was. I would love her if she stayed in that bed, flat on her back, barely breathing, for the next forty years. For the rest of my life. But I wanted my daughter back. I wanted that laughing, smart, witty, vibrant girl to come dancing into our house, filled with plans and energy and excitement.

I wanted to murder the boy who had driven that speedboat. I wanted to put my hands around his neck and strangle him. I wanted to choke the life out of him.

I wondered if Andrew was having these thoughts. If he was, he never said. Of course, I didn't tell him what I was thinking either. My thoughts were too dark. Darker than I even wanted to admit to myself.

My thoughts had gone beyond the emotional out-crying in my head, saying that I wanted to murder him.

I'd gone so far as to plan it out. I'd thought of ways that I might overpower him, if I could catch him by surprise. I considered poison. I'd thought about a handgun, a knife. I had thoughts of luring him to the top of a tall building and pushing him off.

"When is she going to wake up?" I asked.

"The doctor already explained that. When the swelling goes down," Andrew said.

"Do you think she's dreaming?"

"I don't know." He took my hand, squeezing it gently. "Please try to relax. Just picture her being well."

"I want to know what's happening."

"We can't. All we can do is love her and hope for the best."

"Do you think my stalker had anything to do with this?"

He let go of my hand and turned to face me. "It's not a good idea to start thinking that way, Rachel. I know you're upset. What happened to Chelsea is devastating, for all of us. And the person who's been tormenting you all these years is a very sick individual. But I honestly don't think there's any connection between the two. If for no other reason, than it would be impossible to orchestrate something like that."

"It makes no sense! Why would that boy drive his boat into a concrete wall? It's the stupidest thing I've ever heard of. What if someone paid him a lot of money?"

"It was suicidal," Andrew said. "No one does something like that for money. At least not most rational people. And I know a lot of kids that age don't always think rationally, but I think it's much more likely it was the alcohol. Possibly drugs. They should have done a drug test. That was a real screw-up by the police—stopping with alcohol."

Turning my attention back to my daughter, I gazed at her face and wondered if I would ever see her smile again. I wondered if I would ever hear her clear, melodic voice. I wondered if her mind would ever be healthy and whole again.

FIFTY-EIGHT

I felt a sudden intake of breath. I watched them, trying to read their body language. Had they just met? Were they flirting, or was something else going on? I couldn't tell if they were old friends. What was going on here? I wasn't sure it was even possible to tell from someone's body language if they'd just met or if they'd known each other for years. Especially standing in a swimming pool, sipping cocktails at a resort. Sometimes, complete strangers looked as if they'd known each other for half a decade.

They carried on talking and laughing for nearly forty minutes before the man placed his empty glass on the bar, turned, and made his way to the edge of the pool. He walked up the steps, grabbed a towel, dried off, and began walking toward my building.

When he entered my suite, I was sitting on the sofa, waiting for him.

"Who were those women you were talking to?" I asked.

He smiled. Was there a look of condescension in his eyes? I couldn't be sure. It seemed as if he was treating me like I was a paranoid, delusional basket case. If I was, he was the one working overtime, trying to make me that way. I thought I'd done an excellent job of resisting his gaslighting.

"Are you jealous?" he asked.

"Absolutely not. Why are you dodging the question?"

"I'm not dodging the question." He laughed. "Just two women I met at the bar."

"You've never met them before tonight?"

"No. Why do you ask?"

"Did they ask about me?"

"Why would they ask about you?"

"Because I've met them. I've spent quite a bit of time with them."

"Your name didn't come up."

I seriously doubted that. I was sure I'd pointed the man out to them. And I was sure he must have told them something about himself. If nothing else, he would have given them his name. They certainly would have made the connection from that. Unless he'd lied about his name.

I didn't believe a word he'd said. But that was nothing new. Now, I wondered which part I didn't believe. Was he only lying that they hadn't talked about me? Or was he lying about never having met them before?

Unsure whether I was becoming paranoid or if I was being set up in a way that I hadn't realized, I desperately needed to get out of my room. I grabbed my key card and left. I didn't even take my phone. After my call with Bella, there was no one I wanted to talk to. I hurried down the stairs, along the edge of the pool, and went out through the gate to the beach.

I walked to the edge of the water and stepped into the surf, letting the water cool my feet and soothe my mind.

I began walking along the shore. Listening to the surf helped me relax slightly. There were a few other people walking on the beach, but they were so far away, I felt as if I was alone.

I walked for a while, losing track of time. I tried to recall the details of my conversations with Lori and Kendall. I wondered if some of the things they'd said could be interpreted differently than I'd taken them at the time. Had there been any hint that they'd already known my story?

It was strange how they'd appeared so suddenly at the foot of my lounge chair, declaring it was destiny that we meet because we had the same cocktails in our glasses. And then Kendall's parting words. They'd chilled me at the time, and now, I found them even more disturbing—*This isn't about your husband, it's about you.*

She'd said it with such confidence. As if she'd *known*. And then there was the fact that they'd practically kidnapped me. Yes, they'd let me go without too much trouble, but for a few minutes, I'd felt as if they weren't going to.

But if that man was involved with those two women, they'd created something so elaborate, and so sinister, there was no way I would understand it simply by turning it over in my mind.

I stopped and gazed at the moonlight shimmering on the surface of the ocean. After a few minutes, I turned back in the direction I'd come.

I'd only taken a few steps, when I heard the faint sound of a motorboat not far from shore. I looked out again and saw a small boat that seemed to be keeping pace with me. The figure steering it across the unusually calm surface of the water was difficult to make out in the darkness. But one thing was crystal clear. They were wearing a white baseball cap. It appeared to be identical to the hat from the high school where Jay taught.

I couldn't see the logo on the hat, but I had no doubt it was Jay's. I knew it was absurd to believe this. Anyone could have a white hat; the world was filled with white ball caps. But was it really? Somehow, I was absolutely certain it was his. Why else would the boat be tracking my steps, moving slowly, parallel to the shore? I waded into the water up to my knees.

"Jay!" I waded deeper, the water splashing up to my thighs. The surf was calm, but still, the waves slapped my legs. I wanted to swim out to him. I had no doubt it was him. After all this time there he was! Cruising along, just out of reach, watching me. I screamed his name louder. "Jay! Jay!!"

Everything made sense. He'd been there all along. This was why they couldn't identify the body. He wasn't dead! Somehow, someone had gotten his clothes. The man in my room had probably taken them out of his bag and given them to someone, trying to trick me. Those notes *had* been from Jay. He'd wanted to meet me there, but for some reason he hadn't been able to. Maybe that dead man had attacked Jay and Jay had been forced to kill him to defend himself. Now, here he was alive!

The dental records were inconclusive because that body wasn't Jay's. This was why the investigation was going nowhere. This was why everything felt stalled. This was why my life was spinning in circles. I'd gotten it all wrong.

I continued screaming his name until my voice was hoarse. He must hear me. He knew I was there; he was watching me. Why wasn't he answering?

I needed to get to him. He couldn't bring the motorboat to shore. The outboard motor would drag into the sand. He needed me to come to him. I turned away. I splashed out of the water. Back near the edge of the beach was a row of kayaks. I ran up to them and grabbed the first one, dragging it toward the water. As I pulled it across the sand, the paddle fell out. I stopped and ran back and picked it up. I carried it to the boat and shoved it inside. I continued dragging the kayak into the surf.

Once it was in the water, I climbed in and began paddling toward the motorboat. After I'd gone twenty or thirty yards, the swells were larger. The front of the boat rose up and plummeted down. If I'd been body surfing, I probably would have been able to handle them, but the boat behaved differently. The water tossed it around like a cork, making it difficult to paddle.

I pushed ahead, using all my strength, my shoulder muscles burning as I forced the paddle into the water, stroking as fast as I could. After another twenty or thirty yards, I began to tire. Maybe this hadn't been a good idea, but there was no other way to reach him. It was too far for me to swim and I knew he couldn't bring the motorboat to shore. I couldn't let him get away from me.

I wasn't sure I could continue. Spears of pain shot through my back. I called his name over and over, but I sounded weak and the sound of the motorboat likely drowned out my voice. I realized I couldn't hear the motor any longer. As my eyes tried to peer through the darkness, even with the help of the moonlight, I no longer saw the boat.

Had it pulled so far away from me that I couldn't see it? Or were the waves blocking it from view? I didn't think they were because despite how I felt they were tossing me around, they were still relatively gentle. Why couldn't I see him? He had to be here somewhere. I hadn't heard the motor grow louder as if the boat was accelerating away from me.

I stopped paddling. I rested the oar across the kayak. For a moment, I closed my eyes. It was a dangerous thing to do. Sitting out here on the ocean, in the darkness. There were sharks out here. Not often, but it wasn't unheard of. I was exhausted. I couldn't see the motorboat. I couldn't see Jay. I couldn't see anything but dark water and dark sky lit with the tiniest of stars and the milky spot of the moon.

Opening my eyes, I tried to find something to focus on. There was nothing, just the constantly moving water, and the moon above me.

The motorboat was nowhere in sight. Should I return to shore? It was crazy to keep paddling out toward open ocean. I had no destination, and there were no landmarks to head toward. But returning to shore felt like giving up, like I was losing Jay forever, when just moments before, I'd thought we were moments away from a reunion. Only a few moments earlier, I'd believed that my nightmare was over. Finally, finally over.

There was no sound except the lapping of the waves. I had to accept reality. I lowered the paddle into the water on the left side of the kayak and began to maneuver it around toward the shore. Before I could finish changing direction, while the kayak was parallel to the beach, the sound of the motorboat filled my ears again. It grew to a roar as it approached, seeming to come from nowhere. I felt the water churn as the boat raced toward me.

A moment later, the boat slammed into the front of the kayak, sending it flying into the air, flipping it upside down. I slipped out of the cavity where I was sitting as easily as a fish sliding out of glass bowl. I was falling through the water, completely submerged with no idea in which direction the sky was or how far below me the sandy bottom lay.

Thrashing my arms and legs, trying to swim, hoping my natural buoyancy would carry me to the surface, I felt water rushing into my nose and mouth. I clamped my mouth closed, but the water was already inside. I coughed and sputtered, then closed my mouth again, trying to hold my breath, fighting with all my strength to make my way to the surface.

Then I felt strong arms on my shoulders, pushing me down. I was going deeper into the water, losing sight of the surface, my lungs ready to burst.

FIFTY-NINE

CHELSEA

Strong hands pressed down on my shoulders, pushing me deeper under the water. I held my breath, feeling as if my lungs might burst. I kicked as hard as I could trying to aim my feet at the legs of the person holding me, but the water made my legs move slowly. The only contact I made with my attacker was skimming the surface of their legs with my toes, having no impact at all.

When my head bobbed above water, I saw my attacker's head covered with a close-fitting hood, a face concealed by a diving mask, a mouth distorted by the breathing apparatus of oxygen tanks that were strapped to the diver's back. Who was this? It couldn't be the person who'd been in the motorboat. Had there been time to change into full diving gear? Everything felt distorted. Time was dissolving around me. I felt as if I've been in the water for hours, possibly all night. I felt as if my entire life had shrunk to this fight in the water, gulping liquid salt, unsure if I would be able to take another breath.

I was losing. My attacker was stronger. My attacker had the ability to breathe underwater. There was no chance I would prevail.

Paddling the kayak had weakened my arms, draining them of strength. My back ached. I was losing the ability to continue holding my breath underwater for long periods of time. The strong kicks I'd aimed at my attacker earlier were now nothing but tiny flutters.

Any moment, my body would collapse and sink to the bottom of the ocean.

I closed my eyes. I was so tired. I was so tired of everything. What was I fighting for? Maybe for my parents. They would be devastated if my life ended here. Bella might grieve without me. We'd been best friends for more years than I could remember, despite our final conversation. But I couldn't keep this up. I was so very tired.

Closing my eyes wasn't good. I was giving in.

I tried forcing my eyes open, but they filled with salt water. I blinked furiously, but the more I did, the more the water poured across the surface, blinding me. I was sucking in more and more water. I continued thrashing, but I could tell that I was moving more like kelp floating languidly in the water than I was like someone fighting for her life.

My time below the surface was increasing. The moments that I was able to break through and gasp in lungs-full of oxygen were becoming more infrequent. Soon, salt water would fill every cavity in my body. I would sink like a stone. I felt myself growing lightheaded. I felt myself not caring what happened. I felt my mind drifting between panic and a sense of peace and inevitability.

Then, as if some celestial being, perhaps the moon herself, reached down and took hold of me. I felt arms under my own. The rubber-clad sea creature disappeared back into the depths of the ocean. My body rose to the surface, gliding across the water. I was being pulled through the waves. I looked up at the stars, blinking salty water out of my eyes. Tears and the ocean washed down my cheeks.

Soon, waves were breaking over me. Then, someone was picking me up. Someone was carrying me, cradling me like a child.

A few minutes later, I was being placed on a lounge chair. A spasm ran through my body. I shivered as if from extreme cold. But the air was still warm with a tropical breeze, even at this late hour.

"Can you breathe?"

I coughed.

"Shake your head. Yes, or no?"

I gave a single nod of my head.

"Rest for a moment. It might be better if you turned on your side. Here, I'll help you." I recognized the man's voice. I felt his hands on my back and shoulders, gently moving me onto my side. Then his hand was gently rubbing my upper back. "You took in a lot of water. I'm calling the paramedics now."

I felt the weight of him as he sat on the foot of the lounge chair. I heard his voice on the phone, talking to emergency services.

Then he was silent again. I drifted into a state of semi-sleep. I wasn't aware of how much time had passed before I heard the voices of a few other men and women. I felt hands on me, checking my pulse, my blood pressure. Someone was taking my temperature, putting something on my fingertip. They were discussing my condition. They were asking the man questions about what had happened.

After they finished checking me out, ensuring that the water had not in fact gone into my lungs, they raised me slightly on the chair. They asked if I felt up to answering their questions.

I told them what had happened. One of them was instructed to swim out and retrieve the kayak. The others were standing near the shore, scanning the water for the motorboat

I'd reported seeing. After more time had passed, it was determined there was no motorboat in the area.

The paramedics advised me to rest. They advised me not to go to sleep for a few hours. They gave the man instructions for my care. He explained that he was my husband. I didn't have the strength or the mental fortitude to argue, so I remained silent.

Soon, they were gone, and he was helping me back to my room.

I wondered if I had seen my husband in the motorboat. I wondered if Jay was the one who had tried to kill me. Or was it someone else? I even wondered if the man had tried to kill me, then stripped off his gear and rescued me.

I underestimated her strength. I underestimated her determination to live. I'd stupidly assumed that by now, her mental state would have left her weak and unwilling to fight. There was another thing I hadn't considered.

I'd made the assumption that the lingering trauma of her boating accident would have paralyzed her in the water. All those horrifying memories of what she'd experienced only two years ago would have come rushing back, taking over her mind, making her body incapable of fighting.

Fear was supposed to immobilize her. Finally, I would enjoy the sweet taste of revenge.

But I was wrong about everything.

This left me angry, but I had only myself to be angry with.

Then I realized, just like preparing a good meal, or like any form of art, the creator has to be open to new inspiration, new possibilities. Creativity isn't always about following a plan. Adhering strictly to a recipe often leads to something derivative and mundane. True works of art come from flashes of inspiration. Something brilliant is often born out of failure.

And the failure of the scene I'd tried to orchestrate in the ocean waves made me realize there were more things that could be done to make this a more satisfying experience for me, and at the same time, a far more punishing experience for everyone involved.

As I dove beneath the waves, moving silently through the water as purposefully as a shark, my mind was already working. I disappeared into the blackness of the ocean. I was long gone before they even thought to look for me. I vanished as if I'd never existed.

Swimming in the silent depths, my thoughts moved in a new direction. I thought about the pleasure of knowing my true victim was suffering in real time. Despite all my planning, I'd rushed too quickly to the climax. I hadn't been willing to take enough risk.

There's another popular theme that many live by: no guts, no glory.

If I could find the courage to expose myself, I would be able to enjoy the ultimate thrill of knowing my victim was feeling intense pain while remaining utterly helpless. It was an enormous risk but would be so worth the reward I would enjoy. An experience that I could play over in my mind for the rest of my life.

SIXTY-ONE

CHELSEA

I woke the next morning feeling surprisingly normal. I'd expected to have trouble breathing, my brain and the rest of my body squishy with salt water. Part of me had assumed I might feel as horrible as I had after my boating accident. Instead, I felt refreshed from a good night's sleep, even though it had been brief. I'd followed the paramedics instructions to not go to sleep immediately. I'd eat half a sandwich and some fruit and consumed several glasses of water.

The man hadn't liked it that I wanted to lock myself in the bedroom. He insisted it wasn't safe. He said I was risking my life, that he needed to keep an eye on me to make sure nothing happened during the night. At the same time, he couldn't provide anything specific that he thought might happen. It wasn't as if I'd had a concussion and needed to be watched for signs of brain damage.

Ignoring his concern, I'd closed and locked the doors and gone to bed.

After a warm, comforting shower, I went into the living area. He'd already closed up the hide-a-bed. He was stressed, drinking a cup of coffee, his legs crossed. He been staring at the doors to my room, waiting for me to come out.

"How are you feeling?" he asked.

"Fine." I took a deep breath. Because of everything, I wasn't thrilled with what I needed to say next. But I needed to say it. "Thank you for rescuing me." I didn't like that I had to thank him. I didn't like using the word *rescue*. But as I'd taken my shower, I turned it over in my head again and again, and I couldn't think of any better way to say it.

The other thing I wanted to say to him, *he* wasn't going to like.

"I really appreciate what you did for me, and I recognize that you probably saved my life. But at the same time this has to be said. I'm tired of you following me everywhere I go. It's creepy and I want it to stop. Do you understand?"

"You would've drowned."

"I said, I get that. But I'm telling you now, I want it to stop."

"What if something like that happens again?"

"I'm not going to take a kayak out into the ocean at night again. So, it's not going to happen."

He stared at me as if I'd lost my mind. I wondered what he was thinking. But since I had no clue who he was or what he was up to, it was a fruitless thing to wonder. More fruitless than in a normal relationship. I didn't have the tiniest sliver of insight into how his mind worked. After all this time, he was still an absolute stranger to me.

"Did you see the person who was attacking me?"

"Of course not. It was dark, and they were wearing a diving mask."

"You didn't see anything at all?"

"I didn't see anything at all."

"Do you know who it was?"

"Why would you ask me that?"

"Why aren't you answering the question?"

"I don't understand why you think I might know who it was. I saw someone trying to drown you and I went out to help. That's all I know."

"Why should I believe you? You've done nothing but lie to me since the first moment I saw you. I don't believe a word that comes out of your mouth."

He smirked. "Then why are you asking me these questions?"

"Because you know something. I think you know a lot about all of this. I think you might know everything. Somehow you got a key to my room. You knew my husband wouldn't be here, or you wouldn't have ended up in my bed. You have a lot of information about my husband, about me. You duplicated his ID. You didn't just appear here out of nowhere. So, the logical conclusion is that you know everything that's going on here. I think you know who killed Jay and I think you know who attacked me. So why should I trust you at all? You seem kind, you pretend to care about my mother, and you act as if you're concerned about my welfare. But at the same time, you lie to my face and gaslight me every moment of every day."

Why was I asking him any questions at all? Why did I keep banging my head against this concrete wall? It was a waste of time. Whatever he knew he was never going to tell me.

The person in the hat had to be Jay. Or somebody taunting me. Trying to make me believe I was losing my mind. It was not a casual person who had simply found Jay's hat lying on the ground.

I couldn't stop thinking about the police and their failure to identify the body I'd found. Maybe they couldn't identify him because it wasn't Jay. The dental records were inconclusive because they were Jay's dental records, and they didn't match the teeth of the man whose body I'd found. I'd only believed it was Jay's body because he'd told me to meet him there and the clothes belonged to Jay. But he hadn't been wearing Jay's wedding ring. Why hadn't I focused more on that important fact?

What if something had happened to Jay before he was able to meet me? What if he was involved in something I knew nothing about? Maybe my mother had been right from the beginning. I didn't know everything about his background. Yes, we shared a lot about our lives, enough that it felt like everything, but only what we'd chosen to share. Maybe he was involved in something I knew nothing about. Maybe that phone call at our wedding wasn't from a disgruntled parent. What parent called a man on the day of his wedding to complain about a college application issue?

And Jay had been unreasonably upset. Why had he even answered the call? I would have let it go to voicemail if it was only a parent calling to complain. Why had he answered? Why had he left the reception to talk to that person?

I wanted to cry with frustration and fear and grief. I wanted to believe my husband was still alive. I wanted to escape from this never-ending nightmare.

"I have one simple question for you," the man said. "Do you believe me now, that it's not safe for you to go out of the room without me? I know you don't like me following you, but it's the only way I know of to keep you safe."

"Did you know somebody was going to try to kill me out there?"

He held my gaze. I watched to see if his head would nod in agreement. He didn't move at all. He didn't speak.

SIXTY-TWO

RACHEL

Now

The doorbell rang. Andrew would be home with our takeout meal any minute so I checked my phone to look at the security camera app. It was a delivery person. I wasn't expecting a package. The woman was holding her digital device, her gaze solidly fixed on the front door.

After I signed for the package, I took it into the kitchen and sliced the tape with a knife. I tore off the brown paper and let it fall onto the table. Inside was a beautifully wrapped box. I smiled. It must be something to comfort and encourage me during my upcoming chemo.

The paper was pale gray with white clouds on it. A dark gray ribbon was wrapped around the narrow box, tied into a small, flat bow.

I undid the ribbon and tore off the wrapping paper. I lifted the lid off the box. Inside was a framed print of a newborn's tiny footprints done in pink paint.

I dropped the print onto the table. The glass cracked.

This wasn't meant to cheer me up. I was sure this was a cryptic message from my stalker, my tormentor. Again.

I wanted to pound my fist against the glass protecting those tiny footprints, but I feared slicing my hand, slivers of glass embedding themselves in my flesh. I picked up the lid, ready to smash it back onto the box. As I pulled it away from the tissue paper, a small white envelope fell out. I knew the words inside would find a way to frighten me. I shouldn't read them. I should stuff the card inside the box with that print and carry the whole mess out to the trash.

Slamming the lid onto the box, I was satisfied to hear another crack in the glass. I picked up the package and carried it to the back door. I pressed down on the handle and pushed the door open with my hip. I walked outside and went to the enclosed area where the trash cans were located. Just as I was about to raise the lid on the bin, I was overcome with a desperate need to know what my stalker had said to me this time.

I turned away from the trash bins and went into the garden. I sat on the bench under an ancient oak tree that was the pride of our backyard. Slowly, I lifted the lid off the box for the second time. I picked up the envelope and opened it. The words on the card stunned me.

The card slipped through my fingers and fluttered to the ground. The breeze picked it up, turned it onto its edge, then blew it across the yard, carrying it into the freshly watered soil under my white roses.

It didn't matter to me if the card rotted in the garden. The words, just like the words on all the other letters and cards I'd received over the years, would live inside me forever.

You thought this gift was for you, but it's for your husband.
Andrew, when you toasted your bride-to-be at your engage-

ment party, you said she had tamed you. Everyone laughed. You, the hardest of all.

You certainly had many women before you settled down, didn't you? How many children did your countless one-offs produce? You don't even know, do you? Did you ever give it a moment's thought?

You thought Chelsea was the only child who needed you. The apple of your eye. Because of you, I lost my daughter. Now, it's your turn.

Rachel, it was never about you! But you have the over-inflated sense of self-importance to think it was!

I pressed my hand over my mouth to keep myself from screaming, rousing the neighbors who would surely come running to help. Who *was* this person?

For all these years, for a reason I couldn't explain, I had assumed it was a man. But this note made me realize it was a woman. A woman who had been in love with my husband. Was she suggesting she'd had a child with him?

I felt sick to my stomach.

I bolted off the bench and rushed across the yard, grabbing the note out of the damp earth. I brushed clumps of wet soil off the card and pressed it against my jeans to pat it dry. The note said she'd lost her daughter and now it was Andrew's turn. What had happened to her daughter? Was she dead? Was this woman threatening to kill Chelsea?!

Clutching the card in one hand, crumpling it inside my fist, I bent forward, sobbing.

A short time later, when Andrew came into the kitchen with the bag of Chinese food, I was sitting at the table with a glass of wine in front of me. It would be my final glass of wine for quite a while, once chemo started. Right now, I needed it desperately.

"Did you have a child, or get someone pregnant, before we

were married? Is it possible you might have a child you don't know about?"

"What are you talking about?" He placed the bag of food containers on the table.

I showed the note to him, tears starting to fill my eyes again, clogging my throat. I had no appetite. I hadn't had much of one anyway, and with the contents of that note, the veiled threat against Chelsea, my stomach was overflowing with bile. I sipped my wine, hoping it would calm me, stop my hands from shaking, my heart from racing so fast I could hardly breathe. "Can you recall anyone who might have gotten pregnant? Any relationships that had messy endings where maybe you weren't told everything? I don't know. I'm trying to figure out who this person *is!*" I began crying. I pushed the wineglass away from me.

He dropped the card onto the table. He sat down on the chair across from me, giving me a stunned look. "I have no idea. If I did, I would tell you." He reached for my hand. "You know I would. With everything right now..." His eyes turned red and he blinked hard, breaking his gaze away from mine. "I don't know. Of course I had other relationships before us. You know that. But nothing after we got together. You know that, too!"

I refused to let him take my hand. I trusted him, but I wondered if his mind was landing on a particular girl, or woman, even as he looked at something across the room. "You need to go and bring her home."

"I can't leave you! Your chemo starts Monday."

"I know that. But this person sounds like she's threatening her life! And Jay... and that man."

"Katherine's there."

"You need to go."

"I'm not leaving you, Rachel." Now he was holding my hand with both of his.

"Do you know who she is? You have to tell me." Wouldn't

he tell me, with this note threatening our daughter's life, if there was something he'd kept from me all these years?

"I don't know!"

"You're telling me the truth?"

"Yes!"

"Chelsea's life might depend on this."

"I'm telling you the truth. And it hurts that you're asking me that question."

"I still think you should go."

"We can call Katherine. Tell her they need to come home. Now. There's nothing to be gained with me going."

"What if she—"

"They can be on a plane and halfway home before I could get there," he said.

I pulled my hand out of his and left the room without saying more. I needed to breathe, and I couldn't do it sitting in the same room as him.

SIXTY-THREE

CHELSEA

The man was still staring at me, refusing to tell me anything. He looked calm, as he always did, as if my questions were casual inquiries about what kind of wine he wanted. As if not answering was a matter of little importance.

My cell phone buzzed in my pocket. I pulled it out. When I saw my father's face, my heart fluttered slightly. He and I were close, but he rarely called. We usually texted each other.

Sliding my thumb across the screen, I went into the bedroom and closed the plantation doors to the main room. I walked to the glass doors facing the balcony so I could look out at the view while I talked to him.

"Hi, Dad. What's going on?"

"Just checking on you. How is everything?"

"Mostly the same." I wasn't sure which parts to tell him, and I couldn't begin to tell him everything that had happened, so it was better to tell him nothing. Of course, he didn't believe me that things were as calm as my voice pretended.

"Something's come up," he said.

"Is Mom okay?" My knee-jerk panic made my voice rise an octave.

"Yes. Yes, she's fine. Starting chemo next week. I didn't mean to sound the alarm. Everything's good with her. I'm not calling about that. I just... I wanted to know how you're doing. I'm really concerned, we're all concerned, about that man in your room. I can't accept that there aren't any other options. There's always another option," he said. "I don't want to criticize, but are you sure you pushed hard enough?"

"Yes, Dad. I pushed them hard." Why was he bringing this up again? After all this time?

"I just wonder if there's more to this than we realize. If someone put him up to this. If there are others involved. If..."

"If, what?" He didn't sound like himself. It wasn't like him to hesitate in the middle of what he was saying. I could feel that something was on his mind. Why was he being so vague? "What's going on?" I imagined him sitting at his desk as he always did when he made phone calls. I pictured him taking the pens out of his top drawer and lining them up in order of color and size, as he always did when he talked on the phone.

He was silent.

"What is it? Is something wrong with Mom? Is there something you're not telling me?"

"No, no. I told you, she's fine. Everything is good. This is... I guess she told you about that person who has been harassing her over the years, right?"

"Yes. Did something happen?"

He sighed. "It's hard telling you this." I'd never heard him like this. I'd understood why my mother was upset about the letters she received over the years. But it was shocking to hear the undercurrent of fear in my father's voice. He'd never been afraid of anything or anyone.

Even though my mother had been worried and suspicious of my relationship with Jay at the beginning, those fears had developed as a result of my boating accident—both from the manic behavior of Brent, and the endless days when she'd thought I might not recover. She hadn't been that way throughout my life. She hadn't been one of those overprotective parents, always trying to prevent me from doing what I wanted. In fact, it had been the opposite. She'd always pushed me to go out and experience my life, and the world, to the fullest.

As I gazed out at the coconut palms and the ocean beyond, my father began telling me about the package my mother had received. He described the framed infant footprints. He told me about the threatening note that seemed to suggest a woman from his past might be planning to kill me in a demented attempt to punish my father.

I recalled the boat ramming my kayak, the hands pushing me under the waves, salt water in my lungs. I couldn't tell them any of that. It would terrify them, and it wouldn't make me any safer.

"Do you understand why we're so afraid for you?" he asked. "Your mother and I respect you, Chelsea. We trust your judgment. You know that. But we're having trouble understanding why you've allowed this man to stay in your room. We've always thought he was dangerous, and now, we're concerned, in fact, we're certain he's connected to this woman. Whoever she is. It's likely he'll allow her into your room, and one of them will do something to seriously hurt you, or worse. You need to get him out of there, or you need to leave. Immediately."

"Do you have another child?" I asked softly.

He was quiet for a moment, obviously embarrassed to hear that question from me. "No. I don't... not that I was ever told about. And I've never cheated on your mother. It's..."

"Well, then this person is deranged."

"That's what we're afraid of. And maybe there's something I don't—"

"Katherine will be here soon. And once the police identify Jay's body, I'll come home. Okay?"

"Your casual attitude really concerns me." His voice was so loud, I had to move the phone away from my ear.

He'd never spoken to me like that and it was shocking to hear. It made me realize how frightened he was. The note must've upset him even more than I'd realized. Hearing about it was disturbing, reading it, while looking at those tiny footprints, must have been terrifying. "I'm not being casual," I said. "It's just a gut feeling. He's never behaved in a threatening way." Even as I said the words, I knew they were a lie. He'd been menacing in subtle, but very clear ways.

"That doesn't mean he won't."

"I know what I feel, what I can sense. I need to find out about Jay. How many times do I have to say that?"

"A psychopath is very good at pretending they're someone they're not. Or, I should say, *something* they're not. Because they're hardly human."

"I honestly don't think that's what he is."

"Do you have a degree in psychiatry?" he asked.

I sighed.

"I'm serious. It's clear from this note that someone is threatening your life."

"Katherine will be here today."

"Can you go somewhere until she arrives? Stay in a public area? Please? I'm begging you. We're begging you."

"I'll try."

"Chelsea. You need to—"

"Please don't worry. You can trust me to take care of myself."

He fretted for a few more minutes, and I continued to reassure him, knowing my words weren't penetrating his worry. Finally, we said goodbye and I promised to text when Katherine arrived.

After I finished talking to my father, I walked along the balcony and entered the main room. The man was stretched out on the sofa, his ankles propped up on the arm, his head resting on a pillow. He was looking directly at me, as if he'd been waiting for me to return and finish our earlier conversation. But it hadn't been a conversation. I'd asked him questions that he refused to answer, as always, so, I wasn't sure what he was waiting for.

"A friend of my mother's is coming to stay with me," I said. " There's not going to be any room for you once Katherine gets here."

He sat up. He looked slightly anxious.

"Did you send a gift to my parents?"

He stared at me as if he couldn't make sense of the question. "Why would I send a gift to your parents?"

"Why would you do any of the things you've done to me?"

His expression was unreadable. "Why is your mother's friend coming?"

"To keep me safe."

"If you say so."

"That means this is probably your last chance to tell me what's going on. It's your only opportunity before the police get seriously involved. Because once Katherine gets here, things will change."

He held my gaze, but for the first time, I saw a flicker of fear in his eyes. Or had I imagined it?

SIXTY-FOUR

CHELSEA

Despite what appeared to be a moment of weakness flashing across the man's face, that flicker in his eyes that suggested he might be afraid, he said nothing. After a few minutes, I grew tired of the standoff. I grabbed my purse and left the room.

I knew the wise choice was to go to the breakfast restaurant or one of the coffee kiosks for a luscious drink loaded with caffeine, but I wanted something to numb the jittery, confused feelings I had after talking to my father. I went to the Golden Rim and slid onto a stool at the bar. I ordered a Bloody Mary. The moment it arrived, I stirred it and took a bite out of the celery, followed by a long, spicy, cold sip.

Placing my phone on the bar, I opened a text window and sent a joint message to Lori and Kendall.

> Sipping a Bloody Mary, our synchronous drink.
> Want to join me?

They both responded immediately with hearts. I smiled. My lure had hooked them. Finding out if they knew the man in my room, or why they'd become such fast, eager friends that first day, might not be quite as easy. But Kendall's remark that everything that had happened was all about me and had nothing to do with Jay wouldn't stop poking at my brain. And I needed to find out why they'd all looked so incredibly friendly, laughing and sipping drinks in the swimming pool bar a few nights ago.

Within ten minutes, they were seated on either side of me. Five minutes after that, a Bloody Mary was perched on the bar in front of each of them. We clicked our glasses together.

"Cheers!" I said.

"Does your good mood mean they found the person who killed your husband?" Kendall looked at me with eager, excited eyes. She blinked, then smiled.

Her expression caused me to think I'd misjudged them, despite their cozy time with the man in my room. She looked and sounded concerned. She gave the same vibe they'd both projected the day I'd met them. But then, they'd put something in my drink, taken me to their room, and tried to keep me there.

"Is that man gone? Lori asked. "Was he arrested?!" She sipped her drink.

"He's still there. They still haven't identified my husband's body, and as far as I can tell, they haven't done much at all to investigate his death." Hardly pausing for a breath, I continued. "I saw you talking to the man in my room the other night. In the pool bar. Do you know him?"

"What?" Kendall asked.

"The man pretending to be Jay, my husband. I saw you in the pool with him. It looked like you three all knew each other."

"What man?" Lori asked.

"You were at the bar in the swimming pool. You were laughing and talking to a guy. Kind of hot, he has dark hair, just a little over six feet. He wasn't very tan, even though he's been here for over a week." I laughed. "You don't remember? He didn't tell you his name?"

"Oh. Yes, okay," Kendall said. "No, we never exchanged

names. He just started talking to us, asking where we were from, how long we were staying. The usual."

"You don't know him?" I asked.

They stuck their straws in their mouths and sipped their drinks, shaking their heads in unison.

Did I believe them? They looked sincere. They sounded as if they were telling the truth. I tried to remember what I'd seen that night. Had I read more into than was there because I was paranoid? Or were they lying now? I couldn't be sure. Something didn't feel right. They were looking at me with wide, round eyes, as if they were waiting for me to say more, as if they were studying me, watching to see what I would do.

"It feels like you're not being straight with me," I said.

"We don't know him." Kendall moved her nearly empty glass to the side. She signaled the bartender for another.

"Did you put something in my drink? The night you took me to your room and I passed out?"

"We were *worried* about you!" Lori said. "That man—"

"So you kidnapped me?"

"We didn't kidnap you," Lori said.

The bartender placed another Bloody Mary in front of Kendall, asked if anyone else wanted a second, then left when we shook our heads.

"And drugged my drink. I just feel... I thought you were just friendly when we first met, and now I feel like you're setting me up. I don't know why, or for what, but I'm already losing my mind. I thought you had my back, and I don't understand why you would—"

"Okay." Kendall held up her hand. She stirred her drink furiously, ice clinking against the glass. "We were worried, yes. We shouldn't have..." She slid one of the olives off the stick balanced across the glass. She ate it, then took a bit of celery.

"What?" I asked. "What is it?"

"The manager—Shep. He thinks you're a little..." She

laughed. "I'm sorry, I hate saying this. He thinks you might be unhinged. I know him. I've stayed here before. Twice. We hooked up once." She blushed slightly, then recovered. "He asked if we would keep an eye on you."

"What the hell does that mean? And why? For what... Why would you do that? And what right does he have to ask you that? To ask anyone? And who does he think he is making that kind of decision about me. There's nothing wrong with me except that something horrible is happening in my life. And half the problem is because of him, and the resort refusing to help me!"

Kendall pushed her drink away. She placed her hand on mine. I tried pulling my hand away, but she held on tightly.

"I'm so sorry. We shouldn't have. We should have said something. Or, I don't know... It didn't seem like a big deal. Just being friendly. And when we heard your story, we were scared for you. We honestly were."

"We still are!" Lori said.

"But we don't know that man. And we wish we could help. And I'm really sorry," Kendall said. "It seemed like the right thing, at the time. Like it wouldn't hurt anything. But might help you."

"We thought you needed friends," Lori said.

They were right about that, but I wasn't going to admit it to them. I felt betrayed. I couldn't trust anyone.

"Sorry," Kendall said.

I signaled the bartender and gave him my room number.

"We'll pay for your drink," Kendall said. "No worries."

I gave her a grim smile.

"Sorry," they said.

"A friend from home is coming. I need to get back." I walked out of the bar. What they'd done wasn't the worst thing in the world, but I still felt betrayed. And I wasn't entirely sure I believed their story. I wondered what the man would have to say if I asked him once again about whether he'd met Lori and Kendall before.

I also realized I'd told him to leave our room. Had that been a mistake? Once he was gone, I would lose my opportunity to get him to talk. Despite a week and a half of failure, asking about Lori and Kendall might open up a new possibility. And that hint of fear I'd seen in his eyes made me hope he might finally be willing to tell me something.

When I was a few doors away from my room, I saw a white envelope sticking out from under the mat. My heart almost stopped with my feet, as the reaction puncturing my thoughts was that this was another note from Jay. Immediately, my senses righted themselves. I ran to the door and grabbed the envelope.

Inside was a card like those I'd received from Jay.

If you want to know what happened to your husband. If you want to know everything, meet me at the waterfall where you were married tomorrow night at eleven. Alone.

There was no signature. I stared at the words for a moment longer before shoving the card into my purse. After what my father had told me, I would be a fool to go. The note offered the final promise of death. Did this person know me well enough to believe my burning desire to know the truth would overpower my self-preservation? I wasn't sure what I would do. If I went, I would surely end up dead. If I didn't go, I might never find the answers to questions that had gnawed at me since the moment I saw Jay walk out of our reception to take a disturbing phone call.

With a trembling hand, I inserted the key card into the door and pushed it open. Something inside the room felt different. I stepped into my suite. The room looked as if it had been cleaned for new occupants. The man was gone.

There was no evidence he'd ever been there at all. The

hide-a-bed was made up into a sofa. His phone and charger were gone. His wallet and the other odds and ends that he kept on the console under the TV were gone. But it didn't look as if he'd left for a meal, it was clear that he'd taken everything. His flip-flops that he usually kept by the door onto the balcony were missing, as were his other shoes. I checked the closet in the main room and his suitcase was no longer there. The bathroom counter was stripped clean of his products.

My final hope of getting him to talk was also gone.

SIXTY-FIVE
CHELSEA

After absorbing the shock of my empty suite, I turned and left. Maybe I could find him in the lobby waiting for a car to the airport. I yanked open the door and bolted out, running along the corridor past surprised guests who were enjoying the casual pace inspired by the tropical air.

I hurried down the stairs and ran toward the lobby, startled by the fact that I was now chasing after a man I'd spent the past two weeks trying to be rid of. As I passed the outdoor seating area and entered the lobby, I stopped suddenly. Katherine was standing only a few feet in front of me. She gave me a comforting, affectionate smile and let go of the handle of her suitcase. She lowered her shoulder so her purse strap slid off and reached out her arms, rushing forward to hug me.

"Oh, Chelsea." She rubbed my back, tightening her hold on me. "I'm so, so sorry for everything you've been through. What a nightmare. It's horrific! From the bliss of your wedding to... to this! I wish I could do something to fix it."

I held on to her, finally pulling away to give her a limp smile. There wasn't anything I could say, so I asked about her flight. Hoping I wasn't too late, I scanned the lobby for the man, walking out to the front drive to ask the valets if they'd seen him. No one had. Defeated, I led the way to my suite. I ushered her into the room and showed her where she could put her suitcase.

Now that she was here in my room, I wondered what Katherine thought she was going to do to actually help with my situation. The police clearly had their own procedures that they would follow no matter what anybody said, especially someone from the mainland. It had become clear to me that they didn't appreciate outsiders telling them how to do their jobs. I supposed she was also here for emotional support, which I appreciated, and needed. But it wouldn't change anything.

While she washed up and changed her clothes, I took two tiny bottles of vodka out of the minibar fridge, poured the contents into glasses over ice, and added cranberry juice. We sat on the balcony and sipped our drinks. We talked about all the things that had happened. It did feel good to tell my story again. It was comforting to hear her shock and outrage over the things that had happened to me.

Although it was an absolute relief to have the physical presence of someone on my side, the longer I talked, the longer I listened to her reassuring murmurs of support, the more I wondered why she'd made the trip. The police wouldn't listen to me, they certainly weren't going to listen to someone who had no involvement at all, no matter how powerful she was in her corner of the world. And now that the man had vanished, she wouldn't be able to help by trying to break through his façade where I'd failed.

"You must have been in a constant state of fear." Katherine's eyes were glassy with tears. She took a sip of her drink. "I can't imagine how it's been for you. I can't even find the words to tell you how sorry I am that you've had to live through this, that you're still... that Jay is dead. I'm sorry I couldn't come sooner. And your mom..." She put her hand on my leg and squeezed gently. "How did you sleep at night with that man in your room?"

I swallowed the last of my drink. I told her about the knife, how I'd kept it in my purse, slept with it under my pillow, often waking with my fist curled around it. She nodded, but looked slightly uncomfortable. "It might not have been enough. If he'd —" She shivered.

"I know." Then, I showed her the most recent note I'd received, and again, she expressed the shock I found comforting, especially as I told her about the message to my parents and the accompanying infant footprints.

"Your mom told me about the footprints. And how threatening that note was. You aren't thinking of going to *meet* this person, are you?"

"I—"

"That's insane, Chelsea. He'll... or she... wants to *kill* you. That's clearly what—"

"I have the knife." I knew it sounded completely inadequate.

She laughed, confirming my feelings.

"I have to know what happened... to Jay. Who that man was. I—"

"I could go with you, and not let them see me."

"No. It said—"

"You can't go by yourself. With a *knife?*" She laughed again, more gently this time.

I hesitated. "Maybe you're right," I said finally.

"Of course I'm right, sweetheart. The reason I'm here is to look out for you. That's why your mom wanted me to come. This is so dangerous. Having someone there who's unexpected can only be good. Why don't we go over there after dinner tonight? You can get familiar with the area again. See what it's like at night. And then, tomorrow, I'm going with you. Otherwise, I can't let you do that."

I didn't like her acting as if she was in charge. As if this was about her. But going there first, to get familiar with the area in the dark might not be a terrible idea. I nodded.

"And maybe I can help you figure out who this man is."

"How? He's gone."

"He must be here somewhere. After all that? He wouldn't just—"

"It's too late."

"It's not. Let me help you. He must still be here. We can demand the police take some action."

I laughed. "Good luck with that."

"Strength in numbers."

"I'm sure he's gone. There aren't any available rooms at the resort."

"There are always rooms in a resort this size. In any hotel. No matter what they tell you. Aside from that, a woman might have offered to let him stay with her." She laughed. "Since he's so good-looking."

I told her about Lori and Kendall, about seeing them laughing and flirting with him at the pool bar.

"There you go." The look on her face was one of triumphant relief, as if she'd solved the entire puzzle, including Jay's murder.

As we dressed for dinner, we vowed that we wouldn't talk any more about Jay or the man, about Katherine's plan to find him and make him pay for what he'd done to me. We deemed everything that had happened since my wedding forbidden topics. We would find other things to talk about—memories from the past, stories about the islands, Katherine's work, my plans for law school.

We went to the steak house located in the main building of

the resort. Katherine slid onto the banquette, insisting I take the more comfortable upholstered chair on the opposite side. She held out her hand. "Give me your purse, there's plenty of room over here." She placed my purse beside her and I took my seat.

"I feel the need for some exquisitely rare beef," Katherine said. "Something I can sink my teeth into. Lots of iron... for my hair." She tossed her head and let her long, expertly darkened waves side across her shoulder. "You should too, Chelsea. You look pale and tired. You need to get your strength back after everything you've been through." She reached across the table and circled my wrist with her hand. "You feel tense. You can relax now. You're not alone." She gave me a warm smile.

Katherine ordered a steak cooked rare with a baked potato and a side of baby green beans. I did the same, feeling too tired to make my own selection. She ordered a bottle of Cabernet to pair with our steaks. After it was opened and poured, she raised her glass. "To healing your heart, and better days ahead."

I clinked my glass against hers. She took a sip and placed her glass on the table. She shifted to the side, crossing her legs under the table, and shoving my purse behind her angled legs. She picked up a piece of bread and buttered it. She took a large bite. She held the basket toward me. I shook my head.

Katherine asked me about law school and my plans for returning. After that, she talked about her travels—her most recent trip to India. I liked hearing her stories, and it was a great distraction to the tormenting thoughts that had circled endlessly and repetitively in my head for the previous two weeks.

While she talked, she alternated between sipping her wine and her water, continuously topping off both our glasses.

"You know, sometimes I wonder if the dead man is really Jay," I said. "Because they still haven't identified him."

"Oh hon." Katherine put down her wineglass and leaned forward, looking at me with pity. "Don't do that to yourself."

Tears filled my eyes. I patted my lower lids with my napkin. "Will you give me my purse?"

She handed me a tissue from her own purse.

"I was thinking, I should text Lori and Kendall to join us for drinks. I'd like to get your take on them."

"This is our time," she said. "We weren't going talk about—"

"I know. But just for one drink. It still bothers me that they acted like they knew that man. And the way they were so overly friendly to me right from the start, as if they... I don't know. You have more perspective. I'd just like to know if you sense anything off about them."

"I don't think that's important."

"Maybe he is staying in their room, like you said."

She took a sip of wine.

"Give me my purse. I'll text them."

"But we..."

I half stood and leaned across the table, pulling my purse from behind her legs. I took out my phone and sent a text to Lori while Katherine sipped her wine and continued murmuring objections, reminding me we were going to the waterfalls where I'd been married.

"We can still go," I said. "Look, they already said yes." I stood again, putting the strap over my shoulder. "I'll go to the bar and order some drinks for us. Espresso martinis?"

"Our server can—"

"I need to make a quick stop at the restroom anyway." I smiled, blinking away my tears again. "I'll be right back. Enjoy the wine. And the rest of your steak." I gave her a watery smile.

As I stood at the bar waiting for our drinks, I slipped my hand into my purse. I unzipped the interior pocket and felt for my bottle of opioids that I'd hidden there when I'd suspected the man of going through my luggage. I flipped off the easy-open cap from the mislabeled bottle and rolled one of the tablets between my fingers.

I hadn't taken them in so long. Not since before I'd met Jay. Ibuprofen was more than enough for my occasional residual pain. But I remembered the great relief they'd provided. And not just from physical pain. They'd had a way of softening my mind, slowing my thoughts, offering a mild sense of euphoria, taking away the sharpness of the hurt I'd felt in knowing that the boy I'd loved had driven a boat straight into a concrete pillar, caring nothing for my life.

In some ways, I felt that now. What had Jay done to put his own life at risk, and as a result, mine? Did he know this person who was so driven to hurt my parents through me? Since the day I'd woken up to find a stranger in my bed, I'd been tormented by unanswerable questions. My mind was worn out from thinking, not unlike the tablet that was turning to powder between my fingers.

A moment later, Lori and Kendall were beside me. They ordered their drinks and we returned to the table. I introduced them to Katherine. They were charming, friendly, and seemed to connect easily with her. There wasn't a whisper of deception in anything they said, or in any of their mannerisms.

When we left the restaurant forty minutes later, Katherine agreed. "They seemed like they really cared about you. Maybe that man messed up your sense of reality so much, you're having a hard time trusting anyone."

I nodded. She gave me a quick hug and we started back toward my suite.

* * *

We changed into comfortable clothes and athletic shoes. We tied our hair into ponytails. Katherine sat down for a moment, telling me the wine and martini had hit her harder than she'd expected. I told her I would order an Uber while she drank some water. While we waited for the driver, my heart tightened with pain, recalling the last time I'd been to the Hibiscus Garden, seeing flashes of my wedding in my mind.

I dreaded entering that beautiful garden, hearing those waterfalls, plunging over a hundred-foot cliff to a secluded cove that opened to the ocean below. I thought about the beauty and the love that had filled that day, and the horrid contrast to what was coming now. Then, I shoved those memories out of my mind, focusing on this moment.

When we arrived at the wedding venue, the gates onto the property were still open. The posted sign said the garden area closed at 10 p.m.

As we walked along the narrow path toward the garden where Jay and I had been married, I was flooded with memories of that day. It seemed like another lifetime. Even though it was dark now, the path was familiar. The aroma of the flowers surrounding me was the same and the ground under my feet felt as if I'd walked it many times before instead of just a few times for our rehearsal and the wedding itself.

The garden was strung with fairy lights, which provided a soft glow that enhanced the moonlight and the stars twinkling overhead. The dark clouds from earlier in the day had poured out a few brief showers, then been swept away for now by warm, tropical breezes, as they often were.

"It's good that we're here," Katherine said. "It's important to refresh your memory, don't you think? That way, we'll have the upper hand."

I nodded, unable to speak. I was overwhelmed by feelings of what I'd held in the palm of my hand for such a brief time, and the enormity of what I'd lost. Truthfully, I hadn't lost it at all. It had been snatched away from me.

Katherine took my hand and led me farther into the open space, pulling me closer to where I'd stood when I said my wedding vows, when Jay had taken my hands, looked into my eyes, and promised to stand by my side for the rest of his life.

Neither of us had guessed his life would be over in a few short days.

Katherine was still holding my hand. She continued to pull me gently toward the side of the garden, closer to the falls, where a group of palm trees grew in a cluster of three. The roar of the falls was louder here. She asked me a question, but I couldn't hear.

She spoke again, raising her voice. "Are you feeling okay?"

I nodded.

"You're so quiet," she said. "You look a little disoriented. Are you sure you're not going to pass out? I should have brought some water. Maybe it wasn't a good idea to drink all that wine, and an espresso martini." She laughed softly. "Is this too much for you?"

I shook my head. She was right, I wasn't feeling well. But it wasn't the alcohol. It was everything else. It was all too much.

"Do you want to sit down?" she asked.

"No, I'm fine."

"Come over here," Katherine said.

I let her tug my hand, pulling me toward the palm trees.

"Lean against this tree," she said. "It will make you feel solid. You can put your arm around it if you feel like you're losing your balance." She swayed slightly, then laughed. "I'm feeling a little unsteady myself. I think I drank that last martini too fast."

I leaned my back against the stately palm tree. The solid column supported my back. It felt good to have something holding me up. The sound of the wind moving through the fronds overhead was like musical instruments, a soft clattering that echoed the falls, an orchestra warming up, conducted by nature.

"Just rest," Katherine said, her voice softer than normal, as if she was being swallowed by the sounds of the wind and water.

I felt her push me against the tree, leaning into me.

"What are you doing?" I asked.

"This is it." She opened the large bag that was slung over her right shoulder. She pulled out my knife and held it close to my throat. "If you believe in an afterlife, you and your husband will be together very soon, just as you promised when you stood here the first time."

SIXTY-SIX

KATHERINE

Chelsea began whimpering like a baby. She'd been through a lot, poor thing. It might not have been fair that I was hurting her as a means to punish her father, but there was no other way to do this. They say the children suffer for the sins of the parents.

Despite the fairy lights, I couldn't see much of Chelsea's face in the darkness, but I absolutely sensed her fear. I felt her confusion. She had no idea what was happening. She didn't understand why her mother's best friend was holding a knife to her throat. She barely understood how I'd come to have possession of that knife; the knife I'd pulled out of her purse so easily while she allowed herself to get caught up once again in wondering whether Jay might yet be alive, sipping wine and fantasizing, rather than paying attention to what I was doing.

"Please," Chelsea whimpered. "Why are you—"

"Your father knew me as Katie," I said. "Of course, you've never heard that name. You don't even know who that girl is."

"Katie, who?" Chelsea asked.

"My mother was his family's live-in chef for almost twenty years."

Chelsea stared at me as if I were talking about strangers, a family she'd never heard of.

"Your father has chosen to forget me. I was fifteen when I fell in love with him. He was nineteen. I was a girl he used and discarded before he went back to college. He didn't know he also left a baby behind."

Me and my precious baby girl. Thrown away like leftovers from a dinner he hadn't particularly cared for.

Chelsea was still staring at me, as if I hadn't made it clear. Was she as dense as her father after all? I'd always thought she was a bright girl. Maybe I needed to shock her into understanding.

"When I was fifteen years old, your father fucked me. In his family's guest house. Of course, that's not what I thought it was. Because he seduced me with beautiful words in the weeks before that. And because I was young, with stars blinding my eyes. So, so young. And so naïve. I thought he loved me." I laughed. The hysteria swelled inside me, my laughter piercing the night sky.

"I don't think he—"

"I'm not *finished*. It happened several times, the fucking," I said. "That's what really pulled me in. That's what made me believe I was *the one*." I laughed. "The things he said swept me away. You know how it is, Chelsea. You've heard men whisper those things to you when you're naked and vulnerable, as if you're the most precious creature on the planet. I won't bore you with them now. Because of course, they were lies. They don't even deserve the dignity of being called lies. They were nonsense. Words that were said to make me bend over and welcome him. And then, that was it. He was finished with me."

"But you're my mom's best friend. And I thought you loved my dad, as a *friend*... you're friends with our family. I don't understand."

I laughed. "That was later. I grew up fast. I became an adult when I was fifteen years old and my baby started growing inside me. But I didn't realize what was happening, until it was too late. My mother sent me to live with my aunt until the baby came."

"Why are you so close to my mom? You're her best friend! Didn't my dad—"

"He had no clue who I was by the time I cultivated your mother's friendship. Success and confidence change a person. Money changes a person. By the time I walked into your mother's life and offered her my friendship, I was an entirely different person. Your father didn't recognize me. He'd forgotten all about meek little Katie. Successful, confident, savvy Katherine didn't resemble that girl at all. Besides, he'd put her so far out of his mind, she was nothing but a shadow. A smudge he could wipe away with his thumb."

"What does all this have to do with me? You sound like you hate me. I thought—"

"That's how self-absorbed you are. All of you." I spit the words at her. "None of you understand anything."

"What don't I understand?" Chelsea asked.

"I loved my baby. I loved her as much as your father loves you. But my baby was ripped out of my arms because she didn't have a father! Because he wasn't there. Because he forgot I even existed! They handed me a piece of paper with her tiny little footprints, and then they took her away. Her father wanted nothing to do with her."

"But he didn't know she existed."

"His mother knew. His father knew."

"I'm really sorry that happened to you. It sounds terrible. But why are you blaming me for something that happened more than thirty years ago, something I didn't know anything about? I wasn't even alive. It's not my fault you gave up your baby."

"No, it's not your fault. But he chose you over our child. It's his fault that he had sex with me and told me he loved me and acted as if he wanted to be with me and then threw me away like a piece of trash. His parents knew! They knew he had a daughter with me! The only reason I came out of it so well was because my mother blackmailed his father."

"It sounds like this is your mother's fault. She made you give up the baby—"

"It's not *the* baby! She was my tiny, precious daughter! Your grandfather wanted nothing to do with me. He didn't even believe me! The only reason he gave my mother money was because your *grandmother* believed me."

"I'm sorry he hurt you so badly. Teenagers have lots of relationships. I'm sorry if you took it for more than it was. Everyone has hard break-ups when they're young. You told me that, Katherine. Don't you remember? We grow and become stronger, that's what you said. Please let me go. Why are you doing this?"

I grabbed Chelsea's ponytail. I yanked her head back, exposing her pale, white neck. I raised the knife. The fairy lights reflected on the blade.

A guttural sound came out of her throat, strained and tight.

"Don't hurt me! Please! What do you want?" she cried.

I laughed. "That's a very good question. What do you think I want?"

"I don't know! It feels like you're... like you're losing your mind. I thought you were my mom's best friend. I thought you *loved* me! You need help. My mom, my family can help you, if you'll let us."

"I don't want your fucking help."

"Then what do you want?"

"Haven't you figured it out?"

"How would I figure it out? You're crazy. Writing those cruel letters to my mom all these years? I assume that was you?"

"Very good, Chelsea. You're one step closer."

"Please, put down the knife."

"You haven't answered my question. What do you think I want?"

"I don't know!"

I laughed. "Your mother needs to suffer for what she did—taking him away from me. Torturing her all this time, knowing he was trying, and failing to comfort her has been an absolute *delight*. It's given me years of pleasure. Not that I care about him anymore. But I did... once. He was everything. I loved that boy with all my heart. I gave my body, my mind, my soul... I gave everything to him. I gave him *everything*. And he threw me away like I was nothing. He threw our baby away like she was nothing. I want him to suffer! They're going to have their baby torn out of their arms just like I did! This has been so worth the wait. I thought that brainless boy was going to steal it all away from me when he crashed the motorboat. But he didn't." I laughed, throwing my head back, overcome with the thrill of victory and by how very long, and with such great patience I'd waited for this moment. I swayed slightly, feeling euphoric, then lightheaded. I needed to remain calm. Just a while longer.

"Please." Chelsea's voice was soft, meek. She sounded as if she thought she could reason with me. "We can talk about this— you and my dad. My mom, too. Whatever you think would work best. So everyone can understand your pain, what you've been through."

I remembered the things she'd said during dinner about becoming an attorney. I wanted to laugh. She thought she was going to argue me out of this. I could sense her starting to prepare her words, thinking she could persuade me. Suddenly, I was tired of talking. She would never understand. Andrew was the one who needed to hear this. And he would, once his daughter was gone, swallowed by the waterfall. Then, he and I would be on even footing—two grieving parents.

All that would be left was his relentless suffering. Our pain would be equal once Chelsea was ripped out of his life, just like my baby girl had been torn out of mine.

SIXTY-SEVEN

CHELSEA

Feeling that large knife touching my throat, my very own knife, the one I'd kept close beside me all this time to keep me safe, now made me terrified even to swallow. In the darkness, with tiny lights sparkling across her skin, Katherine no longer looked like herself. It felt as if a stranger held my knife, ready to cut my throat in one clean stroke.

I couldn't kick her. I couldn't grab her arm. Any movement meant driving myself into that blade.

After all her talking, I still couldn't understand what the man who had been staying in my room, pretending to be Jay, had to do with any of this. All she'd done was talk about the past. I assumed she'd murdered Jay, but she'd said nothing about what had happened to him, about how that man had come to be in my room, or mentioned who he was.

Before I could ask, as if thinking about him had conjured him, I saw the man.

I couldn't be sure what made my eyes dart in that direction. Maybe it was my survival instinct, heightened by the knife at my throat, raising all my senses to peak awareness of my surroundings, as if I were a wild animal, smelling another creature's scent on the soft breeze.

He was clearly trying to keep himself hidden from view. And in the darkness, it wasn't difficult. Maybe I caught sight of him because my eyes were the only part of my body that felt safe to move. And so, I found myself looking around as if I might somehow find a way to escape from a position in which I felt utterly immobilized.

The man was about twenty feet away, standing close to a small shack made of bamboo and dried grasses. Then, as I watched, he moved away from the building and began walking toward us. His stride was confident and relaxed.

"Katherine," he said.

"You're late," Katherine said.

"I don't think you have this under control." He continued toward us.

"I wanted you to record what I told her. So Andrew and Rachel could hear it all, before..."

"Don't come any closer." I felt her grip on me loosen slightly. The knife wobbled. "I don't..." She moved her hand, pushing harder where she was forcing my shoulder against the palm tree.

I was overcome with the sensation that time had stopped moving forward, terrified that any minute, Katherine would slash the knife across my throat. She hadn't, yet. Why not?

My thoughts seemed disconnected from my body. I didn't understand how I could be having logical, linear thoughts when each breath might be my last. In some ways, I felt as if I had floated out of my body, as if I were up near the fairy lights, looking down at myself, watching to see what would happen.

"Is a video necessary? It's kind of cruel and—"

"I'll tell you what's cruel, Drake!" Katherine was screaming, but her voice was weak. She gasped for air, the knife shaking, moving closer to my jaw.

"Are you okay?" he asked. "Maybe this isn't... You don't have to do this. It's okay to change your mind."

Droplets of sweat had formed around her hairline and across her upper lip. *Had* she had lost her nerve? She'd known me all my life. She was as close to me as an aunt, a godmother. Did she really hate me so much that she would be able to slit my throat as if I were an animal and she was a butcher, adept and comfortable with slaughtering cattle? I couldn't believe that about her. Even hearing the things she'd said, I couldn't believe she was that cold-blooded. Or throw me over the cliff into the thundering waterfall, as the man—Drake—had suggested.

I understood that she wanted my father to experience the pain of losing his child. But what about me? She'd loved me since I was an infant, hadn't she? I'd always felt that she did. She laughed with me and played with me as a child. She read stories to me and looked after me when my parents went out for the evening, or away for the weekend. I'd confided in her as a teenager.

Was this the same person? Had she looked at me with secret loathing during every moment she'd spent with me? Even when I was a little girl? It didn't seem possible. How had I never noticed?

Drake began moving closer again.

"Stay back," Katherine said. "Where's your phone? You need to start filming."

He continued walking. A moment later, he was standing beside me. "Just breathe, Chelsea."

"Don't talk to her," Katherine said.

"Give me the knife," Drake said.

"You're supposed to be *helping* me. But never mind. Just leave us alone. I don't need you! I've waited all my life for this!" She stifled a yawn. "I'm just so..." She shook her head slightly and moved the knife closer to my collarbone. "I can do this. I will do this." She sounded elated. "Andrew needs to pay for what he did to me. He's never paid for it!" Tears filled her eyes. She blinked them away.

Drake stood silently. His breath was warm on my face. I knew she felt it too. We were all within inches of each other. Our breath commingled, our eyes rarely blinking, watching the others.

Then, in one swift move, so fast I felt the shift in the air before I saw his hand, Drake grabbed Katherine's wrist, wrenching it away from me, twisting her arm back until the knife was behind her body. He held it that way, pushing harder until she cried out in pain.

I stumbled back, scraping my arm on the palm tree.

"Stop! What are you doing?" Katherine lunged toward him, trying to grab the knife. "Now she's—"

Drake shoved her hard and she fell onto her back, silent for a moment as the wind was knocked out of her.

Katherine pushed herself up, twisted to her side, and grabbed Drake's ankle with both hands. She yanked his right leg to the side at an awkward angle, sending him sprawling onto the ground with a thud and a painful-sounding grunt. The knife flew out of his hands, disappearing in the darkness, landing with a whisper on the soft grass.

"I had her!" Katherine screamed. "Now she's going to run!" She struggled to her feet, groaning. "What's wrong with me? I feel..." She stared toward me.

Drake didn't respond. The moon and the fairy lights showed his eyes half-closed. He groaned again.

I did as Katherine had suggested and began running, but she was surprisingly fast. Even though she was almost thirty years older than me, I was still fuzzy-headed with alcohol and incoherent with the things she'd said, with the shocking realization that she'd hated me and my parents all my life, that she intended to kill me.

As I ran toward the path leading out of the garden, she

grabbed me and began dragging me back toward the cluster of palm trees and the edge of the cliff that overlooked the two waterfalls.

"You acted as if you loved me all my life!" I cried. "Why are you doing this?"

"You already know the answer." Her voice was cold, but her words were slurred.

She continued dragging me, both hands around one wrist. I pulled against her, but her strength felt almost superhuman. It felt as if my arm was going to come out of the socket at my shoulder joint.

"Did you hate me every time you looked at me, every time you held me on your lap?"

She laughed. She sounded demented, like someone in a horror movie, locked up in a lunatic asylum. Had she always been this way and kept it hidden, or had something cracked open and let this monstrous side out while we'd been struggling in the dark?

"There's a difference between your pain and the pain you'll cause my parents," I said.

"What are you talking about?" She grunted, dragging me closer to the edge of the cliff. We were now only a foot or so from the edge. The sound of the water was deafening, forcing us to shout to be heard above it.

"My father and mother will know that I loved them. You'll never know that. You'll never hold your baby and you'll never feel any love for the rest of your life. So you can't hurt them the way you think you can. They'll always have something you never had, and you never will."

"Oh!" She clutched her chest with one hand as if I'd shot her. "You're vicious." She let go and threw herself at me, reaching for my neck.

I ducked and punched her knee. She screamed. I slammed my fist into her other knee, hearing the crunch of cartilage. She stumbled, almost falling, but managing to stay partially upright.

"What a cruel thing to say," she whispered.

Still keeping my body in a half-crouch, I shoved her away from me. She grabbed for my shoulders, trying to keep herself from falling again. I straightened and pushed her as hard as I could. She flew backward. Her lower leg hit one of the small, woefully inadequate rocks that formed a border along the cliff edge. She toppled over it and fell backward, disappearing into the darkness below.

The thundering waterfall swallowed the sound of her screams.

SIXTY-EIGHT

CHELSEA

Drake was standing beside me. I had no sense of when he'd walked up to the edge of the cliff or how long I'd been there, staring into the dark far below me where the water thrashed violently, the only thing visible, the white foam that glistened in the moonlight. There was no sign of Katherine's body.

After a while, I turned away. He hadn't spoken, and I was grateful for that. I didn't want to hear his voice. I didn't even want to hear my own thoughts, recalling what she'd told me, or the imagined scenarios of what might happen now.

Finally, he took my hand and placed the knife in my palm. "No one has to know about this," he said.

"Some people do." I turned and began walking back across the garden.

As we started down the path, he took my wrist. "There are things you don't know."

"It's a little late now."

"I can explain."

"I don't want your explanation now. You had a hundred opportunities." I was lying to myself. I wanted to know everything. But not now. I was numb, too shocked by what I'd done. I was still trying to process what Katherine had said. And I was beyond furious that now, after all this time, he wanted to explain everything to me.

He was suggesting he was going to cover this up for me. Was that what I wanted? I stopped walking. Had I committed murder? Was that how the police would view this? I'd been fighting for my life. There was no other choice. But the police, and nearly everyone who knew me on this island, believed I was mentally unstable. I imagined trying to tell my story now. My missing, murdered husband. This strange man whom I'd allowed to stay in my room. Our closest family friend, a psychopath who had tried to murder me, who was the likely killer of my husband.

Was it easier to do it his way? Simply walk away? Once her body washed ashore, they might assume suicide. There would be no evidence that anyone else had been here. Unless there were footprints in the grass. How would we know? I looked up at the sky. There was a decent chance, given the weather that afternoon, and several clouds that had drifted back to cover the stars, that more rain would fall before morning. How many days would it be before someone reported Katherine missing?

It seemed risky.

How long would it be until her body floated to the surface? It might never. The cove wasn't large. Before long, the current would begin pulling her body out to sea.

As if the island itself were providing an answer for me, I felt a few raindrops on my face.

I followed him to his rental car and got inside. We pulled out of the parking area and turned onto the highway. He didn't offer again to explain anything. I held my knife on my lap and we drove back to the resort in silence.

When we arrived, he avoided the valet parking. He drove to the parking garage and we walked back, entering the resort area through a side gate.

"I can come to your suite so we can talk," he said.

"No. I need to sleep."

"I understand. I'll text you tomorrow," he said.

In my room, I stripped off my clothes, showered, and went to bed. Miraculously, I fell into a dreamless sleep.

SIXTY-NINE

CHELSEA

When I woke, the first thing I felt was the spaciousness of my suite, having slept with the bedroom doors open to the living area for the first time in two weeks. I relished the peace of having my room to myself. I'd put the security lock on the door before going to sleep, so I'd slept knowing there was no possibility of Drake re-entering the room.

I ordered a light breakfast and sat on the balcony alternating sips of coffee and orange juice, watching the equally orange-stained clouds after the rain during the night. It was reassuring to know that any signs of my struggle with Katherine had been washed away.

The question was—would they be as easily washed from my memories? Right now, it already seemed like a rapidly fading dream. But would it remain that way? Would guilt rear its head at some point? Would a crippling sense of regret that I hadn't given her more time to talk, to help me understand her life and her rage, consume me for the rest of my life? At the same time, if I hadn't done what I had, I wouldn't be sitting here sipping coffee and gazing at the heartbreaking blue of the ocean with its promising sky overhead.

After a while, I picked up my phone and called my parents. I told them everything, holding back none of the hatred Katherine had poured out on my father, my mother, and even me. As I talked, I heard my mother crying softly. Behind her weeping were murmurs of pain from my father.

I couldn't imagine the shock, the betrayal, and all the other emotions that must be consuming them, twisting their hearts into knots. I wanted to be there, to hug them, to provide any comfort I could. At the same time, Katherine had been my mother's closest friend. My father's teenage lover. This wasn't about me. They needed to work through it without me there.

After a few minutes, my mother calmed herself enough to speak. "I want you to come home."

"Today," my father added.

"Not yet. I need to talk to Drake. I want to know everything."

"You can't trust him. What if he hurts you?" my mother cried. "You still don't know who he is."

"He helped me get out of this. She might have killed me if he hadn't been there. And I need to find out... I can't live my life with these unanswered questions. Even though he should have explained himself a long time ago, I need to know the rest of it. And the police are—"

"Don't talk to the police," my father said. "Don't give them any reason to ask you what happened to Katherine. Don't—"

"I want to know what's happening with Jay! They're supposed to be investigating his murder. They're supposed to be identifying his body. How long can it *take?*"

"Let them come to you. And they can do that when you're back home. You don't need to see them face to face."

"Fine. But I need to talk to Drake. I'll book a flight for tomorrow."

After a few final words about Katherine, we ended the call.

I mixed myself a mimosa from the minibar and took it back

out to the balcony. I settled on the lounge chair and raised my glass toward the horizon before taking a sip, toasting my victory over a woman who had taken advantage of my love, and a lifetime of trust.

SEVENTY

RACHEL

Katherine and I became friends when we met at the gym after I graduated from college. I'd just started working at an art gallery in San Francisco, mostly doing grunt work—packaging artwork for shipping, answering phones, and dusting the pieces on display.

I signed up for an aerobics class and we connected right away. It wasn't long before we were going out for a glass of wine after class. It was absolutely counterproductive to be drinking wine after sweating in an aerobics class, but we laughed about it and sipped more wine.

She didn't boast about how she'd gotten all her money. All I knew was that she'd been lucky enough to be one of the early employees at a highly valued tech company that had gone public, turning her into one of those Silicon Valley overnight millionaires.

Because she was in the tech industry, she'd traveled all over the world. She'd never been married, but she'd had several long-term relationships with *fascinating* men. We talked about men and careers. We talked about working out and clothes, movies and books and friendship.

Katherine was there at our engagement party, giving Andrew and me an emotional, heartfelt toast. She was the maid of honor at our wedding. And she looked after our cat while we spent our honeymoon in Italy.

When I got pregnant, Katherine was thrilled. The moment I found out we were having a girl, she began buying us adorable outfits and offered to be our number one babysitter.

Once I stopped working at the art gallery, Katherine seemed to have a lot more free time as well. Of course, I was busy with Chelsea, but I swapped childcare with other friends which gave me time to go to the gym and continue my wine dates with Katherine after our workouts.

She and I had lunch together once a month. Once Chelsea started school, those lunches turned into weekly three-hour affairs. We shared a bottle of wine and talked. We could talk for hours without the slightest pause in the flow. We understood each other perfectly. Part of it was that Katherine was a great listener.

One of the things I cherished about Katherine, was that as Chelsea got older, I found myself holding some things back from my friends who had children Chelsea's age. I didn't want to betray Chelsea's confidences to the parents of her friends. It felt good to have a friend with whom I could share absolutely everything.

When Chelsea had crushes on boys whom I didn't care for, I could talk to Katherine about it. I could pour out my heart to Katherine over cliques among the girls at school, or issues with bullying because she didn't know the people involved. I wasn't betraying anyone's confidence, and none of it would come back on Chelsea. I was free to share my thoughts and feelings without reservation.

By the time Chelsea became an adult, the pattern was set.

I blame myself. I should have stopped talking about my daughter. She was another adult now. Equal with me. I shouldn't have been talking about the intimate details of her life to another person, no matter how much she loved my daughter, no matter how close we were.

But I didn't. I continued sharing confidences with Katherine. I told her all the details of the boating accident. I talked to her about Chelsea's recovery, about the medication she was prescribed, and my concerns over a possible addiction to the opioid painkillers. I told her about my hatred for the boy who had driven his boat into that concrete pillar.

And then I told her about my fears regarding online dating. I told her how scared I was for Chelsea, that her life seemed to have shrunk to her computer screen, as she sat at home recovering.

I told Katherine about the men Chelsea met online. I told her about Jay. I shared details of their relationship. I told her about Jay's career, about his interest in sailing. Of course, Chelsea was also close to Katherine. She shared a lot of her own stories, telling Katherine why she was leaving the high-tech industry and why she'd decided to pursue a law degree.

I told Katherine Highsmith every single thing about my daughter's life—I shared Chelsea's thoughts, her feelings, her hurts, and even many of her private conversations with her fiancé that Chelsea had shared with me.

And then, my closest friend took every secret, every point of vulnerability and used them to nearly destroy my daughter's life. She used that information to entice Chelsea's husband out of their honeymoon suite and murder him. She used it to coach a man who would pretend to be her husband, driving my daughter to doubt her own sanity, tormenting her for weeks before finally trying to lure Chelsea to her death.

But my daughter is a strong woman.

SEVENTY-ONE
CHELSEA

In the afternoon, I sat on the beach for a while, watching the waves, reliving the past twenty-four hours. Lori and Kendall had turned out to be friends after all. Their weird attempt to hold me captive in their room had made me wonder about them, but in the end, their willingness to meet me and Katherine for a drink had given me time to sprinkle the crushed opioid into Katherine's espresso martini. They provided the distraction I needed so that Katherine believed I was still her gullible victim.

I thought about what I'd done to Katherine. Despite her decades of perfect lies, she'd made the tiniest mistake when she told me a woman might have offered to let Drake stay in her room *because he was so good-looking*.

When she'd said that, Katherine had never seen the man in my room. I'd never told my mother he was good-looking. It wasn't important. Her comment startled me. I started to wonder. And then, the look of absolute relief on Katherine's face when I offered her an out by telling her how aggressively Lori and Kendall had flirted with him was truly one of triumph, an expression disproportionate to the situation.

After watching her protective care of my purse during

dinner, more pieces clicked into place. I realized she was on her way to removing my knife. Looking at her lips across the table, the stain of red wine, her teeth tearing into the rare steak with fervor, it was almost as if I could see the years of lies spilling out of her mouth.

When I went to the bar, I rubbed the opioid tablet in my fingers until it was powder. I sprinkled it into her drink where the taste was overpowered by the strong flavor of espresso and Kahlua.

Pushing her off the cliff was easy once the opioid mixed with alcohol took hold of her body. I would have escaped from under the knife blade even if Drake hadn't shown up to interfere.

After a shower and a light dinner, I texted Drake, telling him to come to my suite. As we'd parted ways the night before, he told me he'd gone to Katherine's room, when he'd moved out of mine. Now, I wanted to hear what he had to say. I wanted to understand why he'd spent all that time and energy gaslighting me. I needed to find out how he knew Katherine.

The first thing he did when he walked in the door was to hand my wallet to me. I took it without a word. The proof that he'd had it all along told me everything.

I suggested we sit on the balcony. A bottle of wine stood on the table with two glasses beside it.

I filled both glasses and took a sip, hoping the wine would calm my amped-up state. I hoped that sitting on the balcony gazing up at the night sky, hearing the soft whoosh of the waves in the distance would soothe me. The things this man had to say should have been said a long time ago.

"I want to explain," he said.

"You're insanely late, but go ahead." I took another sip of wine.

"I know you're furious. You have a right to be," he said. "But I'm not what you think I am."

I let out a sharp laugh. Maybe he expected me to thank him for having my back with Katherine.

"There's a reason for the things I did," he said.

"There's always a reason for the things people do. That doesn't excuse it."

"I'd like to explain it to you."

"You're taking a long time to get there."

"I met Katherine quite a few years ago. Even though she's nearly two decades older than I am, we fell for each other. We connected on other levels. Our ages didn't matter. We had a wild time together and I was completely hooked into her before I saw her dark side."

He coughed softly. "My sister is developmentally disabled. It was my dream for a long time to open a world-class occupational therapy clinic for people with intellectual disabilities. I've been the sole caretaker for her since our parents passed. I love her so much." His voice caught. He paused and took a sip of wine. After a moment, he continued. "She's the most important person in my life, and I wanted to do this, not just for her, but as a legacy in her name."

I felt slightly disoriented. What did this have to do with anything? Why was he telling me?

"Katherine invested one and a half million dollars in that dream."

"Oh. That's—"

"Yeah. It was a lot. But she was crazy in love with me. At least that's what she said. It's what I thought. Now I know she wasn't capable of loving anyone. But for a while, it was good. We traveled. We seemed to be in sync with each other. But then, this dark side began to show itself. Every night in bed, I had to listen to her talk about a boy she'd known when she was a teenager. She would talk about him for hours. *Hours*. There was so much bitterness. And *hatred* in her. She went on and on and *on* about the baby she had to give up, how her baby had been *ripped out of her arms.* How she'd loved this guy with all her heart. How she'd given him everything and he'd treated her like a piece of trash. The only good thing that had come out of it was that his family had made her a wealthy woman. Every *night,* for *years* I had to listen to this. I started to think she was mentally ill."

I took a long swallow of wine. I wasn't sure I wanted to hear any more of his story. It didn't have anything to do with me. Except for telling me more of what I already knew about Katherine.

"I tried to break it off. But she wouldn't have it. And she'd wrapped a one and a half million dollar noose around my neck. I couldn't even think about paying her back. Not only did I owe it to my sister, and to the people I was trying to help, but I had employees depending on me." He gulped his wine. "Then things got even darker."

He didn't have to tell me that. I'd lived it.

"She told me what she'd been doing to your mother over the years—sending those terrible letters. Then, she told me what she wanted to do to you, how she was going to punish your father once and for all. And use you to do it—first by tormenting you, all of you, with Jay's disappearance, then his death, and then by killing you. I told her to leave me out of it. But she tightened the noose."

"You were going to commit *murder* for her?" I stared at him, but he wouldn't meet my gaze. "Why didn't you go to the police?"

"I would have lost everything. My sister would lose the support services she depends on. My employees would be let go. All the people who rely on my clinic to improve their lives would be abandoned. But mostly... my sister, Emily. The most sublime creature on this planet."

I felt his pain. But I still didn't understand why he couldn't have found a way to talk to the police.

"So, I came up with another idea. I told Katherine that I would pretend to be your husband. I would stay with you twenty-four seven. I would make sure you didn't return home and that you didn't do anything to prevent her from getting to you when the time was right. I thought I could use my constant presence to keep you safe instead. I thought if I stayed with you I could, somehow, stop her from killing you. I know it was a weak, ridiculous, poorly-thought-out plan. It was doomed to failure. But it was all I had. And I thought *maybe* I could make it work. I had no idea how, but it was the only thing I could think of."

"Okay." He was right. It was weak and poorly thought out. It sounded like a joke.

"You have to understand that, at first, I thought she just wanted to punish your parents by scaring them. I had no idea she was planning to murder Jay. I had no idea she was planning to murder *you*. Not at first. Do you understand that? You have to believe me."

I shrugged. I took several sips of wine. He was staring at me with such intensity, his eyes pleading with me to embrace his feeling of helplessness. It seemed as if he wanted me to be on his side. He wanted me to accept all the things he'd done.

It was all too much. The entire two weeks had completely drained me, leaving me empty and numb. I was grieving the brutal, ugly death of my husband. The things this man had been through with his lover, a woman who I thought had loved and supported me all my life, were close to irrelevant.

"Please understand," he said.

I still didn't speak.

"Will you try?" he asked.

"It sounds as if you were in a difficult position. It sounds like you really love your sister." I wouldn't say any more. That was all I had.

SEVENTY-TWO

RACHEL

Now

I was still trying to come to terms with what my lifelong best friend had done. That she'd tried to murder my daughter. I was trying to process the fact she *had* murdered my son-in-law, and that she'd known my husband as a teenager, given birth to his child, and never told my husband or me.

I wondered if there'd ever been any signs that Katherine hated me so deeply. Were there subtle hints I'd missed over the years? How had she kept such bitter loathing hidden through countless hours spent together?

The realization that she had so much hatred and darkness inside she could easily orchestrate incredible torment for Chelsea, murder Jay, and plan the same for Chelsea, made me physically sick.

I wondered how long it would take me to heal from the betrayal. It made me feel as if I couldn't trust anyone. I still trusted my husband and daughter. But there was an anxiety lying beneath every thought that passed through my mind. Aside from my family, I felt as if I was questioning everyone and everything. Nothing anyone said could be taken at face value. What dark secrets lay inside every human heart?

It was incomprehensible to me that someone could hold on to such a desire for revenge her entire life. And the way her pain and bitterness had bled into the lives of others!

Somehow, along with feeling rejected by Andrew, and the pain of having her baby taken away, her twisted mind blamed *me* for taking Andrew from her. How was it my fault that Andrew had fallen in love with me? He met me long after he'd misused and rejected Katherine.

I didn't want to think about it. I didn't want this to consume my life. I didn't want to question the motives of everyone I knew. I didn't want to become a distrustful person. I didn't want a dark outlook on the world, believing that everyone was lying to me all the time.

Shaking my thoughts to the side, I dragged myself off the sofa and went out to get the mail. When I saw the pale pink envelope, I collapsed to my knees on the front lawn. She was going to torment me from beyond the grave. I knew it before I opened the envelope.

Andrew and Chelsea would tell me not to read it, to burn it. But the moment I saw it, I knew I couldn't escape the desire to hear her final thoughts. The envelope was postmarked from Hawaii. I now knew Katherine had remained there after the wedding, luring Jay from the honeymoon suite, murdering him, and sending notes to my daughter. She'd obviously mailed this before she tried to throw Chelsea into the waterfall that had taken her own life.

Rachel,

Your instincts about Jay were correct. They say a mother always knows. But you were right for the wrong reason.

Jay never loved your daughter because I was the one who

found him. I hired him. I coached him and helped him create a persona that Chelsea would fall in love with.

The man of her dreams was a fantasy. I created him from all the juicy details you've shared with me over the years. Sleep well knowing that the happiest day of your daughter's life was a lie.

Jay Davis was a figment of Chelsea's imagination. He never loved her, not for a single moment. Just as Andrew never loved me, not even when he looked into my eyes and said his heart belonged to me forever.

SEVENTY-THREE
CHELSEA

After Drake told me how Katherine had controlled his life, he said he had more he needed to tell me, but I was suddenly tired. Of everything. The adrenaline had washed out of me like a tsunami—the ominous retreat before it comes crashing through, destroying everything in its path. I was sick of him, but he begged me to let him stay until morning, so I let him sleep on the sofa one last time.

I woke early the next morning. I would be checking out before noon and I wanted to enjoy my final sunrise from the balcony. There had been far too few opportunities for me to relax and drink in the beauty of my surroundings.

Taking a tiny bottle of champagne and a small container of orange juice out of the minibar, as well as a champagne flute, I went out to the balcony, closing the glass door behind me so I wouldn't disturb Drake. I wanted to be alone to think about my phone conversation with my mother the night before. A text from her had caused me to cut short his monologue. Letting him stay on the sofa was a matter of urgency. Her message was alarming:

Call me immediately.

Now, I mixed myself a mimosa. I toasted the pink and orange sky and took a sip.

When I called, my mother had been sobbing. She'd received a final letter from Katherine. She pleaded with me to come home immediately, to not spend another moment waiting for confirmation that the body I had found belonged to Jay Davis.

"He doesn't deserve another moment of your time, even in death. You need to be home where you can heal and put all this behind you," she'd said.

"Don't say that. I want his body treated with dignity. I owe him—"

"I hate that I have to tell you this over the phone, but you need to know. Now. Before you waste any more time thinking about him."

"Why are you—"

"I don't want you to spend another moment of your life grieving for a man who wasn't who he said he was." Her voice was strained and raw, as if she wasn't sure she could get the words out.

Then, she told me what Katherine's letter had said.

At first, I didn't believe her. I didn't *want* to believe her. Why should I? Why would my mother? Katherine had spent her entire life lying to all of us. Everything about her was a lie. Now, she was telling my mother something about Jay when he wasn't there to defend himself. Had Katherine only said that to drive her knife deeper into my mother's heart one more time? She'd expected to be alive when my mother read those words. She'd expected I would be dead.

I sipped my mimosa as my mind began racing back, a film silently running in reverse, through every moment of my relationship with Jay. Was it possible he'd made himself into someone I wanted to see, a man I'd wanted to love, with Katherine's expert coaching? I'd been so broken, so vulnerable when I met him. Maybe...?

Finally, my rapidly reversing thoughts landed on the phone call Jay had received at our wedding reception. I knew now, the call must have come from Katherine, telling him to meet her. Jay hadn't shown up on the security cameras because the police had searched for a man leaving the property alone. They hadn't focused on couples leaving the property. If he already knew Katherine, if they were tightly connected, they would have breezed right past the notice of the police and the resort personnel who had reviewed the footage.

With that, another memory surfaced, not unlike the koi poking their mouths out of the water, grasping for morsels of food. When Katherine crashed into me as I'd pursued Jay, sending my phone hurtling into the pond, sinking below the swarm of fish, it had seemed like a clumsy mistake on my part. But knowing her now for the elegant and practiced liar she was, I saw that event with different eyes—a deliberate attempt to keep me from overhearing her voice on Jay's phone, to rid me of my own phone at the same time, keeping me incapacitated in the hours after Jay first disappeared.

How had I been so easily misled? How had I fallen in love with a man who had fed me what I wanted to hear, who had shown me what I wanted to see? It was humiliating. I wasn't sure if I was nursing a broken heart, or a shattered ego and a damaged sense of who I was. Maybe all of it.

The sky was blue now, filled with light. It promised another spectacular day in paradise.

I heard the door behind me open. Drake stepped onto the balcony carrying a mimosa of his own. "Mind if I join you?"

I lifted my mimosa in response.

He pulled one of the chairs closer to mine and sat down.

"Did you know that Jay was Katherine's creation?" I asked. "He catfished me, with her help."

"I know."

I sipped my mimosa.

"There's something else I want you to know." He took a long sip of his drink, as if to fortify himself. "All the time that Katherine was sending me messages and emails, giving me information about your life, your personality, telling me your dreams, describing your goals, to prepare me for pretending to be your husband..." He paused for a moment. He looked out toward the ocean, then spoke in a softer, slower voice. "I found myself slowly... falling in love with you."

I laughed.

"It's the truth," he said. "It felt as if I was getting to know you. Each detail made me feel as if you were coming alive right before my eyes."

He was quiet again for a few minutes. "So, what I wanted to say, is... now that you know the man you thought loved you was simply playing a game. Worse than that, he was setting you up, he was leading you to your death. Now that you know this, do you think you could... do you think you would consider... staying in touch? Giving me a chance to prove that I'm the real deal? I'm not in a hurry. I know you need a lot of time to work through everything that's happened. But after that...?"

I took a sip of my drink and placed it on the table between us.

I turned to face him. His expression was calm, but hopeful.

"If you thought gaslighting me was the way to get to know me, you don't know *anything* about me. For all the *facts* you thought you knew, you didn't understand a single thing about who I am."

"Was I gaslighting you, or showing you the truth? That he wasn't your husband."

His words irritated me. They made me angry. But I couldn't avoid admitting there was some truth in them. Had there been an element of *too good to be true* about Jay? If someone ticks *all* the boxes, if they're absolutely perfect for you, maybe something's wrong with that picture. A human being, a life partner isn't something you order custom made.

I raised my glass toward his and offered him a welcoming smile. He could take it as he chose, but I would absolutely stay in touch. It was time for him to pay for what he'd done. I was confident I could figure out a way to punish him without hurting his sister. A law degree would help. It would take some time, but I would figure it out.

They say revenge is a dish best served cold.

A LETTER FROM CATHRYN GRANT

Dear reader,

I want to say a huge thank you for choosing to read *Not My Husband*. If you did enjoy it, and want to keep up to date with all my latest releases, just sign up at the following link. Your email address will never be shared and you can unsubscribe at any time.

www.bookouture.com/cathryn-grant

Thankfully the shocking experience Chelsea had when she woke up two days after her wedding never happened to me, or to anyone I know! But the idea came to me partially from that experience all of us have had—of waking in an unfamiliar place, and for a moment, not knowing where we are, forgetting for the briefest moment what happened in our lives the day before. Although her life was turned upside down, it was satisfying to watch her fight her way out from a web of lies, to be transformed into a woman more determined than ever to build a life centered on truth.

It's always a little sad saying goodbye to a group of characters when I write the final page. I love knowing that they've also lived with you for a short time, and I'm so honored that you invited them into your life.

I hope you loved *Not My Husband* and if you did I would be very grateful if you would write a review. I'd love to hear what you think, and it makes such a difference, helping new readers to discover one of my books for the first time.

I love hearing from my readers—you can get in touch on social media or through my website.

Thanks,

Cathryn

www.cathryngrant.com

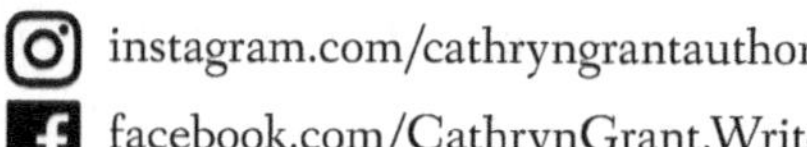
instagram.com/cathryngrantauthor
facebook.com/CathrynGrant.Writer

ACKNOWLEDGMENTS

It's been a fabulous creative experience working with Helen Jenner on *Not My Husband*, my second novel with Bookouture. It was such a thrill to hear her reaction to the concept for this story. I still smile when I remember her shock. I'm incredibly grateful to have such a talented editor and team who are as excited about my story as I am.

To my family, for absolutely everything, always, especially for listening to me talk far too much about murder and crimes of all sorts.

Most of all, to my husband, who has read, and reread every word I've written. My first reader, my biggest fan, and my soul mate. Thank you for all the cups of coffee, tea, and bowls of popcorn. The man who wonders about the *why* behind crimes as much as I do.

And to my readers. Thank you for reading. You will never know how honored I am that you choose to spend your precious time escaping into the lives and worlds of the characters I create.

PUBLISHING TEAM

Turning a manuscript into a book requires the efforts of many people. The publishing team at Bookouture would like to acknowledge everyone who contributed to this publication.

Audio
Alba Proko

Commercial
Lauren Morrissette
Hannah Richmond
Imogen Allport

Cover design
Aaron Munday

Data and analysis
Mark Alder
Mohamed Bussuri

Editorial
Helen Jenner
Ria Clare

Copyeditor
Laura Gerrard

Proofreader
Elaini Caruso

Marketing
Alex Crow
Melanie Price
Occy Carr
Cíara Rosney
Martyna Młynarska

Operations and distribution
Marina Valles
Joe Morris

Production
Hannah Snetsinger
Mandy Kullar
Nadia Michael
Charlotte Hegley

Publicity
Kim Nash
Noelle Holten
Jess Readett
Sarah Hardy

Rights and contracts
Peta Nightingale
Richard King
Saidah Graham

Dear Reader,

We'd love your attention for one more page to tell you about the crisis in children's reading, and what we can all do.

Studies have shown that reading for fun is the **single biggest predictor of a child's future life chances** – more than family circumstance, parents' educational background or income. It improves academic results, mental health, wealth, communication skills, ambition and happiness.

The number of children reading for fun is in rapid decline. Young people have a lot of competition for their time, and a worryingly high number do not have a single book at home.

Hachette works extensively with schools, libraries and literacy charities, but here are some ways we can all raise more readers:

- Reading to children for just 10 minutes a day makes a difference
- Don't give up if children aren't regular readers – there will be books for them!

- Visit bookshops and libraries to get recommendations
- Encourage them to listen to audiobooks
- Support school libraries
- Give books as gifts

There's a lot more information about how to encourage children to read on our websites: **www.RaisingReaders.co.uk** and **www.JoinRaisingReaders.com**.

Thank you for reading.

www.ingramcontent.com/pod-product-compliance
Lightning Source LLC
Chambersburg PA
CBHW031319210726
48287CB00005B/1606